A DREAM
COME TRUE

Dear Deb
Enjoy :)

Shaa Dickson

ALSO BY S.L. DICKSON

Kirk's Promise

Hidden Diary

Lost & Found

A DREAM
COME TRUE

A Novel

S.L. Dickson

William James Publishing

—A Dream Come True—
This is a work of fiction. Names, characters, places and incidents are a product of
the author's imagination or are used fictitiously. Any resemblance to actual
persons, living or dead, business establishments, events or locales is entirely
coincidental.

Published 2018 by S.L. Dickson

ISBN: 978-1-7752485-7-6 (Print edition)

Design and cover by Su Kopil, Earthly Charms
Copyediting by Ted Williams

 Created with Vellum

DEDICATION

This book is dedicated to my husband Bill Dickson who has always been my hero. Also dedicated to all my Canadian and American family and friends.

ACKNOWLEDGMENTS

To my dear friend, Laura Dixon, who has given me constant support throughout my writing career. You have faithfully read every page of my manuscript and provided invaluable input which helped me polish my stories so readers can enjoy them. You are an inspiration. Laura, we did it again. Thank you.

To my first reader and friend, Diane Webb, who encouraged me to add in more scenic details to this story, to make my location and geography come alive.

To my writer friend, Kate Gilbertson, whose point of view is opposite, but has made our conversations about my romantic stories fun.

To my fellow writers and authors from CaRWA and ARWA, who have all been an enormous support. A sincere thank you to each and every one of you, both near and far, for your encouragement and support. A special thank you to fellow author, Shelley Kassian, for helping me get this book to print. Shelley has been a tremendous support.

A special thank you to my writer friend, Deb Smith, for her help in making my monthly trips to Calgary possible and enjoyable.

PROLOGUE

$\mathcal{E}$ight years ago, while heading up to Calgary, Alberta on a family vacation, Amanda (Mandy) Joy Riley and her twin brother, Jason Mackenzie, from Utah, USA, were in a motor vehicle accident taking the lives of their parents', Steven and Joy, and their older brother, Martin. The twins remembered the filthy, drunk driver, who slurred his words and smelled of cheap whiskey as he came to the open van window and peeked in. Terrified, they clung to each other for dear life. Relief took over when the drunken man turned and disappeared.

A more terrifying experience seized them as they witnessed blood gurgling from their father's neck, the stillness of their mother as she fell against their father, and brother Martin taking his last gasp of air. Shock set in when they realized they were covered in their own blood, from injuries they didn't know they had. Sheer panic filled their hearts when a man tried to separate them, as people in uniforms covered their parents and brother with white sheets confirming they were all dead. Fortunately, a man in a suit came forward and issued orders that they were to be kept together.

Richard Riley, their father's youngest brother and his wife,

Maggie, from Calgary were contacted. Jason was released after closing the gaping wound with twenty stitches to his right arm. Mandy on the other hand was admitted to hospital and treated for head and leg injuries for five weeks which took its toll on her both physically and emotionally.

Adoption papers were drawn up and arrangements were made for them to live with their aunt and uncle in Calgary, Alberta. The separation and loss they all had to deal with was emotionally exhausting. A complete life change from living on a large cattle ranch in Utah, to settling in a major city was an additional challenge for Mandy and Jason. However, true love within the Riley family, would conquer all adversities.

CHAPTER 1

Minutes before two o'clock, Amanda Joy Riley drove up the Triple M Ranch road and was immediately awestruck by the wealth and magnificence of the two-story log home. A stone fireplace graced the center of the house from ground level up and beyond the second story. Large windows with forest green shutters flanked either side, giving the house a warm welcome feeling. A well-manicured lawn and flower garden beautified the yard. Grabbing her purse, she got out of her blue half ton and stood beside it admiring the pleasant view.

A huge smile crossed her face when she spotted several horses lazily grazing and enjoying the early summer Alberta afternoon behind a white fenced corral. Beyond the yard, miles of rolling hills and majestic mountains lay to the west and vast prairie land to the east. It gave her a sense of total freedom and peace. With one last glance around the yard, Amanda walked towards the house noticing several lawn chairs clustered around the garden area. The mature oak tree in the middle would certainly give some welcome shade on a hot day.

Beside the wide steps leading up to the front porch which

ran the entire length of the house, was an unfinished wheelchair ramp. Briefly, she wondered who needed the ramp. Holding on to the sturdy porch railing, she walked up the four steps and towards the heavy glass front door.

"May I help you?"

Mandy's hand flew up to her chest as her heart flipped at the harsh baritone voice which seemed to appear from nowhere. She turned and came face to face, or rather face to broad chest, forcing her to look up. A tall, dark-haired man stood inches away from her. A mixture of faint masculine cologne, leather, horses and sweat, teased her senses and gave her an instant thrill. There was no smell in the world she liked better. She stepped away from him and bumped up against the deck railings. His dark, questioning brown eyes cruised over her. Her pulse quickened. Who was he and where had this man come from? She was positive there had been no one in the yard when she drove up.

"Aha... yes, Sir, I have an appointment with Mr. McBride." Mandy watched the muscle in his strong jaw tighten as curious brown eyes studied her from the tips of her toes to the top of her head, then met her gaze. His thick black collar-length hair, gleamed in the sunlight. Rugged features, a square jaw and dark tan, along with a five o'clock shadow at two in the afternoon gave him an all-male look.

"Oh yeah." He backed up allowing much needed fresh air to rush in between them. "You from Calgary?" His eyes cruised the length of her with cold unfeeling dark brown eyes.

Mandy tilted her strong yet feminine chin forward. "Yes." This couldn't be the man she had talked to over the phone. Could it?

"Figures." He shook his head slightly as his large hand wrapped around a metal, carpenter's level, to wipe away damp sand allowing the yellow bubble tube to be exposed.

With rattled nerves, she forced herself to turn and focus

on the corral where several horses grazed. "I'm here for the Nanny position." She turned back to watch his large strong hands wipe the damp sand off of his jeans. Why would an expensive carpenter's tool have damp sand all over it in the first place?

Muscular dark tanned arms dropped to his side while holding the level tight in a fisted hand. "Go on in." His thin lips hardly moved as he stepped back down the steps, knelt on one knee, put the level against one of the many dowels, which ran the length of the ramp. He turned and reached for his black Stetson, which sat beside a large red tool box, and shoved it on his head, then looked her way. "We saw your truck pull up. My brother's expecting you." Ignoring her, he continued back to work.

"Thank you." *Glad you're not interviewing me.* Mandy turned the door knob and let herself in to a wide foyer and closed the door. Curiosity made her look through the glass panel at the dark black cloud working on the ramp. His open shirt flashed a broad, tanned chest. His shirt sleeves were rolled up exposing muscular forearms and biceps. Well-worn jeans covered thick rugged thigh muscles. This image alone was enough to send warmth to her cheeks. There was something exciting yet frightening about this handsome, rugged, yet irritating man. A frown creased her forehead when she caught a glimpse of a beer bottle beside him causing a lump in her throat. She turned away from the window and stepped farther into the foyer. "Mr. McBride?" she called out.

An antique grandfathers clock chimed on the hour, letting her know she was on time. An oak side table with carved ornate legs sat under a large oval mirror along the entrance way. A brass dish held a few coins, a pocket knife and a couple of wrapped red and white mints and a set of keys. Mandy stood in front of the mirror and feathered her bangs and covered the long scar on the left side of her face before turning towards heavy booted footsteps.

A slightly heavier set man with a sparkle in his eyes and a broad sincere smile greeted her. "Miss Riley, welcome to the Triple M Ranch." He extended his hand. "I'm Cole McBride. We spoke on the phone." He released her hand. "Please, come into the den and meet my family." He turned and led the way.

Mandy entered the living room. The high vaulted ceiling with its natural log beams and large antler chandelier with frosted glass lights was impressive. The spacious open concept living room had style, yet still had coziness about it, with its soft brown leather sofa, which was littered with toys. Two matching love seats with colorful toss cushions sat across twin large soft brown, leather rocker recliners. In the center sat a long maple coffee table with a brass horse and rider in the middle and a family Bible beside it. A stack of children's books on the bottom shelf begged to be read. A dark green rocker recliner sat away from the family area and close to the large floor-to-ceiling window. The view was magnificent and for some reason Mandy believed it was *Mr. Dark Cloud's* favorite chair. The home looked clean enough to be healthy, but messy enough to be full of fun.

The stone fireplace was impressive, with its slab of marble for the mantel. Mandy's eyes again caught the younger man through a window working on the ramp. His strong forearm swiped at the perspiration from his brow. He stood and jammed both hands into his front pockets while he inspected his work. Her eyes wandered to his large buckle and below, causing her internal organs to suddenly feel weak. Warm. She forced herself to turn away. She wasn't going there, she was here to work and work only.

The large oversized dining room suite with its double pedestal oak table, matching chairs and detailed carved oak buffet, hutch and side board caught her immediate attention. The workmanship was exquisite and she wondered if by chance, that it might be her grandfather Bailey's design.

"As you can see, the children's stuff is in every corner of the house." Cole chuckled as they left the dining room then pointed to an open door. "That's the play room." He pointed.

Mandy peeked into the bright, spacious and cheery room. Stuffies, dolls, trucks and other toys overflowed the toy box. A game/toy/book shelf stretched from one end of the wall to another interested her and wondered if they had any of her already published books.

They entered an airy, bright, open combination den/games room. A bow window faced west toward a grand view of the mountains beyond the rolling hills. A card table with a chess board on top looked like someone was in the middle of a game. Mandy smiled at a pretty olive-skinned lady in a wheelchair, by a large oak business desk as she approached. Her long dark brown hair was up in a ponytail and her soft brown eyes sparkled with interest. Across from her sat three wide-eyed children on a black leather couch.

"Miss Riley, my wife, Dianne," Cole announced with pride then stepped towards her. "Dianne, meet Amanda Riley." He glanced at the scrap of paper. "Mandy." He nodded.

"Pleased to meet you, Mandy." Dianne leaned forward with a smile and extended her hand.

Mandy accepted it graciously. "My pleasure, Mrs. McBride." She nodded.

"We're not formal here, so please call us Dianne and Cole." Dianne smiled then turned towards their children on the couch. "These are our children Ryan, Crystal, and our youngest, Robert, who we call Bobby."

Mandy glanced at the three children. "Pleasure to meet you all." Each child sat straight and proper on the couch and stared at her with big grins on their clean shiny faces. Cole pushed over a black leather office chair. "Please, have a seat and make yourself comfortable." He nodded then stepped towards a dark leather bar and opened a mini fridge. "Would you like a glass of lemonade?"

"That would be lovely, thank you." Mandy turned to the two youngest children who were waving their hands in the air. Ryan, being older and more reserved, nodded to his father.

"Be patient you two, you'll get some." From a silver tray, Cole handed Mandy a frosted glass filled with fresh lemonade, a few ice cubes and a twist of lemon, then handed the children theirs. "I realize how difficult it is to be sitting with all of us, so I'll start." He handed his wife a tall glass, pushed a few papers to the center of the oak desk and perched himself on top of it. "My wife and I need someone to assist with the children." His hand reached over and touched Dianne with affection. "A couple days ago, Dianne fell off her horse and broke her right leg and twisted the other badly. That's six weeks in a cast and probably another six for therapy." He twisted his mouth with concern then and took a sip of lemonade. "With it still being May, there's still a lot of spring chores to do. Branding, vaccination… we can get into that later." Cole chuckled. "Of course, there's always paper work, which everyone hates doing. I personally would rather shovel shit." He laughed.

Dianne softly took over the conversation. "Which leads us to where you come in. Ryan is nine and in grade four."

Mandy turned to Ryan who was the spitting image of his father with short dark hair and dark complexion. Earphones draped around his neck with an MP3 player in his hand and a case clipped to his belt. "Hello, Ryan it's a pleasure to meet you."

"Hello, Miss Riley," the handsome boy said with maturity.

"Crystal is seven and in grade two," Dianne continued.

Mandy's eyes shifted to the middle child. Her blue, cotton

dress covered her crossed legs. A light blue ribbon already hung down, tying her long blonde hair into a ponytail. Two missing front teeth and a mischievous grin told Mandy she'd be one busy Nanny. "Hello, Crystal." Mandy smiled as the girl wiggled her fingers at her.

"This is Bobby, our youngest. He's two and a half," Dianne added proudly.

Mandy shifted her eyes to the youngest. A little bulldozer she thought and had to stifle a giggle at how his neatly combed dark hair looked out of place. She wondered how on earth Dianne got him to stand still long enough to brush it. His feet were never still and wiggled from side to side. His chubby fingers wrapped around a one-eyed, floppy eared teddy bear and his pockets were filled with bits of string and leather. "Hello, Bobby."

"He's doing very well with his potty training and now only wears pull-ups at night." Dianne winked at her son. "Remember to tell us if you have to go potty."

"Me don't go yet," Bobby hollered out with a grin.

"We need a live-in Nanny…" Cole nodded, "…for the children and to help Dianne out. The kids are starting summer vacation in nineteen days." He chuckled and raised his dark brows. "We're counting. The kids in this area are out mid-June. Anyway, living on a ranch is a full-time job, so I'll be around as much as I can, but I have my work to do. As you know the job is only for twelve weeks. Then again we don't know."

"That's fine," Mandy assured them. "I'm only looking for part-time work right now. My parents were ranchers in Utah and I remember the chores we did, so I understand the work involved on a ranch. We lived there until we came to Calgary eight years ago." She watched two sets of eyebrows shoot up with interest.

"Bonus," Cole said with enthusiasm and slid off the desk.

"Your understanding of ranch life is a real plus. We've never had a nanny before, ah..." he shrugged. "...I don't really know what to tell you, except we need someone to help out."

Mandy realized the interest in her had shot up to a hundred percent. "I brought my resume with me." She opened her purse and handed him a white envelope. "And references."

He reached over and took it with enthusiasm. "Thank you."

Dianne leaned forward. Her eyes wide with interest. "Like Cole said, we need help. I can't bath and dress Bobby and at times Crystal needs help with her hair. Ryan can pretty much do for himself." Dianne turned to the two youngest who were giggling and poking each other. "Hey, Crystal, Bobby, please, sit still and listen."

Bobby's fat little fists dug into his dimpled cheeks as he squealed. "Crysil ticky me, Mommy." He stood up and jumped on the couch.

Mandy tried to control a chuckle but failed, when Dianne started to laugh.

"Ma, I'll take Bobby outside for a while." Ryan got off the couch and took his little brother by the hand. "Nice meeting you, Miss Riley."

"Thank you, Ryan. It was my pleasure."

"Thanks, Son," Cole said. "We won't be long."

The two boys scurried out the door with Bobby hugging his treasures close to his chest.

"We took Ryan and Crystal out of school this afternoon to be part of the interview," Dianne informed. "Now, where was I?" She clicked her tongue. "Oh, yeah, you'll find Ryan a big help after school and during the weekends, but he has chores to do with his dad and can't always be here with me." She shrugged. "What else?" Dianne wiggled her brows. "Oh yes." She chuckled. "Sorry, interviewing is a little nerve-wracking for me. We usually have two cooks, one for here and the other at the cookhouse. Della, who used to cook for the hands, retired so, Betty, who cooks for us and has been here for many years, is now cooking for the ranch hands. Now with me breaking my leg we haven't gotten around to hiring another cook yet, so Betty can get back here. However, we still need a nanny for the children because Cole's had to come home early to help me."

"Uhm, I can help too," Crystal hollered. "I can help with a whole bunch of cooking. Our cook, Betty, says I'm a big help, but I hate cleaning out the barns because there's horse poop and it stinks."

Cole laughed deep and loud with a surprised grunt. "Sweetie, we live on a ranch."

"I know, Daddy and I love it and I love my horse and I love brushing her and feeding her. I take care of her lots, but I still don't like cleaning up horse poop." Crystal frowned. "I still do it, though." She grinned. "While Mommy is in the wheelchair, I can help in the kitchen til she's better." Crystal put her hands on her hips. "And Bobby can sit and watch from his high chair so he won't be a pest."

Dianne laughed softly. "Oh, Sweetheart, you're already a big help to me." Dianne nodded at her daughter then turned to Mandy. "Just to finish off, I'll need you to run to town at times, but the important thing is we need a Nanny."

Cole piped up. "I see here you worked at the new Carlson Memorial Hospital as a private secretary."

"Yes, I worked on the children's ward, under the supervision of Doctor Sean Maguire. He's the head pediatrician there and he also started the library." Mandy shrugged. "It's a big hospital and I miss country living."

"I totally understand." He flipped the page. "You mention reading in the library."

"Two and a half years ago I started a program called, 'Story Time with Friends.' It's a program where I read to the children and their families three times a week after supper in the hospital library. The parents and their children have told me they found it relaxing, so I found someone to replace me before I left. Anyway, all I can promise you, if I get the position here, I will do my best."

"That's all we ask," Dianne said and looked at Cole as her eyes flashed with eagerness. "We'd like you to take the job."

A quick sharp rap on the den door caused Mandy to turn and watch tall, handsome, 'Mr. Dark Cloud' enter.

"Uncle Adam." Crystal scurried off the couch, raced over to her uncle and bounded into his arms. "Miss Riley is going to be our new Nanny." Her voice bubbled over.

"That's nice, Honey," he said, his voice low and soothing as he kissed her forehead.

Crystal patted his shirt pocket. "Ohh, you got mints." She peeked into his pocket. "Can I have one, Uncle Adam?"

"Of course." He knelt down and put his hand into his pocket and unwrapped a white and red striped candy. "Here." He stuffed the wrapper into his pocket. "Now, go over and help your Mom and Dad and I'll see you later."

Mandy studied the relationship between the powerful man and the little child. His broad smile was sincere and his eyes twinkled with love and tenderness.

"Thanks, Uncle Adam," Crystal hollered, raced back to the couch and plunked herself down. "See, Mommy." She took the mint from her mouth and held it up in between her index finger and thumb, then popped it back into her mouth.

"Uncle Adam spoils you." Dianne reached over and patted the little girl on the knee.

Well, it seemed that the dark cloud had a silver lining, Mandy thought for a second before he glanced back at her with a cold, dark, untrusting look, giving her a reason to believe her presence was not welcome on the ranch. Why would he regret her being here? She turned away.

"Cole, the new hired hand is here, so whenever you're finished, come to the bunkhouse."

Mandy sensed a friction between the two brothers. An uncomfortable silence after the door was shut fell over the room.

"Excuse my brother." Cole shook his head. "Adam's a good man, but he's been out of sorts lately and doesn't particularly like outsiders." Cole slapped his hand on his leg as he got off the desk. "Anyway, if you take the job we'll pay six hundred a week, plus room and all the food you can eat. The catch is, we can only give you Sundays off." Cole flipped his hand palm out, then rested it on his upper thigh, suggesting an apology for not being able to give her more time off.

"Oh, that sounds fair. Thank you." Mandy nodded. "When would you like me to start?"

"Now," Cole and Dianne said in unison.

Mandy smiled. "All I need is to collect my clothing and personal items then I can come back after supper. If you'd like me to."

Dianne clasped her hands together. "That would be awesome. And another thing, Mandy, do you still ride?"

"It's been a while."

"Would you like to get back into the saddle?" Dianne asked.

"Well..." she paused, "...yes."

"Usually on Saturdays we pack a picnic lunch and ride to the south pasture. The kids enjoy it, so if possible, I want those Saturdays to continue. Cole will pick out a nice mare for you and it will be yours for as long as you're here."

The anticipation was all too exciting, but Mandy wondered how well she'd do after eight long years. "Thank you."

"You're welcome. Now, on Sundays we try to get to church, but sometimes it's just not possible."

"God loves us anyway," Crystal shouted out loud and clear.

"That's right, Honey, He does." Dianne smiled at her daughter then focused back to Mandy. "We are quite open with our faith."

Mandy was pleased she was with a family who believed. She smiled at Crystal.

Cole stood up. "Well, we'll let you go home and get packed, and I'll have your room ready by the time you return,"

"I should be back by seven o'clock." Mandy gathered her purse and rose.

"Can I call you Mandy?" Crystal spoke up.

"No, Crystal," Dianne said. "You're to address her as Miss Riley, please."

"Oh, okay." Crystal giggled. "I'm glad you're going to be our Nanny, Miss Riley."

"Thank you, Crystal. I'm glad, too." She glanced at Dianne, smiled and nodded, then followed Cole out to the front porch.

"Just walk in the house, Mandy, in case I'm busy with the kids," Cole instructed.

The grandfather clock chimed a full-length tune telling everyone that an hour had passed, surprising Mandy how quickly the interview had gone. "Lovely chimes."

"Yes, they are. It's been in the family for three generations now."

"Thank you again, Cole." With her spirits lifted, she unconsciously pushed her hair all the way up and back, exposing her long thin white scar. "I'll see you at seven."

A chill raced up her spine as if someone was watching her. She turned as Adam walked up the steps. Their eyes met and held steady until he bent down to pick up the red tool box. He was the most rugged, good-looking, heart throb of a man she had ever seen. His tanned, flawless complexion and perfect features for some reason terrified her. Consciously, she quickly combed the left side of her hair forward and fluffed up her bangs with her fingers. *Did he see my scar?* Not wanting to see any facial reaction on his face, if he did notice, she nervously glanced away and focused on the finished wheelchair ramp.

"Accept the position?" he questioned with a low tone.

His body was so close, she felt small. Her stomach knotted. His face dark and unyielding. "Yes, Sir, I did." Cole had told her he was a good man, but then he was his brother. When his eyes cruised her body from head to toe a second time before he walked away, it made her feel uneasy.

Aware her limp was noticeable because of sheer nervousness, Mandy walked to her truck as casually as she could. Driving away, she glanced into the rear-view mirror to see Adam watching. Maybe this wasn't a good place to work.

CHAPTER 2

*T*he Triple M was going to see some changes in the next twelve weeks. Adam shoved the red tool box into the back of his silver, three-quarter ton, Dodge Ram. "Damn it, Cole, you know I'd help you and Dianne out. We don't need outsiders," he grumbled as his thoughts turned to the pretty, graceful Miss Riley. He rubbed his forehead as if he wanted to erase her from his mind. He had enough of women. They all wanted something from him, especially those city gals. They were all infatuated with the idea of a cowboy or rancher, but they didn't have a clue what they were made of.

Adam's dream of having a wife and children of his own had been shattered. Women like Libby and Nina weren't in love with him. They were in love with whom he represented. The romantic West. A fantasy of times past and present. Women like that were in love with an idea. Because of women like that, trust and love were no longer in Adam's vocabulary.

Adam was one of the most eligible bachelors in Alberta and his phone never stopped ringing. He hated it with a passion. He wanted one honest good woman. One who would love what he loved and that was ranching. One who wanted to know him for who he is.

Turning twenty-nine last month, he wanted what his father had, and his brother, Cole, had now. A strong loving relationship with a woman he could share ideas with, have fun, laugh together and yes, even argue with and make up later. Would he ever have that or, was he just a lonely rancher. A lone cowboy who loves his horse, the trail rides, the night watch and the midnight campfire with other loners.

Adam's mind spun back to Miss Riley. She was beautiful with her soft oval face, cream-colored complexion, baby blue eyes and long honey-blonde hair. Her shyness and gentle voice intrigued him as he remembered the soft fragrance when he walked past her. She seemed different from any of the women he had gone out with. Miss Riley's nails were neatly trimmed and natural and she didn't wear makeup or eye shadow. Her long hair looked soft and untouched from dyes or tints and her pretty pink, full lips were innocent of lipstick.

Adam shook his head and walked towards the house to get Cole, so they could finish the interview with the new ranch hand. *Looks can be deceiving*. He picked up the empty beer bottle from the front porch steps, along with his favorite, extra-large to-go-mug. His favorite, one-of-a-kind thermo-mug, with the green frog on it and a sturdy twist on lid and a thick, solid handle. The mug only he used when he worked around the house and barn. He entered the kitchen, rinsed his special mug, and poured himself a fresh, strong, black coffee.

Warm laughter from the den, just beyond the kitchen and on the other side of the dining room, irritated his eardrums. He followed it, then stood in the doorway and leaned against the door jamb with his legs crossed at the ankles. He watched the enthusiasm from his family bounce off the walls.

"Adam, come join us." Cole jerked his head towards one of the leather chairs. "Relax a bit."

"No thanks." He took a sip of the hot black brew. "Have you forgotten we have to interview the new fellah?" Adam pushed away from the door jamb and headed down the hallway towards the front door. He stilled when Cole called to him.

"Adam, you know Dianne and I need someone to help us with the children."

Adam backed up a few steps and turned to face his brother. "No, you don't. I told you I was more than willing to help you both with the chores and the kids." He grunted then took a swig of coffee. "You don't need a Nanny. You need Betty back at the house and a new cook for the hands."

"Well, she's hired. Mandy is a lovely person and the children were just saying how much they like her already. We'll deal with a cook later."

"Fine. I'm happy for you," he snapped as he saluted with his mug in hand. "Just don't expect me to help her when she needs anything. Guaranteed, that little city gal will ask me for something." He turned abruptly and walked away. "I've got things to do in town, so let's get this interview done with." He picked up his truck keys, the pocket knife, a few coins, and a couple of mints from the brass dish that sat on the oak foyer table.

RYAN TUGGED on his dad's shirt sleeve. "Doesn't Uncle Adam like Miss Riley?"

Cole turned. "You three go and play for a few minutes, I want to talk to your mother."

Ryan held back. "Well?"

"Well what?" Cole shrugged.

"Doesn't Uncle Adam like Miss Riley?" Ryan stepped forward.

"I'm sure he does, but right now Uncle Adam has a lot on his mind and just has to get to know her." Cole glanced towards Dianne then back to Ryan. "Go on outside and finish your chores."

"Okay, Pa."

Cole watched his son leave. "Our son is growing up too darn fast." He turned to his wife. "I wish Adam would get over the failed relationships of his. He used to confide in me, now he's so peeved and distant all the time. To top it all off, I think he's drinking."

"Oh no, just hold on minute, Cole," Dianne said defensively. "Yes, Adam has some serious issues with his exes and he's not taking it well. In fact, he's hurting. I don't know what the problem is, but, I know he will come to you when he feels the need to, because he loves you. Give him time and when he comes to you, be there for him. As far as the drinking, I don't agree. I know he likes a few drinks occasionally with the men, but, he isn't drinking any more than you or your dad are."

Cole nodded. "Okay, I hope you're right. Oh, and between you and me our head foreman, Chuck, told me the other day he's worried about him. He knows he's trying to help his friend Hank with his drinking problem, but he can't understand why he's working himself to death. He's not delegating out the workload anymore and he's trying to do it all himself."

"Like I said." Dianne rolled her wheelchair away from the desk. "He's got issues to work out and the only way Adam knows how to do that is to sweat it out."

Cole shrugged. "I understand sweating out serious issues, but helping Hank out, he's got to realize he's a rancher not a counsellor."

"Give him time."

Cole smiled. "I don't wish Mandy on him, but maybe he'll realize not all women are like his exes. He should know better. Mom was the most gentle, loving lady ever and they had a special mother and son bond and losing her affected him deeply. I understand, because I loved her, too." Cole plunked himself down on the couch. "And he loves and respects you too, Dianne, so just because he had a couple bad experiences shouldn't turn him against all women."

"Cole, it's only been a month since he broke off with his last girlfriend. Remember, he's hurting and we not only have to keep praying for him we need to be here for him. Whatever happened he has to deal with it, and he'll realize that those women aren't worth making himself sick."

Cole nodded, got up, bent down and kissed her on the mouth. "Mmm." He kissed her again. This time slow, deliberate... and meaningful. "Mmm. Mmm." Reluctantly, Cole straightened. "You're right. That's why I married you." He winked. "I'd better get to the barn before I forget myself." He wiggled his brows.

~

MANDY PASSED various types of saws, wood-working tools, and lengths of assorted hardwood boards to look for her brother. The sweet smell of freshly cut wood shavings enticed her to take in a deep breath as she meandered through the aisles to a dust-free finishing room of her uncle's furniture shop, to where Jason was working.

She opened a hardwood door and closed it. "Jason, I got the job," she hollered with pleasure. "The family's wonderful and want me to start right away. It's only for twelve weeks, but you never know where it may lead." She rattled on about how the interview went, what her job entailed, and her one day off. "Oh, and they're going to give me a horse to ride." She sighed deeply with pleasure.

"Well, Squeak." Jason put down a finishing tool and slipped off his safety glasses. "Good, good for you." He gave her a big bear hug.

She embraced her brother tightly and tighter yet, when he called her Squeak. It was their older brother, Martin, who gave her that nickname when she was a toddler. The name stuck, and after the accident, Jason carried on with it.

"Let's go and have a glass of lemonade before you head back," Jason suggested.

"Okay." Outside, she followed him down a graveled path for several yards, and then past a neatly trimmed hedge which separated the rather large back yard from the shop area. The sidewalk bordered with purple alyssum, led towards a large two-story, soft gray house. There was a small vegetable garden by the fence, a flower garden with a pond, and a fountain in front of a graceful weeping willow. As they chatted they walked up the steps to a large open deck overlooking the yard.

"Sit and relax while I get the refreshments." Jason pointed to a deck chair.

Mandy sat down in one of the wooden deck chairs their uncle had made and gazed over the garden and watched the birds flutter from the feeders to the tree branches. It had been their home for eight years, and the yard had matured just as they had. Love had a way of making all things beautiful.

Jason returned with the lemonade in two tall glasses filled with ice cubes. Her eyes skimmed over the wide, long, white, jagged scar on his right forearm which seemed to show up much more in the summer months. She thought how fortunate she was that Jason hadn't been killed in the accident with their other brother and parents. Jason tried to hide the scar, but as he grew older, he accepted it.

"Do you think you'll be able to finish your children's book?" Jason asked as he took a seat.

"I'm sure when the children are in bed." She took a sip. "Mmm, this is so good. Anyway, the younger McBride acts like a rebel and I don't think he wants me around." She shrugged. "Oh well, the rest of the family's wonderful and they're anxious to have me come back as soon as I can."

"What do you mean he doesn't want you around? He's not going to be a problem for you, is he?"

"Oh, he's just different from the rest of the family." Mandy recognized the concern in her brothers face and wished she hadn't said anything. Throughout the years, she had relied on him more often than she cared to admit. And now, he was too protective. Jason would want to meet him and the family if she didn't change the subject pretty darn fast. "I can hardly wait to see the horse they picked out for me."

"This rebel type person…"

Mandy knew her brother wasn't going to drop the subject so interrupted him. "I'm not working for him." She sipped her drink.

"Maybe you should have stayed at the hospital."

Mandy shook her head. "I liked my secretary job and working with Doctor Maguire, but I need a change. Like we've talked about, I'm still having difficulty working with large groups of people. It surprises me how many of my co-workers and other staff members continue to ask about my injuries. Maybe it's because I was a patient at the old hospital, and the older staff that used to work there, before they transferred to the new one, remembered me and that we were from Utah and the tragedy of it all." She shrugged. "I know they ask because they care, and they like me."

Jason nodded in agreement.

Mandy flipped her hands over then placed them flat on

the table. "Not only that, when I sit for too long, my leg gets stiff. I know I need to exercise it more, but sometimes there's just no time. This job here..." she flipped the newspaper laying on the table, "...is perfect and it's on a ranch where I want to be. I can get the exercise I need, fresh air regularly and not to mention I'd be much more comfortable. If it doesn't work, I'll come back to my old job with you and Uncle Richard."

"Uncle Richard didn't want you to leave in the first place."

"I know. Jason, I want this job, and I really like these people. Oh, they'll probably be the same as everyone else and ask a dozen questions, but at least I'll only have to tell them once, and then they won't have to ask anymore." She stroked her temple to calm herself. "I think this is for me."

"I know, Squeak, and I understand. You know the problem I had when we first came here and I hated it when people stared at my arm. I've accepted it, and there's still times when I'm conscious about it. Especially when, well..." Jason looked down at the long jagged raised scar and traced it with three of his fingers from his elbow to his wrist, "...I know it's harder for you." He gazed at his sister with unconditional love. She meant everything to him. "Ohh... I wish we had a ranch now. All these years, you and I have been saving up for our own dream ranch and it isn't coming fast enough. I wish we could go back to Utah where we grew up," he grunted.

Mandy knew Jason missed his past life as much as she did. Maybe more so. "It sure would, but I don't think I'd go back. I like Canada and I can hardly wait to start our ranch right here in Southern Alberta." A smile crossed her face.

"Yeah, you're right, there's no one left back there anyway. Besides, I wouldn't want to be too far away from Uncle Richard and Aunt Maggie who have been our parents for the past eight years now. And let's not forget all the friends we've made." He sighed. "In some ways, I can't believe how fast time has flown by."

"I know how you feel." She leaned back and put her feet on the wooden stool. Her mind wandered over the past eight years. Some of it was tough. Especially the first year. Tears, pain, separation, dealing with the tragic loss of their parents and their brother, Martin. Living in a big city and having to listen to the noise and the stench of city life. But the love they received from Aunt Maggie and Uncle Richard was unconditional. The physical pain diminished as laughter replaced tears. The love of her aunt and uncle became strong, after she realized they had also lost loved ones, allowing the family to become one. Laughter, hugs, family picnics, Uncle Richard helping with homework, Aunty Maggie's fresh baked cookies after school. It was such a different life, yet the love they all shared bonded them.

"You know, Squeak." Jason placed his elbows on the table. "We probably have just about enough money between us to purchase a small spread."

Mandy took her feet off the stool and leaned forward. "We should tell Uncle Richard about our plans so he can advise us."

"For sure." He smiled. "Mentally calculating our investments Mom and Dad left us, and the money we've saved together, we could buy a piece of land with a small house on it. It would be tight, but we could get a mortgage. We've got good credit that we've built up over the years and I take in a damn good income with Uncle Richard's furniture shop and business. Your involvement in the business with your youth furniture design has brought in a good dollar and your book money is great. Hey, we can't lose."

"Jason, I don't care how small the place is. I just want to get out of the city and get our dream ranch started." She circled the rim of her glass with her finger. "Uncle Richard never kept it a secret that Dad and Mom had left an inheritance and he's always shared that there were provisions made, so he and Aunt Maggie could raise us comfortably and give us our education. And he's told us from time to time that he's invested the money for us so we should talk to him."

"Get settled in your new job and we'll talk to him later, together."

"Okay, well, I have to get packed and I want to talk with Aunty Maggie before I go. Where's Uncle Richard?"

"He's out on a delivery, but he'll be home before you go."

DURING AN EARLY SUPPER, Amanda repeated everything she had told Jason to her aunt and uncle. During a quiet break, she studied her family. Aunt Maggie, a calm quiet, gentle lady was always easy to talk to. Her soft brown eyes twinkled with fun and her smile was genuine and her heart was as big as Alberta itself. She reminded her so much of their real mother. She turned to watch her Uncle Richard who resembled his older brother, their father, Steven Riley. His dark hair, with a touch of gray at the sides, made him look distinguished. He was a serious business man and a good provider. A big man, six foot, two inches, with a good sense of humor, a cleft in his chin and a sparkle in his blue eyes and was quick to laugh.

She glanced at her twin. He was built like their father. His plus six foot two, large frame and broad chest, muscled arms and large hands were the physical characteristics of the Rileys'. Jason also had their confidence. He had a sense of humor, at times, but was much more serious in nature than their father or uncle. His deep blue eyes were intriguing and almost mesmerizing.

"I need a lift to the ranch."

"I'll drive you," Jason piped up.

"Hold on, Jason, Amanda can take my truck," Richard said

and looked at his niece. "It's always nice to have your own vehicle for the first week. It's a security thing."

"Squeak, we don't need our truck this week either," Jason said and stuffed a cookie into his mouth.

"Son, yes, you do." Richard looked directly at Jason. "I changed the delivery schedule just half an hour ago." He chuckled. "You have a couple deliveries on Tuesday and one on Thursday. Sorry, when Amanda started to tell us her news, it slipped my mind." He turned back to his niece. "So, take mine." He took a cookie from the plate.

"Okay, I'll take it." She gave Jason a sassy grin. "My turn to drive Uncle Richard's new truck." She laughed when Jason rolled his eyes.

A half hour later, Amanda threw her back pack and suitcase into her uncle's brand-new red GMC, three-quarter ton, diesel with extra chrome. She kissed and hugged everyone, then jumped into the driver's seat and buckled up. A small tear trickled down her cheek as she waved goodbye to her family. A glance in the rear-view mirror confirmed they were all standing in the driveway waving and watching her leave.

CHAPTER 3

*A*dam watched from the front porch as an unfamiliar truck drove into the driveway and parked by the other family vehicles at the side of the house. "Crap. Company." He sighed and sat straight up in his large wooden deck chair. His jaw dropped when Miss Riley got out, walked to the back, unlatched the tailgate and gathered her luggage and flipped the tailgate up again with absolutely no effort. He watched her as she walked up the steps to the porch with her purse and duffel bag over her shoulder and a wheeled suitcase towed behind her. She didn't have a lot of luggage, but it was enough. Enough to tell him that she was staying for a while.

He couldn't stop his eyes from cruising over her slender body. The pink, cotton sleeveless top she wore brought out the gentle blush of her cheeks when she spotted him staring at her. Adam had to admit, she was a pretty little thing with her crystal blue eyes, dark long lashes, natural-looking long, dark honey-blonde hair and fair skin. Her slim figure and trim hips and what looked like perfect breasts underneath the soft cotton fabric would turn any man's head. She had turned his and he didn't like it one damn bit.

Being a McBride, he stood up and walked towards the door to open it for her. Being close, he inhaled the light fragrance of her perfume. It teased his senses and played havoc with his body. Awareness hit him like a brick when his hand accidentally brushed against the soft bare skin of her shoulder.

"Thank you, Mr. McBride." She smiled quickly, as she adjusted her shoulder bag, and entered the house.

Her voice was soft and gentle. Angel-like. Adam could have listened to it for hours, but he wasn't about to continue the conversation because he liked the sound of her voice. Correction, he loved the sound of her voice. "Don't mention it," he said sharply, closed the door and went back to his chair and banged his fist on the arm rest. "Why Cole?" he grumbled under his breath wishing his brother hadn't hired her. He touched his hand that had brushed against her soft bare shoulder when he opened the door. It annoyed him that his body had reacted to the simple touch.

He turned to look at the brand new pimped-up truck she drove. The chrome itself would make any other man drool, but not him. It made him curious. It was a truck for a hardworking man with a few bucks in his pocket. It didn't fit a Nanny, yet she handled it like a pro, not to mention she looked confident in it. The truck was pricy, so why would she need a nanny job? Something didn't fit and something was definitely wrong here.

Adam got up, threw the rest of his coffee over the railing into the flower garden and headed towards the bunkhouse to talk to the new hired hand, who he figured would be settled in by now. He had too much to do on the ranch to think about little Miss city gal. City women were trouble with a capital T. "Just stay out of my way," he grumbled out-loud. He was thankful it was the end of May and the ranch was busy with branding, castrating and vaccinations. There would be no time to think about a woman.

Especially the stunning, soft-spoken, pretty blue-eyed, Miss Riley.

~

As MANDY STOOD in the hallway, she listened to the thud of Adam's cowboy boots on the wooden porch. Sweet memories spun in her head of her own family home in Utah, where everyone in the family owned a pair. She longed for those times back. Present day thoughts returned to Adam McBride and even though she was not pleased with the way he studied her, watched her, and undressed her with his eyes, there was something thrilling about him. Something made her body come alive when he strolled towards her. His tanned muscular arms, his shirt half-undone, exposed rich dark chest hairs, sent tingles of awareness up her spine. She couldn't stop her own eyes from wandering to his waist and hips. Faded jeans fit perfectly against the hard muscles of his thighs. A hint of male aftershave with male sweat from a hard day's work lingered long after she entered the house. Giving herself a mental shake, she walked through the living room and called out. "Cole, Dianne, I'm here."

"You came back?" Ryan pushed past his father to greet her. "I'm glad you did."

"Thank you, Ryan, I'm happy to be here."

"Let me help you." Cole reached for her luggage. "Your room's ready. Ryan and I moved our belongings to the guest room on the main floor the other day because of Dianne's wheelchair. We prepared our bedroom for you so you'll be closer to the children."

Mandy followed as they passed the den and toy room then headed up the highly polished, circular, hardwood staircase to the second floor.

Cole pushed open the door and put her suitcase beside the bed then made a sweeping motion with his arm. "I hope you'll be comfortable. If you need anything, just ask."

Mandy glanced around the spacious bedroom with awe. One wall papered with tiny blue flowers pleased her. A private bath to her left was a plus, along with a walk-in closet that had ample room for a whole family let alone two people. A beautiful handmade quilt of a black stallion spread across the four-poster king-size bed. The fine tiny stitches showed tender loving care, had been put into the beautiful heirloom. Matching bedside tables, a large dresser and vanity were all cleared for her use. An old-fashioned restored roll top desk caught her eye. "Thank you." She smiled. "I'm sure it will be just fine."

"Can I stay and help you unpack, Miss Riley?" Ryan asked with enthusiasm.

"You sure can." She turned to Cole. "May I use that desk?" She pointed towards it.

"By all means." He smiled then looked at his son. "Let Miss Riley settle by herself."

"Oh, I don't mind," Mandy piped up. "It will give us a chance to talk." She gave Ryan a big smile and handed him her back pack.

"Okay, Ryan, just don't frighten her away." Cole chuckled.

"Oh, Pa."

A half hour later, Mandy had everything organized and her manuscript, laptop, pencils and paper on the old-fashioned desk. She followed Ryan into the hallway where family pictures covered every inch of the wall.

"This is Uncle Adam's room." Ryan hit the half-opened door with his knuckles.

She glanced into the room directly across from hers. "Wow, it's huge and sure is neat," she said without hesitation.

"Yeah," Ryan answered. "Uncle Adam's a neat freak. He

doesn't mind if you go in, and you can borrow anything as long as you put things back. Cause, he gets mad if you don't." Ryan raced to the next room.

I won't be borrowing anything. Mandy followed Ryan.

"This is Bobby's room. Sometimes he lives like a pig, but we cleaned it up before you came back. It was a lot of work."

Mandy chuckled. The little boy's room had a freshly clean look about it. "We'll try and keep it neat for him." She watched Ryan dash across the hallway.

"This is Crystal's." Ryan crossed his eyes and stuck out his tongue sideways. "It's a puke pink color, but she tries to keep it neat." He pointed then darted to the end bedroom. "My room's the best." He waved for her to hurry.

Before following, Mandy quickly peeked into Crystal's room. Soft pink walls, a white and pink bed spread and pillow sham, a cowgirl hat on the dresser, and horse posters plastered the walls. A real mixture of femininity and a Tom-boy which reminded her of her bedroom back home on the family ranch.

She entered Ryan's room where everything was organized for a boy his age. "Just like your Uncle Adam's and it's very nice, Ryan."

"Yeah, I guess I am a bit of a neat freak, too." Ryan laughed and his hand swept in-front of him.

Melanie focused on the wagon wheel lamp which was the main accent, on top of his dresser. Several horse shoes were nailed to the wall with different colored bandanas draping over some. Of course, typical electronic games for his generation sat on the desk plugged in and ready to use. "That covered wagon lamp looks familiar." She studied the unique fixture.

"There's only two like it. Grandpa McBride made them. There's lots that are similar in gift shops all over Calgary, but not like these," he said with pride. "I've got one and Uncle Adam has the other."

"Oh." She felt her cheeks grow hot. How could she have forgotten from one room to another? "Yes. It's very nice." She placed her fingers on the bridge of her nose and sighed quietly.

"Grandpa's room is just across the hallway. I have trouble sleeping sometimes. I don't know why, I just do. Occasionally Grandpa and I sneak downstairs for hot chocolate at night after everyone goes to bed. He told me that when he was young, he had trouble sleeping, too. He told me, it was because we have big brains and they work overtime. That's why we stay awake."

Mandy smiled at the very informative young boy.

"We had better get downstairs and talk to my mom." Ryan raced down the hall. "That's the kids bathroom," he hollered and pointed. "All the adults have their own, but the kids have to share."

Mandy peeked into the clean bathroom that the three children shared. A variety of towels were hung separately on towel racks. She could tell by the color and pattern which child they belonged to. As Mandy passed Adam's room, she glanced in. There it was, the matching chuck wagon lamp on top of his solid wood maple dresser. She left quickly. It would be her luck for Adam to catch her peeking in his room.

Down in the living room, Cole got off the soft brown leather love seat as Mandy entered and motioned for her to join the family. "I'd like you to meet my father, John McBride, Pa, Amanda Riley. Mandy for short." She watched the senior McBride get up from the large soft brown leather rocker recliner and step forward.

The family resemblance between the men in the family was uncanny. John McBride was a big man with rugged features. His hair still dark with gray at the temples. His barrel chest and arms stretched the fabric of his brown plaid shirt. The only difference between him and his sons besides his age, was his waist was thicker and the permanent lines around his eyes gave him a wise look which his sons had yet to develop. His eyes twinkled with sincerity and his smile could charm a grizzly, she thought with a grin.

"Welcome, Amanda, it's a great pleasure to meet you." He offered his hand.

"My pleasure, Sir." Mandy took his hand firmly and gave him her best smile. He made her feel welcome, just as the others did. She liked him. A slight movement by the long window on the other side of the fireplace, caused her to glance over for a brief second. Just long enough to catch Adam watching her. Tingles of apprehension boiled in her stomach. Again.

"Miss Riley, you said you liked reading, so could you read us a story?" Crystal handed her a book.

"Let Miss Riley relax tonight," Dianne suggested.

"Really, I don't mind." Mandy sat down on the matching soft brown rocker recliner next to John. At that moment, Crystal climbed up onto her knee, just as she saw Bobby come racing over wanting the other. Being a big boy for his age, his chunky frame, with his yellow t-shirt, reminded her of the big yellow bulldozer her brother Jason had when he was little. Her left leg wouldn't take the pressure for too long. "Why don't we sit by the hearth in a circle while I read." She gently nudged the children off her lap and stood up and stepped towards the fireplace.

"Gee whiz, Crystal, do we have to listen to your silly Cinderella book again?" Ryan threw up his hands and crossed his eyes. "Let, Miss Riley, read Call of the Wild, Treasure Island, or Robin Hood."

"What other type of books do you like, Ryan?" Mandy turned her attention to the frowning boy as she made herself comfortable and sat cross-legged on the floor.

"My favorite books are about the north country by Jack London. But I like super hero adventure books, too. And books about different times and places."

"How about we read one of your books tomorrow evening since Crystal has this one now, and then Bobby next. We'll rotate."

Ryan twisted his mouth into an agreeable grin and clicked his tongue. "Sounds fair, I guess." He settled down on the floor beside his sister then quickly moved over as his little brother shoved his thumb into his mouth, then plopped himself right in between them.

As the story went on, the children listened with great interest. Mandy knew she could hold their attention even if it had been the daily newspaper.

ADAM LEANED BACK in his green velvet recliner, that stood alone by the window on the other side of the fireplace and stared at the stunning Miss Riley. Her voice was captivating, like songbirds in the morning. Sweet, soft and gentle. Everything in the room became silent. The clock on the wall didn't tick as loud and the radio had somehow turned itself off. His family seemed to be in a trance while she read. Her mouth formed each word perfectly and the tone of her voice whisked his family into the story book.

The desire to kiss her mouth, to touch her soft peaches-and-cream cheeks surprised him. He wanted to caress her slender neck with his mouth. His body reacted when his eyes fell upon her chest. He imagined her soft breasts close to him as she took in quiet breaths, making them move underneath the soft silky blouse she had changed into.

He licked his lips and swallowed hard. His jeans became tight at just the sight of her, to the point he couldn't get out of his chair and run. He couldn't, or wouldn't, embarrass himself. *What the hell's the matter with me?* He rubbed his forehead to desperately try to get control over himself and to get this city gal out of his mind. He didn't want to get to know her. Didn't want her around. She was a stranger in his home.

Soft clapping and praises brought him back to reality. *What's going on?* He jerked his head towards the grandfather clock. Was the story finished? "Five after nine," he muttered in surprise. He hadn't heard the chimes go off.

"Amanda," John McBride said. "I've never, in my entire life, heard Cinderella read with such passion. You read beautifully, and I for one can hardly wait until tomorrow evening."

"Thank you, Mr. McBride." Mandy smiled.

"Please, call me John."

Adam watched her interact with everyone. He felt his jaw tighten when his father made a fuss over a silly story and every one of his family agreed. This woman had been in his home for less than three hours and already won their hearts. He watched her eyes sparkle with delight over his family's compliments. A soft pink washed over her delicate cheeks.

"Adam." Cole gave Adam a brotherly whack on the back. "What's your opinion on having a story hour every night?" Cole asked sincerely.

He shrugged and stood up, ignoring the question. "I've got night checks to do." His head turned to Mandy's angelic voice, as she spoke to the children and told them she was going outside for a moment, so they could spend a few minutes with their parents before going to bed. He watched her get up off the floor. Slowly and carefully. Her chin tilted slightly, her eyes focused forward, as if she wanted to ignore him while she headed towards the front foyer. He grunted to himself, shook his head slightly, and headed towards the same door several feet behind her.

Adam closed the front door just as Mandy reached for the handrail and walked down the steps. The motion yard light turned her hair golden as the glow of the soft yellow light hallowed around her. His eyes focused on her slender legs. There was something not right in her walk. He studied her gait and noticed that she favored her left leg. Although slight and hardly noticeable, there was a limp. He sauntered over to his favorite chair and sat down and closed his eyes.

A sweet fragrance surrounded him as he inhaled deeply. He realized the western breeze from the mountain had caught her scent and softly brought it directly to where he was sitting. The thought of her soft warm body cuddled next him crossed his mind. The heavenly fragrance she wore continued to caress his senses, causing havoc to his body. Adam opened his eyes quickly. He didn't want to start fantasizing over the pretty little filly who was only ten yards away. It was best to ignore her any way he could, even as he inhaled her scent that gently fenced him in.

SITTING TOO LONG on the floor spelled trouble. Mandy rubbed the top of her thigh to ease out the ache, then walked the length of the garden and back. Eyes bored into her back as she prayed he wouldn't notice her limp, but reality was, Adam would notice. She believed nothing would escape him. Then again, with the sun already behind the mountains and the yard light being a soft yellow, there'd be slight chance he hadn't noticed. Nevertheless, if he didn't see it by now, he would in time. Mandy knew her slender frame gave her a fragile look and it would probably irritate Adam, having a gimp on the ranch.

Adam McBride would be the type of man who wanted a stronger, more capable woman. One who could handle anything from hauling bales of hay, to cooking up a storm. She knew women like that. They were strong and competent, yet beautiful and feminine. She imagined how beautiful his women friends were. A man, especially like Adam, would have someone who would complement his strength and good looks.

She found herself contemplating how she could impress him. Win him over. She could still ride a horse and after a few days of practice, she'd be fine. In time he'd find out she was a hard worker and quite the rancher herself. However, she'd always have her limits.

$\sim$

FIVE A.M. came all too soon, yet Mandy remembered getting up early with her family back home, but with living in the city for the past eight years, seven o'clock was now the norm for her. She threw the covers back, got up and did her morning leg exercises before her shower. After putting on her jeans and a light blue t-shirt, she was ready for the day. Passing the mirror, she quickly arranged her hair so it would hide the scar then fluffed up her delicate bangs.

In the kitchen, she found a kettle, filled it with water and turned on the stove. Searching the cupboards, she found a box of green tea and a variety of mugs and tea cups. An extremely large strong plastic, happy-faced, green frog, to-go-mug caught her attention. Liking frogs, she smiled at the huge mug then twisted off the lid. "Mmm, awesome. I won't have to come back for a refill." Not being a true connoisseur of tea, she tossed in a tea bag and filled it with boiling water. While it steeped in the special mug, she looked around the kitchen. She turned to the oak breakfast nook with a padded leather bench seat and the four, stubby leather padded stools.

As she reached over to pick up the green twist-on top, she pictured the family sitting around the nook before the children went to school. A cozy family chat in the morning, planning out the day in front of the large bay window. The kitchen reminded her of home where her mother always had delicious raisin oatmeal cookies for her and her brothers after school while they did their homework. Delicious smells of home-cooked meals and fresh baking was just one of her many memories she'd always cherish.

With the tea ready, she plucked out the tea bag and screwed on the lid. The day began with a lovey large mug of delicious green tea. She grabbed the thick sturdy handle, raised the mug to her eye level and smile at the frog face.

Outside, she turned to the west and gazed up at the majestic peaks of the Rocky Mountains. The morning was breath-taking. A few quiet peaceful moments surrounded her as she remembered her childhood years. Her eyes focused on several little birds singing in the various shade trees as she scanned the manicured yard with the large oak tree centered in the middle. A picnic table off to the side with a few lawn chairs around it. The basket of wilted flowers, shovel, spade and rake were still under the tree, had been left after Dianne's accident. A chore she would enjoy doing.

The front door opened and shut. Mandy turned towards it and watched Adam take in a deep breath as his eyes focused directly at the giant green frog coffee mug she was using. She glanced at the smaller to go mug he had in his large hand and would have bet her first paycheck that she had his personal mug. It took all the willpower she had not to have a good belly laugh over the dwarfed cup in his hand. Her first morning and she had already ticked him off. She looked up towards him. "Good morning, Mr. McBride."

He took in a deep breath and slowly exhaled. "Yeah," he said gruffly and walked down the steps and turned towards the barn.

She'd bet she was sitting in his chair, too.

CHAPTER 4

"*D*amn, an early riser," Adam grumbled as he walked briskly to the barn. "Not only does she use my favorite mug, but she's in my chair to boot. Does she even know what a day's work is like?" He finished his coffee in one gulp and wanted another, but damn if he was going back for a refill to get a glimpse at her lush mouth on his coffee mug and her petite firm body sitting in his chair. He put the little mug down on a bale of hay, just inside of the barn doors, grabbed his chaps off a hook and put them on. He glanced back to the porch as his thoughts flashed to the Nanny's lovely curves, slight frame and long legs. He couldn't help but wonder what sort of men she dated, how old she was, and most importantly, did she have a boyfriend? And, why did she want to be a nanny? His eyes narrowed at the flashy decked-out truck.

He strolled to his horse's stall, stopped and looked at the beer bottle cases in front of the tack room floor from last night's party the men had to welcome the new hand. "Jeez, Hank." He turned and headed towards the corral to retrieve his Dodge Ram. "Clean up your own mess." He got in, flipped the visor for his keys, started it, backed it up to the tack room doorway, stacked the boxes into the back, pushed up the tailgate.

Adam went to the barn to get his horse, Zircon, his sixteen-and-a-half-hands-high, gray stallion which he'd had since he was sixteen years old. The one creature on the ranch he could count on. "You should see that new Nanny, Zircon," he said to his horse as he put the blanket then the saddle on his horse's back. "You didn't hear this from me, but I'd love to feel the texture of her long honey-colored mane." He chuckled as he adjusted the girth then stroked Zircon's neck. "Well, boy, we've got work to do." He took the reins in his hands.

"Hey, Adam, you ready?" head foreman Chuck Larson hollered out. Chuck was a strong man in his mid-forties, with dark blonde hair. A true cowboy who had worked for the McBrides since he was a young kid.

"Yup, I'm ready now. The damn empties weren't put away." Adam secured his rope to the horn of the saddle then mounted as he nodded at Chuck who had been waiting for him on his sixteen-year old, dark gray quarter horse. Zircon's older brother, Diamond.

"Yeah. I'm getting tired of it myself."

Both Adam and Chuck mounted their horses and left to check on the hired hands to see how they were doing. Castration, branding and vaccination began today and it was going to be a long week. It was good to be busy and it would help Adam to keep his mind off of what it was on.

MANDY SAT down for breakfast with everyone in the family except Adam. Did he dislike her that much he'd miss breakfast with his family?

During breakfast, Mandy learned a lot about each member

of the McBride family. John McBride had been a widow for the past three years and still grieved over his wife, Helen. He was a tall, healthy man and still the head honcho. His hands were as big as ham hulks, yet he was a gentle, kind, understanding man, who would give anyone a chance, but also a no-nonsense type. He believed in doing the job well, and demanded the ranch be run properly.

Dianne was thirty and had grown up on a ranch east of Black Gold, a small town an hour west of Calgary. Her two brothers still lived at home with her parents and were well-respected ranchers. Ranching was her life and she thought of nothing else.

Cole, now thirty-two, graduated with honors then went to college to take business, which helped to run the business end of ranching. Adam, she learned, had just turned twenty-nine last month. After graduating from high school, he went to University and took education, majored in geology, and got his degree in teaching. He taught geology for one year, in a junior high school, but missed the ranch life so came home.

After breakfast, Mandy and Dianne sat with the children for a few minutes until it was time to catch the school bus. As the chimes chimed, Ryan and Crystal picked up their back packs and left by the back door. Mandy took Bobby's hand and walked out to watch the two children run across the patio, jump over a planter filled with flowers, slap the wings of a solid, wooden blue jay, to make it spin, then skipped down a graveled path, until they reached the front driveway, then race down the road. A big yellow school bus pulled up and opened the door as Bobby waved bye to his siblings.

Mandy walked with Bobby to the back of the house, where a large sandbox sat on the patio close to the hexagon wooden picnic table with a large green umbrella offering shade. She watched as the little boy moved a plastic log house, from one end of the sand box to another. He jammed a couple plastic horses and a super hero figure in the sand.

Mandy wrapped her arms around her knees as she sat on the little corner seat of the sandbox, and glanced around the yard. From where she sat, she could view a good portion of the front yard. The wilted flowers by the old oak tree made her heart weep. If they weren't planted and watered soon, they'd die. Determined to do something about it, she turned to the little boy. "Want to help plant some flowers for your mom?"

"I'elp." The little boy jumped up and dashed past the junipers beside the house and straight towards the unfinished flower garden and picked up a hand spade. "I... I ready."

Fortunately for the snapdragons, pansies, orange marigolds, and white alyssum, the garden was already prepared and the still moist earth was smoothed out. In each little hole Mandy prepared, Bobby deposited a tiny plant. He covered the roots with fresh earth while she guided his hand. After the plants were all done, she stood back with his little hand in hers. "I'm sure they're thirsty." She looked at his little mud-streaked cheeks. "What do you say we give them a drink?"

"K, me 'elp."

"Okay, we'll get the hose." She unraveled the hose, made sure the nozzle was off, then turned the tap on then readjusted the nozzle. Bobby giggled while a slight breeze caught the fine spray as Mandy watered the petite flowers.

"It get me wet," Bobby hollered with laughter as he jumped towards the spraying water. "Get me gain, Miss 'iley."

Mandy turned off the water. "That's enough for now, Bobby." She nodded at the excited little fella as they stood back after they had finished watering each dainty plant. "They already look perky after the fresh drink we gave them." She turned and checked her watch. "Oh, my goodness, it's lunch time." She chuckled. "You know what, Bobby, this has to be the shortest morning I've had in years." She smiled. "I'm glad I'm here and this job is not only going to be fun, but a piece of cake." She smiled at the messy face that looked up at her with a big grin.

Taking Bobby by the hand, she headed towards the house. "You're going to have to have a good face scrubbing before your mom sees you." She grinned. "Oh, wait a minute, we'll water the flowers by the deck before we go in." She released his hand and stretched the hose to the end of the patio, flipped the hose to make it longer, then grasped the nozzle. "Darn, it's stuck." She looked behind her. "Oh, oh... it's kinked." She moved the nozzle away from the boy with one hand, stepped towards the kink, then flipped the hose with a hard whip.

"Hey, watch it."

Mandy turned at the low angry growl.

"Ahhh."

"Sorry, ohh..." Her fingers gripped the nozzle to turn it off, but failed. A full spray shot out. "Ohh, ohh… sorry."

"Hey... stop... point it... the other way… Stop... jeez... Stop it."

Mandy stepped back to move the hose away from the ticked off, tall, dark, handsome man. "Sorry." To her horror she watched the soaking wet Adam shake his head, as he did a war dance, during a desperate attempt to get away from the spray. Water droplets flew from his thick dark hair in every direction. His hands flew in the air as if to stop the water from hitting him.

"Damn it, woman." He stepped back.

"Sorry... sorry." She jerked the hose, giving him one final blast of cold water before finally being able to turn it off. "I... I'm... so sorry. It's... stuck... it... won't..."

"Forget it. Just forget it." He raced to the back door.

Mandy watched him stamp his feet on the concrete pad, reach for the screened back door knob and enter the house, leaving her standing there holding the hose. Mortified by what had just happened, she turned to the squealing child.

"Do me, do me." Bobby jumped up and down clapping his hands.

She kinked the hose just below the rusty nozzle, then with a hard twist turned it off. "Enough water for the day." She dropped the hose. Thank goodness there was no sign of her victim when she entered the house to get Bobby a snack.

After a quick clean-up, and needing some quiet time, Mandy took the large, froggy-faced to go mug, filled with tea, and Bobby back out to play in the sandbox. Peace and quiet had no sooner surrounded her when a dark shadow crept behind her. There was no need to turn around to know who it was, as she reached for a hammer that wasn't a toy. Chills raced up her spine. Was he still ticked off with the cold-water shower, she had given him? She kept her head down and peeked through her bangs to watch him kneel down and take his nephew's hand. He had changed into a crisp fresh western-cut blue shirt. His damp dark hair gleamed in the sunlight. He looked absolutely delicious.

"Hey, Sport." He put down a white plastic bag, then picked up a screw-driver, a level, and the vice grips and put them aside. "Having a good time?"

"Me got a orsey, Unky Dem."

"I can see you're playing with a horsey and here's a cow and a dog." He placed two little animals by the small ranch house then reached over to the end of the sandbox and picked up a few more animals. "Here's a little white goat and a lamb and a mommy horse and here's a baby horse." He stuck the rest of the animals in a row then picked up a few sticks which lay outside of the sand box. With the twigs, he made a little corral.

Mandy shivered when he glanced at her. His voice gentle, as

he spoke to the child. His eyes turned dark when she met his gaze.

"See these tools?" He spoke to the child, but glared at her. "These aren't toys." He looked back at the boy. "Your daddy and grandfather and me, need them. Okay, li'l Buddy."

"Wyan said, me pay with dum."

"I know what Ryan said, and I'll talk to him later. Here, you play with these." Adam reached for the white plastic bag and emptied out an orange plastic hammer, a large plastic yellow flat head screwdriver along with several other play tools and a green plastic level with large yellow bubbles.

"Oh tanks, Unky Dem." The little boy got up and threw his arms around his uncle.

"You're welcome, Sport." Adam patted the boy's back and kissed him on the top of his head. "Uncle has to get back to work now so I'll see you later."

She watched Adam stand up. His height made her feel small.

"You may not realize, Miss Riley, but these tools are expensive so if you're a Nanny like you say you are, you would know the difference between toys and tools," he huffed and took the hammer from her out-reached hand.

Mystery solved about the sand-covered levelling tool he was cleaning the day she came for her interview. She stood up and squared her shoulders. It was time to take a stand and no one was going to push her around. Besides, he should have put the tools away. "I know the difference," she said firmly, looking way up at him. "If you had put them away last evening, after you finished the ramp, instead of leaving them unattended by your chair, there wouldn't be a problem. And… you wouldn't have had to brush the sand off the levelling tool before you used it." She watched him take in a breath. His broad chest expanded. It was obvious this powerful man was used to being in control. What surprised her the most is how she handled herself. Especially to Mr. Dark Cloud. His eyes narrowed. "Aren't you supposed to be with the herd?" she asked sweetly as she watched his eyes dart a glance at his large green froggy mug she had sitting next to her.

"Hey, don't start telling me how to do my job." He turned and walked away.

"Cranky, are we?" Mandy mumbled under her breath, yet he must have heard her, because he stopped for a moment, but didn't turn around. He looked rugged, wild and risky. Warm shivers raced up her spine. Her heart beat hard and fast.

ADAM STOOD behind his dining chair and studied Miss Riley, as she watched everyone take their place at the dining table for lunch. He glanced at the chair directly opposite him. "Oh, good lord," he frowned. "At least you don't have a garden hose in your hand." He pointed towards the chair and nodded for her to take a seat. Her smile was quick, yet sweet. He took a second look at her perfect full mouth.

Sitting down himself, he reached for Bobby's hand then turned to Crystal and took hers. Before he lowered his head, he darted a glance at Mandy and wondered if she was going to join in with the grace. To his surprise and he had to admit relief, she took Bobby's and Dianne's hands and lowered her head while his father said a prayer. After the blessing, he helped himself to a thick, hardy, roast beef sandwich, then scooped up some fresh crisp garden salad and piled it onto his plate. His eyes darted to her white cotton sleeveless blouse that fit nicely and showed off her lovely bust and trim waist. He wondered what she was wearing under it. Lace and silk? Not that it mattered; the way he spoke to her earlier, he didn't have a chance in hell of ever finding out. But he could imagine and he had one helluva imagination. Yup, just as he had thought, the next three months were going to be rough living with that woman in the house.

His eyes darted to her left hand. There was no ring and her hands seemed dry and slightly reddened. This morning they were soft, pink and pretty. What had she done to cause them to look sore? He grunted. Maybe some work. Laundry, plant a flower or two, give a kid a bath, play in the sandbox? *She'll find out what work's all about, then maybe she'll quit.* As he bit into his sandwich, he still wondered why she'd take a position like this? A city girl living out here? Was she hiding from someone or something? Did she have a boyfriend and would he be around in the evenings? Where will she go on her day off?

His thoughts confused him. He wanted her out of here and away from his family and the ranch, yet there was something about her that intrigued him. Or irritated him. Which was it? Her voice sent him in a trance while she spoke to his youngest nephew. Her lip movements gave him urges he hadn't had for a while.

"Adam Scott, did you get all that?"

His father's voice, loud and strong, broke into his wayward thoughts. He jerked his head towards the head of the table. "Sorry, Pa, I had other things on my mind." Jeez, why the hell would I care if she's got a boyfriend or whether she wants to be a Nanny? He focused his attention on his father, and kept it focused.

"Son, we need to check the mares in the east pasture today. You know the two that are late with their foals this year. I want them rounded up and put in the corral by the first barn so we can keep a closer eye on them," John McBride said with a slight frown, because of repeating himself.

"Yeah, I know," Adam said quickly. It was his job to supervise the branding, castrating and vaccinations and had been for the last few years now, so why did his father change the plans? If he had been smart, he should have stayed out with the herd with Chuck and the men. But oh no, just because everything was going along fine, he had to find more work to do, like come back and organize the toolshed and check on his friend, Hank. What a morning. With the look his father gave him, he figured he'd leave well enough alone. "I'll meet you at the first corral." His eyes shifted to Mandy. *She can get a man into trouble just by looking.*

◇

MANDY SMILED and could have sworn there was a hint of color in his cheeks when his father had to raise his voice to get his attention. It had served him right for watching her and not concentrating on the family business. She wiped off Bobby's face as she watched Adam watch her. Nervous at his stares, she tossed the washcloth down onto the table. "Oh, ohh, ohh," she stammered as the washcloth hit his full glass of milk, tipping it over. In horror, she watched it splash over Adam's shirt and jeans.

"Ahh, jeez." He stood quickly.

"Oh...oh... I'm sorry, I'm so sorry." She grabbed a clean napkin, pushed back her chair, darted around the high chair, over to his side of the table, and began to wipe the spilled milk off his shirt then his belt buckle.

"Never mind." He backed up trying to get away from her.

"I'm so sorry." She stepped forward. Her fingers hooked onto his belt loop, then went for him again with the napkin. "I... I am so... so... sorry."

"Forget it." He stepped farther back and pushed her hand away as he tripped over one of Crystal's dolls. Losing his balance, he threw out his arm and braced himself against the wall.

"Be careful." Her hand grabbed his. An electrical current jolted through her fingers. Waves of heat seared her hand, up her arm, and down her spine making her gasp and jerk her hand away. The heat from his hand surprised her. Shocked her. What was it with this man that made her feel this way? Aware of his unstable balance with Crystal's toy under his foot, she reached for him again, catching his shirt sleeve. "Careful."

"I'm fine. I'm fine." He twisted out of her hold. He moved the toy with his foot and walked towards the stairway.

Mandy watched him take the stairs two at a time. Gut-wrenching howling laughter from the family turned her head. Even the children were caught up with the milk overflowing onto Adam's shirt and jeans. She cooled her hot cheeks with the milk-soaked napkin as everyone continued to laugh. Needing fresh air and more room to hoot 'n' holler, the family left the table. John McBride walked away, doubled over with a stitch in his gut. Dianne laughed so hard she had to move her wheelchair away from the table. Cole wiped the tears from his eyes as he put his sandwich on a napkin, tossed it onto Dianne's lap, and helped her escape the scene of the incident and headed to the back patio where his father and the children had already retired to.

Mandy plunked herself down in the chair Adam had deserted. "What a disaster on my first full day." She turned to the boy who was the only one who hadn't abandoned her. Then again, he was busy taking apart his sandwich and poking holes in the bread. "Ha, it's only one in the afternoon and I've already taken your uncle's mug, sat in his chair, showered him with cold water, and now given him a milk bath." She put her elbows on the table and rested her chin on top of her knuckles and continued her conversation with the little boy. "Your uncle must be accident prone. It's not me."

She looked at the hand that had touched his. It still tingled. She shook her head. "Time for a nap, little fellah." Ignoring the day's events to the best of her ability, she took the toddler upstairs.

By the time she came back to the dining room, there was no one in sight, therefore she made herself a cup of tea and sat back down at the table by herself. Mandy realized everything was cleared away as she picked up a note from Cole telling her that he had Crystal and Ryan with him and not to worry. She sighed heavily in disbelief that she had grabbed Adam's belt buckle. She put her head in her hands. "Glad his family thought it was funny," she mumbled under her breath.

CHAPTER 5

A fenced-in area of the east pasture, not far from the bunkhouses exclusively used for pregnant mares, Adam and his father located the two quarter horses that were ready to be brought back to the main barn. Adam enjoyed quiet time with his father, but today, his father was on the curious side and Adam wasn't in the mood to answer questions and would rather be out working with the men.

"Our mares are pretty much right on time with their due dates." John McBride jerked his head forward. "Stacey, the little chestnut, is due any time now."

"I see, and Dee isn't far behind." Adam jutted out his chin to the little brown mare.

John scanned the area. "Yeah, and look, there's three more for next week."

Adam pointed to three more mares. "With last week's mares and these ones coming up, we'll have a nice crop of foals this year." He chuckled. "It makes me think we should go into the horse business instead of cattle."

"Not such a bad idea, our horses bring in a pretty good income," John confirmed.

Adam and his father leisurely walked the horses back towards the barn.

"Stacey is slowing down," Adam said.

"I suspect she'll deliver today."

"Yeah."

John turned to his son. "You in a hurry?"

"No, just want to get back to the herd."

"Cole's there. Son, the ranch is too big for you to be everywhere at once."

Adam shook his head at his father then looked over the land.

"What's wrong, Adam?"

"Nothing." He turned to his father. "Why did you change the plans today? You know I usually organize the branding. Cole, or any of the other hands could've come out with you to get these mares. Huh, you could have done it yourself."

"Adam, something's bothering you and I thought I'd give you a break this afternoon. Enjoy yourself. Relax. You're so wound up lately."

"I have a lot on my mind."

"Son, you used to talk to me."

Adam sighed. He and Cole were the fourth generation and were proud to be ranchers. He looked at his father. "I don't know. The last couple of months I've been thinking of a change."

"What do you want?"

"I don't know."

"What sort of change? You've always loved ranching."

"You know I still do. I don't know, Pa." He lied. He wasn't in the mood to share his feelings with his dad about wanting to start a family of his own. Every day he watched Cole and Dianne and saw how their relationship continued to grow. He wasn't jealous, he was happy for his brother and sister-in-law, he just wanted what they had. He wanted a woman who could understand him. To share what he loved. To confide in. To love. His thoughts went back to the mess he was in with his last few relationships. If all women today were like them, he'd be better off staying single. "Maybe specialize…" he shrugged, "…in llamas. They're valued for their soft woolly fleece and make good pack animals." If his life wasn't so messed up, he'd laugh at his father's priceless expression. He sent his father a quick twisted smile. "Just kidding, Pa."

John shook his head slightly and gave back a low throaty chuckle. "Son, you know this land is going to be yours and Cole's someday. If you want, you can have your half now. You know, your mother and I often thought we'd build a little retirement home up there in the south ridge. The view is awesome. Your mom loved the ranch and she loved you boys and…" John became thoughtful as he looked in the distance, "…her dream was to spoil the grandchildren whenever they'd come to stay with us." John went silent as they continued to head back home.

Adam watched his father for a moment then grew silent himself. He had his own memories of his mother whom he loved very much. He had thought Cole was going to leave the family home and build his own when he married Dianne. As it turned out, Dianne liked the idea of a big family and wanted to stay in the main house. As far as Adam was concerned, he also liked the idea and the more the merrier. He wanted a big family and hoped someday, his future wife would want the same. He planned to add on to the main house, or he'd build one right next to it with a large additional family room attached. He'd like all the cousins to grow up as siblings. If he got married and right now that was a big if.

Adam took in a deep breath as they approached the barn. "I think we came just in time, Pa." They brought the mares into the barn, put them into the berthing stalls, and went directly to Stacey. "Yeah, it looks like she's in labor."

Adam talked quietly to the little chestnut and stroked her

gently to reassure her all would be fine. A slight movement caught his attention in the next stall where Miss Riley and his nephew were quietly watching with gentle interest. He turned his attention back to the mare and prayed this labor would be better than last week when two of their mares had breeches. It was always tough to watch his mares go through so much discomfort. The contractions started. Adam checked Stacey over. "You're going to be fine, girl."

"She's ready, Adam. This one's coming fast."

Adam stood back to give the mare more room. After a few more contractions and some labored breathing he could see it was almost time. Time was ticking and the little mare was beginning to get restless.

"Is she going to be okay, son?"

"She's fine, Pa. Don't worry." Adam smiled warmly. "Yeah... she's good." Adam watched the contractions closely and within an hour later, Stacey delivered. He helped removed the rest of the torn membrane and rubbed the baby down. "Hey, we have ourselves a little filly." He smiled. "You're fine. Good girl," he cooed, patting the little horse. Adam watched as the mare encouraged her baby to stand. The little filly wobbled back and forth a few times then finally stood up then Stacey nuzzled her baby close to her. The bonding between mother and baby started instantly. He glanced at the stall beside Stacey where Miss Riley and his nephew had been. They were gone.

He leaned up against the box stall for a moment. "Enjoy your baby, Stacey and I'll see you before bedtime." He scratched the foal behind the ears then left the barn.

～

"Well, Mandy," Cole started the evening conversation after the children went to bed. "How's your first day?"

"Great, I've enjoyed it. Bobby and I stood and watched Stacey for a while, but when she went into full labor I wasn't sure how Bobby would react so we left."

"Adam said she's doing fine and it was a good delivery," Cole reassured her.

"Oh good, Bobby and I are anxious to see her in the morning." She chuckled. "Speaking of Adam, he's the only person I seem to tick off. First taking his favorite coffee mug, then his chair, spraying him with water then spilling milk all over him. What's going to happen tomorrow?"

"Ahhh, don't worry." Cole laughed. "Adam's a big boy and can handle it."

"Oh, by the way, there's a teachers' meeting so Ryan and Crystal will be home tomorrow," Dianne announced. "Sorry I forgot to tell you, but I had so much on my mind lately."

"Ladies, I'm going to town tomorrow morning." Cole stood and stretched. "Ryan's coming with me to pick up feed, so is there anything we can pick up for either of you?"

The back door opened and slammed shut with a bang. Heavy thud of boots being kicked off as they hit the wall and floor in the back hall caused Mandy to freeze in her chair. Her heart flipped.

"Lay odds Adam's picking up after Hank again." Cole sighed deeply looked at his wife then turned to Mandy. "He's one of our foremen who needs treatment or an A.A. group," he added and looked at Dianne. "Adam's got it in his head he can help him through this drinking stage Hank's going through. Well, I've known a few drinkers in my years and it seems that drinkers have to reach rock bottom before they want to get better. Adam is just adding to the problem by being a, ohh… what do you call it… ahh… when someone allows all this to… go on… keep letting it happen?"

"An enabler," Mandy said with a straight serious face.

"Yeah, yeah, that's what he is and well… he's got to stop. We have a ranch to run and Hank needs to get professional help." Cole shook his head. "He's got to let Hank go. I just hope Adam's not drinking with him."

"You know why he won't let Hank go, Cole, and I can understand Adam," Dianne argued. "And for the record, he doesn't drink with Hank. He may have a few, but he chooses who he drinks with and that's not often."

"Yeah, okay, Di, you're right, and I know Adam doesn't drink much, but Hank's drinking has to be dealt with, before he or someone gets seriously hurt."

Just as Cole headed for the bedroom, another heavy slam from the back door was heard. Heavy booted footsteps came through the kitchen, past the dining room, and into the living room. Adam stilled for a quick moment as he glanced at his older brother then turned and walked to the other side of the dining room and into the den.

Mandy watched him closely. Dianne was right, he didn't look like he had been drinking and he'd been with the mare most of the evening. Instead, she thought how self-assured and masculine he looked with his shirt sleeves rolled up and the top buttons undone. He looked good. Real good. But where had he gone after delivering the foal? Deep male voices were lowered, but loud enough she could hear every word. She put her knuckles to her mouth. Her heart pounded painfully.

"You know I've got a problem with anyone drinking on this ranch, and I'll tell you, I won't have it continue," John's voice carried throughout the house.

Cole took a step towards the den.

Dianne reached over and grabbed his hand. "Cole, leave them be. This issue has been a sore spot for your dad, too, and they need to work it out. We know Hank needs help and Adam is his closest friend. Reminder, we're Hank's friends, too."

"I just need to..." Cole took a step forward.

Dianne held on tighter. "No, you don't just need to do anything."

Cole placed his hands on his hips. "I know, Honey, I know he's our friend, too, but he won't quit and he won't take our help. And just in case you haven't noticed, Adam isn't an Addictions Counsellor any more than we are. He's a rancher like the rest of us so he'd better get back to ranching and call someone else to help Hank through these rough times. Friend or not, Hank is going to cause an accident around here and someone's going to get hurt." Cole turned his head towards the den where the yelling continued.

"Damn it, Adam," John yelled. "What's your problem lately? You've been giving way too much time to Hank and his drinking over the last few months and by George, it's going to stop. You're going to have to tell him to get his sorry butt to a Detox Center and get help, or I will."

"Hank needs me," Adam interrupted. "He needs help from friends. I'm not going to send him away to some stranger. You damn well know why he's drinking and I'm going to help him with or without your support." Adam's voice was loud, clear and angry. "You don't understand and I'm tired of everyone on my back over it."

"Son, you're not a counsellor. You're a rancher. Got that? What the hell do you know about counseling someone with a drinking problem. Especially a problem as big as Hank's." John continued. "If you want to help him get him professional help. If you had been paying attention to your chores, we wouldn't have lost that calf. If Hank had been sober..."

"The calf was already dead," Adam yelled. "There wasn't a damn thing we could do."

"Adam, listen to me. It's not just the calf. Hank's become a liability around here and we don't need any other accidents,"

John's tone lowered. "Son, we all want the best for Hank and I've told you we will help him and get him the best treatment there is. You know I care for him as much as you do, but we don't have the skills here, so let him go."

Mandy heard a thud of some kind in the den. A fist on the desk, a kick from a boot, she wasn't sure, but she couldn't take any more, so got out of her chair. "Good night, Dianne, Cole."

"You, all right?" Dianne asked quietly.

"Yes, I... I'm fine. I'm j... just tired," she stammered and went upstairs.

Before Mandy got to the top of the stairs, the front door slammed hard. After locking her bedroom door, she did her evening exercise routine, washed and got ready for bed, then slipped under the cool cotton sheets and leaned back against the headboard with her notebook. Her mind went over the whole family conversation. Fear tugged at her heart. A drunk on the ranch. Adam angry. What had she gotten herself into? She brought her knees up to her chest and hugged them as she thought of Adam's gentleness with the kids and the baby foal. For now, she'd stay out of Adam's way. Angry men scared her as much as drunks did.

Mandy's passion for writing was a gift and she was motivated. Determined to finish her book she grabbed her pencil. Her editor and readers were counting on her and she had an obligation to them. She began to sketch out Penny, the little black and white pinto who was the main character in her story. The children in her book had put a little cowboy hat on Penny and a red bandana around her neck. It was parade day at the local school and their little pinto pony was going to be the number one attraction. Mandy was finishing off the final touches to Penny's red halter when her concentration was interrupted by heavy footsteps in the hallway, then a slam of a door.

Adam had returned.

She understood John's concern about the calf and other accidents that could happen. Ranch life was tough and hard, so everyone had to work together. Everyone had to watch out for himself and for the person beside him, or there would be more accidents. She questioned just how much time Adam spent with this Hank character and was Hank a bad influence? And why won't Adam let Hank go to a Detox Center where there are professionals to help him?

So many questions.

Mandy's eyes grew heavy with sleep. Her pencil slipped through her tired fingers, yet her mind pushed forward the memory of the drunk driver who killed her parents and older brother. She recalled how he reeked of cheap whisky and could hardly stand, let alone speak and when he did, he drooled all over himself. He was filthy and unkempt. Her eyes flew open. Her arms flung in all directions to protect herself. Her manuscript dropped to the floor and her pencil flew in the opposite direction. Her pulse raced hard and painful. The memories were so vivid, she could almost see and smell him.

Tears trickled down her cheeks as her thoughts returned to Adam. She wanted to believe he was doing the right thing for his friend, yet she knew the only help Hank was going to get was through professionals. And only if he wanted to. Long after the accident, she'd become angry when her uncle would have a drink. It was Uncle Richard who had taught her that people had a choice whether to abuse alcohol or not. The man who killed her family abused it. Uncle Richard constantly reassured her he would never drink to the point of harming anyone. He kept his promise and as the weeks, months and years went by, Mandy began to tolerate it when he had the occasional drink. At times she had to admit that on hot days, a glass of ice cold beer, with its rich amber color in a tall frosted glass, looked inviting, and had tempted her taste buds.

However, she was content to stick with her lemonade or iced tea instead.

Mandy put her manuscript on the bedside table, shut off the light then shifted down into the sheets. All was quiet across the hall. "Good night, Adam," she whispered before sleep claimed her.

CHAPTER 6

"*D*amn it." Adam shifted his weight on the saddle and stared at the dead calf. He didn't know what had got the calf, but his father was right about him and Hank paying attention, so there would be no problems. The calf should have been with the herd. With its mama. *Reality check, mister, you're a McBride and you should've been paying attention.* Adam groaned as he dismounted and laid the calf over the saddle of the other horse. He'd have to get rid of the calf in the lower pasture where there was a small patch of land where they disposed of animals they had to get rid of. He tied the dead calf securely while he thought about everything at home. His father was right about Hank needing professional counseling, but how could he just leave his friend in the city by himself. Hank would go crazy.

After the calf was buried he headed towards his men and the herd. He had to get some work done or his own father was going to fire him. His thoughts again turned to Miss Riley and what she was planning to do to him next. His brain sizzled with the thought of her wiping off his shirt, then his belt buckle, when the glass of milk spilt over him. He grunted at the recollection of her grabbing onto his belt loops and coming after him with the linen napkin. Not once, but twice yet.

His eyes scanned the area. "What the hell?" He rubbed his forehead. "Jeez, where's everyone?" He glanced over the land a second time. Everyone and everything had disappeared. Vanished. "Oh, jeez, damn it all," Adam growled and turned his horse quickly and headed in the opposite direction. The direction he should have been in, in the first place. Adam always took pride in his work and knew his job well. He, like his father and grandfather, could spot good horse flesh a mile away and had a keen eye for good beef cattle. He was born, bred, and lived the life of a rancher and it was totally unlike him to lose a half day's work because he wasn't concentrating on his job, or where he was going. His men would be waiting for him. He hoped his father wasn't.

This was all Mandy's fault. She was in his head, in his thoughts, and if he could get her out of his head he could concentrate on his job. But she was in his head now, and he had a feeling Mandy was going to stay there.

"Boss, where're y... ya b-been?" Hank slurred out the words with a silly grin on his face.

"Busy, got a problem with that?" Adam said with a sharp tongue, then noticed the other men back off without a word.

"Got women p... problems 'gen?" Hank laughed. "Or is it, da new Nanny. Isn't she taken care of ya?" He laughed louder and harder. "If ya don't wan' her. I'll take her."

Adam turned his horse to face Hank and studied him for a moment. His friend was usually a mild-mannered man who respected others, but depending on what he drank, and how much, he either got too friendly or turned ornery. "Do you have any idea what time it is?" Adam's eyes narrowed.

"Uhm... w-why... ya.. ask-in?"

Adam watched Hank shift nervously in the saddle. He wavered. "You get back to the bunkhouse and sober up. Don't come back until then."

"Aw, c-come on, b-boss, I's… fine."

"You're not. Now get. I don't want to see your sorry butt until you're sober and… cleaned up. Understand?" Adam reined his horse forward.

"I's doin' da.. job," Hank hollered as he turned his horse. "Y-you… was la la…late." Hank took off towards the bunkhouse.

Adam scrubbed his face hard and hoped Hank made it back without falling off the saddle. He waved a young cowboy over and instructed him to take the little bay mare he had with him back to the barn and make sure Hank got back safely. Adam worried about Hank, after all, he was his friend. Through thick and thin he was going to help him through these troubled times. The real question was, what was he going to do with him?

Disaster hit Hank two years ago when his beloved wife, Nancy, fell off her horse and died. Hank tried hard to adjust to life without his loving and best friend, Nancy, but the pain of losing her wouldn't go away so he gave up and turned to drinking. He stopped caring about anything or anyone and the bottle became his friend. Adam rubbed his forehead hard. Maybe getting a professional to help was the responsible thing to do. Maybe his brother and father actually did know how much help Hank needed.

By the time Adam and a few of his men were relieved and got back to the barn it was dark. It had been a long hard tough day and he needed a hot shower to wash off the dust from his tired body. After putting his horse away in the stall, he checked on Stacey and her foal then went to the tack room where he found another empty case of beer. "Jeez, Hank." He checked the box then the cooler where he found one cold one left. He twisted off the cap and strolled out to the corral. With his foot on the first rung, he took a long swig as he watched Mandy leave the house and get into her fancy truck. Saturday night and she was off. Where would she go? Who would she see?

As AGREED upon during the interview, if the children were settled Mandy could go home late Saturday night. Halfway home she recalled watching Adam from the rear-view mirror as she left the driveway of the McBride ranch. He had been standing by the corral with something in his hand. A bottle of some sort. His head tilted back. His elbow bent. Typical movements of a drinker. She groaned long and deep at the thought. Had the shadows of dusk played tricks on her eyes? Yet, his head was held high and his walk was steady as he went back to the barn. He definitely didn't resemble someone who drank too much.

She got home shortly before midnight and was greeted anxiously by her aunt and uncle. After several hugs and kisses, she entered the living room and flopped down on the love seat and straightened her legs.

"Good to see you, Honey," Uncle Richard said. "How was your first few days?"

"Hectic, but great," she said as her eyes glanced around the living room taking in dozens of family pictures on the far wall and more on the fireplace mantel. Her toes wiggled into the thick plush carpet. "But still good to be home and I missed y'all."

"Yo, Squeak. We missed ya, too." Jason walked into the living room with popcorn and iced tea. He kissed her on the forehead and placed a bowl in her lap and a glass of iced tea on the end table. "We want to hear all about your first week." Jason sat across from her on the green plush couch and put his feet up on a soft foot stool. "We all figured being Saturday 'n' all, we'd have a midnight party. Just the four of us." He fisted a handful of popcorn from his bowl.

Aunt Maggie tucked her feet under herself in her favorite armchair with a cup of tea, while Uncle Richard took the large dark brown rocker recliner, put the footrest up and took a big swig of cola. Jason wiped his hands on a napkin then took a gulp of his iced tea. She could see her brother was getting ready to ask questions. It was going to be a long night.

"So, start from the beginning, Squeak," Jason said then took another handful of popcorn and stuffed his face.

Mandy puffed out her cheeks. Her brother wanted details so she ignored him. "I never realized how hard it was to chase a two-and-a-half-year-old bulldozer around, playing peek-a-boo and hide-n-seek. It's tougher than I ever imagined." She crunched on a few pieces of popcorn then told everyone about the whole week. "The one thing that's relaxing, is that I read every night to the family."

"We know how you've always enjoyed reading, Amanda," Richard said.

"Hey, Squeak, how's that other man, the reb, what's his name?" Jason asked.

Not wanting to think about Adam, or the fact that he might be a drinker, she wished Jason hadn't brought him up. "Fine, I guess, I've hardly seen him and his name is Adam." She decided to keep to herself how Adam made her feel and how excited she got just at the sight of him. Drink or not, it didn't change the feelings she got when he walked passed her. The aroma of his aftershave took her breath away, his lean body and watchful gaze sent sensations up her spine. She couldn't tell Jason how her body trembled by just the sight of him.

Mandy changed the subject in hopes Jason would drop it. "By the way, Uncle Richard, your truck is still in perfect condition." She chuckled. "Thanks again. I didn't need it, but like you said, it was a comfort to have it there my first week. Oh, and by the way, did you or grandfather ever sell a dining room suite to a John McBride?"

"I don't recall."

"During the interview, I noticed their dining suite. It looks like your design, but there's a slight difference, and I thought maybe Grandfather Riley made it."

"It could be. We changed the design a bit about two years before your grandfather passed away. I can check the files."

"Don't worry, someday I'll ask." Maybe I'll ask Adam and break the ice, she thought to herself.

THE SHORT WEEKEND with her family went far too fast and Mandy was torn between her family and her new job she enjoyed. As she drove back in her uncle's truck, she fantasized about the attractive Rebel Adam. His perfect mouth made her's water. His dark complexion, lean muscular body sent chills of anticipation up her spine. His dark brown eyes made her shiver when he looked at her. A sudden urge to get to the ranch swept over her, so pressed on the gas pedal.

Mandy sensed Adam didn't always have a negative attitude, or issues, or whatever his problem was, and there was a gentle side to him. She had seen it when he was with the children and her feeling was that he could be warm and kind to her. Maybe she was dreaming, but someday she hoped he'd hold her in his arms and show her his tender side.

She drove up at exactly five forty-five, parked Uncle Richard's truck, went in and made tea. This time she took out one of the average-looking, every day, to-go-mugs, filled it with hot water, plopped in a tea bag then headed out to the porch to sit down in the big chair. His chair. A few moments later she watched Adam come out with his extra-large, froggy to-go-mug in his hand. When he turned towards her, a wave of heat hit her as she watched his eyes cruise over her. There was no smile on his face, but his glance still pebbled her skin with tiny goose bumps. She reminded herself that he wasn't her boss and she didn't have to worry about her job. His penetrating gaze made her nervous, yet at the same time, thrilled her.

"Good morning, Mr. McBride," she said softly, wanting him to give her a chance, but his look didn't hold much promise. And his gaze went directly to her own to go mug.

"Don't call me Mr. McBride. If you're going to be living here, call me Adam," he snapped but this time he tried to snap softly. It wasn't her fault his brother and wife wanted a Nanny. He glanced at the truck she drove then back at her. That vehicle and the Nanny still didn't fit. "Nice truck." He walked away and headed towards the barn. "Damn woman, another week of her up early and sitting in my deck chair. Hell, only another eleven weeks to go. Damn it," he grumbled. "I'll have to make another." He looked at his favorite froggy mug. "At least I got you back." He took a sip of his strong black coffee.

Instead of going to the barn, Adam turned towards the workshop and set to work to make another deck chair. For her. One the same as his, but smaller. He pulled out the cedar boards that he had left over from other projects.

With the best of electric saws and tools, he had it cut,

sanded and screwed together before noon. All it needed now was a coat of stain and the chair would be sitting on the porch by early next morning. He hoped. He looked at the chair that would fit her perfectly and found himself getting anxious about finishing the project.

Time to check on the horses, he closed the woodworking shop and headed to the barn. He walked slowly and inspected every stall and patted every mare and checked every baby.

"Adam." Chuck came around the corner of the tack room.

"Yeah, Chuck, what's up?"

"It's Hank." Chuck groaned. "I got a call from the hotel manager in town. Hank's drinking and they can't get him out."

Adam sighed from deep within and checked his watch. "Ahh, crap. It's only twelve-thirty."

"We couldn't stop him and we couldn't find you. And Cole is already gone." Chuck shrugged. "You want me to go...?"

"No." Adam gave off a big groan. "Thanks, Chuck, I'll get him."

~

Twenty minutes later Adam entered the local hotel and headed straight for the table Hank usually sat at. Adam shook his head when he saw Hank making a fool of himself.

"Gimme a kiss, dolly," Hank slurred his words as the waitress jerked her hand away.

Adam sighed heavily then sat down opposite his friend. He pushed away a pile of torn off labels from the bottles to the end of the table. "Jeez, Hank, you can't even drink without littering."

"Welllll h...howdy, boss." Hank slapped Adam's forearm. "How's ya doin?" His mouth crooked. "Hey, Mmm..issy." He waved his hand to the waitress. "Bring one for me fr..friend, ah, A.a.a dam. Uh da, boss."

"No." Adam shook his head at the waitress. "Hank, let's go." Adam got up and pulled Hank to his feet. "You stink." He turned his face away from Hank's. "Come on, time to go home."

"Ugh, boss, j... just one more."

"No, put it down." Adam reached for Hanks bottle.

"Wait. Le'me f..f..finish dis." He hung onto his bottle and tilted his head back.

Since there was no use arguing with a drunk, Adam waited as Hank swigged down the remainder of the beer.

"Uhaa, dat's good," he slurred his words. "Sure ya, ah...don't want one?"

"Definitely not. Jeez, Hank, it's high noon and we have work to do, or at least I do."

"Yeah, I forgot, uh, dose horses for ya." Hank grinned. "Right, b..boss." He burped. "Or is I on cattle t...today?"

"Breathe the other way," Adam ordered. "Two coffees to go," he called out to Connie, the head waitress, who had been working in the same bar for years. Connie was in her mid-fifties and had three grown children who worked at the feed lot. He guided Hank towards the door. "Black." Adam walked Hank to the truck, opened the truck door, and stuffed Hank into the passenger seat, then turned to Connie, who had brought out the strong black coffee to them.

"I put in an ice cube into each cup to cool it faster."

"Thanks, Connie. Is his tab paid?"

"No." Connie shook her head.

"Jeez, no more tab for him. Connie, have your manager call me when he comes in," he commanded. "I know there's been a change in management around here, but if he doesn't call me, I'm going to ban my men from coming here. You tell him that, okay?" He sighed and looked at the older woman whom he'd known all his life. It wasn't her fault his friend couldn't hold his liquor. "Please and thank you." He smiled and nodded. "And, Connie, thank you for calling me."

"You're welcome, Adam." Connie smiled. "I'll tell the rest of the staff there's no more tab for Hank." She nodded, turned and left.

Adam glanced at the remaining sliver of ice. Not wanting to burn his friend's mouth, he reached for a travel mug on the dash and poured the hot coffee back and forth between the two cups a few times. He sipped it. "Get this down your gut." He practically poured the coffee down Hank's throat then opened the second cup, poured it back and forth, then sipped it. "Sit up," he demanded and held the second cup to Hank's mouth. "Damn it, Hank, you know the rules on our ranch. No drinking." He strapped Hank into the seat belt then went to the driver's side and got in.

"Y-you gonna tell your Pa." Hank turned to Adam. His mouth open. "Huh."

Adam coughed. He opened his window wide and drove home without talking.

Back at the ranch, Adam helped Hank out of the truck and into the foreman's cabin. He held his breath as Hank turned his face into his.

"Ahah, you's a good f-f-fiend... uh... I mean fr..friend." Hank kissed Adam on the cheek.

"Jeez, Hank. Stop that. Your breath is enough to kill me." Adam turned his face away. "Come on, stand up. Straight." He put his friend's arm around his neck and his arm around Hank's waist then practically carried him to the bunkhouse. He kicked open the door and walked him to the bedroom. "Get into bed." Adam released Hank, but to his surprise, Hank held on.

"You's a good man, boss." Hank tightened his arms around Adam's neck. "I love ya, man."

"Sure. I love you, too. Let me help you." Adam pried Hank's

hands off his neck and lowered him into the bed. "No use talking to you now. Get some sleep."

"Nighty night, A..d.d.dam,—me—f..friend."

"Yeah." Adam threw a blanket over Hank and left. His heart was at war with his brain over what to do with his friend.

CHAPTER 7

$\mathcal{M}$andy listened to the McBride brothers talk business over a late lunch. Adam's low baritone voice was soothing, almost hypnotic; she thought she could listen to him forever.

"Adam," Cole called over from the end of the table. "Kenny Baines and his son, Mike, are coming over later this afternoon to look at the young bulls, so could you and Hank bring them to the bull pen?"

"Unky, Dem," Bobby interrupted.

"He's coming today?" Adam questioned.

"Unky, Dem." Bobby patted his uncle's forearm.

"He called before breakfast and wants to head out early to his daughter's ranch," Cole informed.

"Unky, Dem," Bobby got louder.

"Just a minute, Lil Buddy." Adam touched the boy's hand and smiled. "We'll talk after your dad and I are finished." He picked up the little boy and sat him on his lap.

Mandy was positive she saw a dimple in Adam's left cheek when he smiled at his nephew, but he had turned back to his brother before she could get a good look. He loved the children in his life and it showed in his eyes, his voice, and most importantly in his actions. He took time to listen and talk to them. He made time for them individually.

"Chuck and I'll have them in the pen by three. By the way, Cole, are you going into town this afternoon?"

Cole ignored Adam's question and threw another one at him. "Where's Hank?"

"Not feeling well so I told him to go lie down." Adam took a bite out of his sandwich.

"Where did you go about twelve or so?" Cole asked.

Mandy focused on Adam. While he swallowed, his eyes shifted to his father then to Dianne. His mouth twisted with annoyance. She didn't particularly like where the conversation was heading and the subject of drinking always made her nervous. She glanced at John who was watching both his sons carefully.

"Hank needed help in town."

"I'm sure," Cole said rudely.

"Unky, Dem."

Adam stood up, threw his nephew over his shoulder and positioned Bobby so he could see his face. "Come on, Lil Buddy we'll talk outside."

She watched him nuzzle the child's neck and laugh. Bobby wrapped his arms around his uncle's neck tightly. This was not the scene of a drinking or an angry man. This was a scene of a loving, caring, family man.

After a quick conversation with Dianne, Mandy headed to the porch and sat on the steps. She watched Adam play with his nephew in the sandbox. There were no words to describe the love in his eyes for his nephew. His mouth made motor sounds as he pushed the large yellow bulldozer across the sand hill. She laughed softly when Bobby jumped on his back. Adam wrestled the child to the ground. Squeals of delight filled the air. After a few more moments, Adam picked him up by the back of his overalls and made airplane sounds as he lifted him up in the air then around and down and up as he walked towards her. Bobby screeched with total excitement. Adam put Bobby on the bottom porch step. "Buddy, I got to get some work done, so you stay with your Nanny and I'll see you later."

"Me 'elp you." Bobby picked himself up and hugged Adam's knee.

"Later, Buddy." Adam patted Bobby's back. "I promise."

Mandy's heart leapt as his eyes met hers for only a moment. Strangely it hurt when he didn't return her smile. Although his slight nod and tip of his hat was promising he was coming to terms with her being here.

AFTER SUPPER and the chores were all done, everyone gathered around Mandy for story time. Cole and Dianne settled on the leather love seat together, as she took her place on the floor while the children anxiously gathered around her. Mandy opened to chapter one of The Call of the Wild. She hadn't finished the first sentence when Adam and his father walked into the living room.

"Amanda." John held up his hand like a young school boy wanting attention. "Have you started?"

She smiled. "Half a sentence."

He waved his hand. "We're going to wash up and grab dinner, so wait a few minutes," he said with enthusiasm, turned and rushed into the kitchen. "Come on, Adam, hurry up."

Mandy watched Adam's eyes cruise over her, then he followed his father into the kitchen. There was no excitement in his eyes and wondered why he came in and was he going to stay?

"This is turning out to be quite the story hour," Cole said with a huge grin. "Honey, we should get you a fake cast and keep Mandy on full-time. It's been nice being home early in the evenings." Cole laughed.

"I agree, I love it and I haven't had anyone read to me since I was a little girl," Dianne said. "But, Cole, that's why Mandy's here so you can do your share of the chores. Adam's been over doing it lately."

"Don't worry, Honey." Cole grinned. "Keeps him out of trouble."

John returned from the kitchen with a plate full of food and sat down on the leather recliner. "Adam said you can start." He set his plate on his lap and took a bite of roast. "Go ahead," he said with his mouth full.

Disappointment set in when Mandy found out that Adam wasn't coming to be with the family or hear her read the story. Her heart ached with a pain she'd never felt before and the thought of not wanting her around hurt more. A quick glance at the rest of the family told her she'd better put her foolish feelings aside and start reading. The first paragraph went well, when suddenly booted footsteps pounded in her ears. From the corner of her eye she noticed Adam sit down in his chair. Her heart fluttered uncontrollably and she had to pause to control her voice. She would give anything right now to have someone else read so she could just sit and stare at him. Take all of him in with her eyes and then dream all night about him touching and holding her.

ADAM SAT on the edge of his seat with his dinner plate in his lap as Mandy read. All thoughts of his friend, Hank, the chair he was making for Mandy, his chores that needed to be completed, were forgotten. He listened, not to her words as much as to her soft voice that made the story come alive. Each and every word she read gave meaning and color to the story. He'd never in his life heard anything so beautiful. After the last bite of his meal Adam put his plate on the end table, leaned forward, planted his elbows on his knees, folded his hands and pressed his knuckles against his mouth. He couldn't take his eyes off her. Her smile sparkled when she glanced at each child. *Is that lip gloss on her lips? They're definitely kissable.* He inhaled deeply. *Is that her fragrant shampoo I smell? Her hair is so shiny.* He brushed his hand down his face hard. He had chores to do then check on Hank. Had to check the horses. Had a million things to do, but here he sat listening to an angelic voice. Staring at a beautiful woman.

He continued to sit and stare. He wanted to know more about her. What was her background? Where did she come from? Why does she drive that big expensive red truck and work here? They were the same questions he asked himself day in and day out, all week. She wasn't Alberta-born; he was sure of it and detected a slight American accent.

With a mind of their own, his eyes again focused on her lush pink lips. Her mouth formed the words perfectly. How would her mouth form on his? He twisted uncomfortably in his chair. His jeans tightened when she'd licked her lips to moisten them every time she turned a page. He licked his own. He wanted her and wanted her badly.

"What's going on?" he muttered when the kids got up and began to jump around. He glanced up at the clock and couldn't believe the story was over. With rapid eye movements, he took in his whole family, moving, talking and laughing. He focused back to her. "You done?" He coughed quickly to cover his surprised tone of voice.

A strange feeling of discontentment set in and he wanted her to continue reading. It took him by surprise that he enjoyed listening to her sweet voice more than he ever thought possible.

Enjoyed watching her turn each and every page with graceful movements. He rubbed his forehead. *You idiot, she's a nanny and a city girl. Keep away from her. Go do your checks and chores.* But he couldn't move. His eyes stayed fixed on her. She was more than just beautiful. She was intelligent, kind-hearted, good with the children, and had a pleasant personality. She was shy and that intrigued him. Was he admitting to himself he was interested in her? He shook his head slightly. It could never be. They were too different.

If only he could explain all this to his hormones.

"Ryan, Crystal, Bobby, it's time to spend a few moments with your family while I go outside for a stretch."

"Okay," Crystal said and hopped over to her uncle. "Can I please have a mint while I get ready for bed, Uncle Adam?"

"You bet, but don't forget to brush your teeth after."

Crystal held out her hand. "Okey dokey."

Mandy watched Adam take out a wrapped red and white mint from his shirt pocket. The same type of mint he had given to her when she first had her interview. Was it to mask the smell of alcohol, or did he just like them?

With story time much longer tonight, her left leg stiffened up. Aware Adam was watching her after Crystal had left his side, she wondered how she was going to get up without him noticing. As she prepared to stand, an intense pain shot up her leg. There was no need to look his way because her red alert nerve endings told her he was watching. She managed to stand up, but not without tightening her jaw. She stood for a moment, then watched Adam walk out the front door. With him gone, relief swept over her, because now she'd be able to have a few minutes to move without him watching.

Mandy walked out of the house quietly, closed the door, then held onto the handrail and eased herself down the wheelchair ramp. If she had been thinking, she should have gone out the back door where the patio was at house level and she would have had some time to herself. Several feet away from the porch, she bent over and massaged the side of her leg and knee to relieve the pain and work out the stiffness to some extent. With some relief, Mandy straightened and focused west. The setting sun colored the tops of the mountains with reds, purples and pinks, making an unbelievable visual delight. A sight she'd never tire of.

"Leg sore?"

She turned quickly towards the baritone voice. A tall shadow at the far end of the porch moved. Her heart accelerated. How on earth had she missed seeing him? How can one man make her so nervous and insecure, yet intoxicated at the same time? She wondered why he constantly watched her. Her mind went dizzy with questions. Cole had told her he didn't like outsiders, but this was ridiculous. "Just a little." She walked towards the stairs. Using the handrail for the third step she exhaled through her mouth. The pain was still there and she hoped he hadn't noticed. "Good night, Mr. McBride." She watched him move to his chair.

"I told you to call me Adam, or don't address me at all," he commanded.

"Yes, Sir, er… Adam." She entered the house leaving him sitting in his shadowed corner. Why couldn't he treat her like the rest of the family did so they could at least be friends? Then again it was obvious he didn't want that.

Reality was, she wanted him to notice her. Gaze upon her with those dark brown eyes of his. Most of all, she wanted him to take her into his arms and cradle her. Knowing that any relationship she had with the man wouldn't last, but she'd have her dreams of this strong rancher with an attitude to hold on to. Could she be attracted to what Jason called a rebel, especially after what she and her family had gone through over eight years ago?

Mandy touched the scar on her temple. What kind of woman did Adam want? Could she have a chance and did she measure up to any of his other women friends? She shrugged as she stepped further into the foyer. She didn't know what type of man she wanted let alone what kind of women he liked. It shouldn't matter, but deep inside she admitted it did matter and it mattered a lot.

~

ADAM SAT in his chair for a spell longer and stared at the door she closed behind her. His mind loaded up with the same questions he asked himself every day since she came. He sat thinking that her limp might be slight and most people may not notice, but he did. One of the new questions he had was why did she play with her left side of her hair so much and pull it forward? She seemed to do it unconsciously. He wanted to push her hair back and see her whole beautiful face.

He remembered the second day and how she looked him straight in the eye and told him he should have put the tools away. He chuckled. As shy as she was, she stood up for herself. Guilt crept into his heart regarding his harsh treatment. He had already made a decision to be a little more pleasant. So why hadn't he? He could have softened his voice a little and asked her to call him Adam, instead of demanding. He liked the sound of his name coming from her lips and when she said his name she made it sound special.

The very idea of her whispering his name in his ear as she caressed his neck with her mouth sent his hormones raging. His hard-on tight against his jeans. He'd caress her slender throat and would whisper back her name, adding a sweet something women liked to hear. He rubbed his forehead again to get her out of his mind. He had to get back to work and sweat her out of his system.

~

MANDY FELT SO comfortable with the family that time was flying by and it was already close to the end of her second week. As much as she loved spending time with Cole and Dianne after the kids went to bed, she needed that time to edit her manuscript. Again, she was too exhausted to edit, so she crawled into bed and closed her eyes. Like every night, visions of Adam came to her. His strong arms wrapped around her and backed her up against one of the stalls. His moist mouth took hers, as he caressed her body and whispered sweet words in her ear. His large hands stroked her throat and slowly, deliberately, undid one button, then two, then three.

Her eyes flew open. Her lower body hot. Her breasts tingled. Her dream of Adam was so graphic, her body had played tricks on her. No other man had ever made her body respond to a dream. Unfortunately, it was only a dream. She wondered how her body would react in real life.

It had to be a hundred times better. No, a thousand times.

Each morning was becoming a ritual with Mandy having her tea and sitting out on the porch in Adam's chair. With a pretty flowered mug in hand and well aware that Adam would probably be out in a few minutes, she glanced at the fold-up chairs leaning against the far railing then shrugged and sat in his chair anyway. It was the best and the most comfortable. The front door opened. He stood there. Like a Greek god. Freshly shaven.

Clean fresh clothes. His favorite froggy coffee mug in hand. She stood up.

"Aw, sit there for one more morning. I've got work to do." He walked away.

Mandy thought that his voice seemed to have a pleasant ring to it and wondered why he gave her permission to sit in his chair. Since she wasn't a mind reader, she watched him walk past the barn and go into the workshop. He walked with confidence, his stride perfect, his hips lean, his legs strong and muscular. He was, she thought, a perfect specimen of a man. All male.

Back in the house, Mandy got the two older children ready for school, waved them off, rushed through the kitchen and into the laundry room to put her first load of wash in. Checking the dryer, she found Adam's shirts. "Hmm." With Bobby still sleeping and thinking he probably would for another half hour, she took out the rest of his clothes and placed them onto the folding table. One by one, his jeans, shirts and underwear were folded and neatly placed in the corner of the table.

Wanting to do something nice for him, she held up a baby blue, silk, long-sleeved, western-style shirt, with mother of pearl snaps. She'd iron it, hoping to score some brownie points with him. She placed it on the ironing board and tested the iron and began pressing when the phone rang. She dashed out of the laundry room into the kitchen to pick up the phone. "McBride Ranch."

"Hey, Squeak."

"Hi, Jason."

"I know it's early and you're probably busy, but your final pay from the hospital is in. I'm doing the online banking, so should I transfer it to our special account, or keep it in checking for now. In case you may need it living out there?"

"Transfer it. Thanks."

"Okay. How's it going?"

"Good."

"How's rebel man?"

"Fine, Jas. Gotta go. Bobby's up soon. Call you later. Bye." Mandy went to hang up then called out. "Thanks for taking care of the banking. Call you tonight." She hung up and raced back to the laundry room. "Oh no... no..." With her eyes closed she picked up the silk dress shirt. "Please, please be okay." She opened her eyes then cringed as she sucked air between her teeth as she stared at the brown melted silk shirt. "Ohh, no. Why didn't I leave well enough alone?" She rolled it up into a ball and threw it into the lint basket underneath the folding table. Guilt set in quickly and she wondered how she was going to tell him. If he found out it was her that burnt his shirt he'd never, never talk to her. She glanced at the pile of clean, folded men's clothes then sighed and glanced back at the lint basket and hoped it wasn't a favorite shirt. Hoped Adam could be forgiving. Hoped he wouldn't find out. Mandy gathered the children's clothes she had folded and went upstairs to get Bobby up from his nap.

After getting the little boy up and ready for the afternoon, she went back into the laundry room and put down a couple of toys on the floor so he could play while she loaded the washer. She glanced at the lint basket. Guilt and remorse nagged at her as she picked through the lint basket and brought out the shirt and held it up. She stared at the burned spot as she willed it to go away.

Her heart squeezed tight for what she had done. "What am I going to do?" Not sure if Adam had left for the barn yet, she peeked around the corner. She'd tell him about the shirt later, when she knew him better. When she mustered up enough courage to say she was sorry and that it was an accident. She looked at the little boy playing quietly with his teddy on the floor and wondered how much, could he really talk. He loved his uncle, therefore if he recognized the shirt, he just might say something.

Mandy decided to stuff the shirt back deep down into the lint basket. Thankfully there was enough lint, old tissues and used fabric softener sheets to cover the shirt giving her some time to dispose of it when everyone was sleeping. She took a step back from the lint basket and sighed deeply before she left the laundry room with regret and shamed that she couldn't be up front and honest.

Outside, Mandy and Bobby played a game of chase around the back. She stopped abruptly when she saw Adam arguing with a man with a bottle of beer in his hand. The name Hank rang in her ears. Was this the man Adam was trying to help? Her eyes focused on the scruffy man wiping his mouth with his shirt sleeve, whereas Adam was fresh and clean-looking. It confused her to why Adam would continue to enable the man. Like Cole said, Hank should go to treatment so why wasn't Adam listening to his brother? Especially since Adam wasn't a drinker himself.

She watched Adam turn and place his hands on his hips and waited until she retrieved what she needed. For some odd reason, even the drunk was quiet while she did her thing. "I'm sorry to interrupt…" She half-smiled an apology. "We have to get the watering can from the garden shed." She took Bobby's hand, picked up the watering can and left quickly. Her heart hardened against him for being an enabler and not listening to his family.

Silence took over as she watered the garden, while Bobby flicked water at the plants with his fingers and giggled. Normally she'd laugh with the little boy, but right now she had nothing to laugh about. The scene of Adam and Hank played heavily on her mind.

After watering the plants, she watched Bobby as he played in the sandbox. Thoughts of Adam ever having a future with her was only a dream. A silly thought. "You know, Bobby, I'm hoping by next year my brother and I will have a ranch." She took the plastic horse and made prints in the sand as she told the youngster her dream. "One with a view of the mountains and we're going to have horses and cattle just like back home." She brought her knees up and hugged them and gazed at the toy black stallion. "I want a pretty flower garden," she said in a trancelike state. "The house doesn't have to be big, just big enough for me and Jason to start out." She smiled and gazed at the little boy who wasn't listening, but she continued anyway. "I want a porch with a swing, so I can sit and watch the sun set. Someday maybe you'll visit me."

CHAPTER 8

"*A*nyone see my blue silk shirt? The one with the pearl snaps," Adam hollered from the laundry room before sitting down for six o'clock dinner.

Mandy stilled and held her breath.

"No," Cole hollered from the dining room while pulling out his chair. "I put your laundry on your bed while I was tidying up the laundry room. I don't think your silk shirt was there."

Mandy cringed, knowing she had to come clean and tell him, but she had hoped she would have had more time to mull over an excuse of some sort. She glanced at Cole and wondered if he had emptied the waste paper basket when he was in the laundry room. Hoping he had, because living with the guilt would be easier than approaching Adam.

"I've already checked my room and it's not there," Adam hollered back.

"You sure?" Cole turned and hollered again.

"Of course, I'm sure. I've only got one blue silk shirt." Frustration carried in his voice.

Mandy heard what sounded like a fist hitting the folding table. A slam of a cupboard, deep groans and grunts coming from beyond the kitchen then another cupboard door slammed. She gritted her teeth.

"Jeez, what the hell." A low baritone shriek went through the house.

"Adam," John McBride hollered from the dining room. "Come and sit down before supper gets cold and look for your shirt later. And will everyone stop the hollering."

Adam stomped through the kitchen and into the dining room holding up his crumpled, burnt, melted shirt. "Can someone explain this?" His glare went straight to her.

Mandy watched as the dining room turned into a three-ring circus. Again. Everyone threw their heads back with fits of laughter, pointing, stomping their feet and slapping the table as they continued to roar with amusement.

"You taking up ironing, Adam?" Cole teased. "You should set the iron on low." Cole opened his mouth and let out a long boisterous laugh.

"I did it," Mandy confessed quietly, but with all the noise no one heard her. Not even Adam who continued to glare at her. She stood up. "I did it," she said louder. "The phone rang and... I'm sorry." She looked at Adam. "I'll get you another."

"Before tonight?" He huffed and stroked his forehead before he chucked the shirt into the corner of the room. With heavy booted steps he took his place at the table and sat down in his chair. "You're not going to get a shirt like that in this one-horse town." He shook his head.

"I'm sorry." Fighting back tears, Mandy's gaze went to the crumpled shirt in the corner.

"Forget it. I've got another."

Mandy looked at him with confusion. "You said you only have one."

Adam waved his hand. "I've got other dress shirts."

"I really am..."

"Sorry... I know... so you said," he huffed. "Forget it." He shoved part of a baked potato into his mouth and chewed rapidly.

"Hey, Uncle Adam," Crystal hollered with her hand stretched towards his. "You're eating and we haven't thanked God yet."

Adam glanced at Crystal, chewed rapidly and swallowed hard as he took her hand. "Yeah, yeah, Honey, you're right." He took Bobby's hand as he glared at Mandy. "God forgive me," he whispered then became silent while grace was said.

After grace Mandy looked up at him. "Are you going out?"

"Yes. Is that okay with you?" He frowned and looked back at his dinner.

She glanced at all the family members who were still talking and joking about Adam and his ironing. In fact, the whole family had a tough time getting through the blessing tonight.

"Okay. Enough," Adam roared. "Can't we have some peace and quiet at the table?" he grumbled loudly.

"Adam," John said with a deep-throated chuckle in his voice. "It was an accident." He looked around the table. "Joke's over, so everyone, settle down. I don't want to hear another word."

"Accident, my ass," Adam muttered under his breath loud enough that Mandy could hear, but low enough not to disturb his father.

She cringed and leaned forward. "Adam, it really was an accident and I am very sorry that I ruined your shirt."

He glared at her then shoved another forkful of food into his mouth.

Dejected, she leaned back in her chair. "I guess you were going somewhere special." With no answer, she put her fork into a baby carrot and put it into her mouth. Her appetite suddenly disappeared. She glanced at him through her feathered bangs. Where was he going? Who was he going to see? It had been a nice shirt. A shirt a man would probably wear if he was going out on a date. Not that it was any of her business; she was just curious who the lucky woman might be.

An hour later after everything was cleaned up, Mandy brought the kids out from the toy room for story time. Surprise and shock hit her to find a thick plush royal blue velvet floor cushion in front of the hearth where she usually sat to tell her stories. Instinctively she turned to Adam. One shoulder lifted to a nonchalant shrug telling her he didn't care, or was it to tell her, it wasn't from him? Her inner feelings told her different and he had placed it there for her to use.

She was so astonished that he'd thought of her comfort, she stared at him with her mouth gaping open as she wondered why he was being so nice to her? His staring gaze caused a scorching heat to rise to her cheeks, forcing her to turn away. Was this the reason he had gone to town after dinner? No, a man wouldn't have put on a silk shirt just to go and buy a floor pillow. How silly of her to think of it. There had to be another reason.

She glanced back at him and pointed at the luxurious cushion and opened her mouth to thank him, then clamped it shut when he waved a stiff hand across his throat. Okay, point taken. He either didn't want any thanks, or he didn't want his family to know he'd given it to her. Mandy glanced around the room at his family. No one noticed the silent conversation, except for his father who apparently missed nothing.

She traced the soft pile with her fingertips. Her heart warmed by his charity and thanks to Adam's thoughtfulness, her leg would not suffer any stiffness. As grumpy as Adam was, he was also a kind and generous man.

She turned to the children as she opened the big story book and began to read.

～

"Leg feel better?"

Mandy turned sharply to see Adam already lounging in his chair with his extra-large coffee mug in hand. His low baritone voice vibrated into her body, shaking her insides. Butterflies fluttered in her lower belly as she turned and walked over to the railing. A spark of hope for his friendship bubbled in her veins as she gazed at the mountains. Like the other evenings, the sun was just setting, the dark of night hadn't totally arrived, yet it was late enough to cast eerie shadows. "Yes, thank you, Adam." She turned to face him as her fingers stroked the wooden railing. "The cushion is very comfortable."

"I didn't tell you I put it there," his voice hushed.

"You're the only one who knew my leg gets stiff from sitting on the floor so long," she said turning her head back towards the west. Her hand stayed clutched to the railing.

He shrugged. "I don't know why you don't sit in a chair in the first place if your leg bothers you so much."

"Well…" She turned back to face him. "Children have a habit of sitting on knees when someone reads to them. So, again, thank you." She gave him a quick smile. "It was sweet of you."

"I'm not sweet, Mandy, so get that out of your pretty little head. You want sweet, stick with my brother and his family."

"Why did you get it for me, then? And why did you see to my comfort if it doesn't matter?" It was still light enough that she could see his eyes roam over her. Red alert signals pebbled her skin. His eyes were hungry yet were still filled with contempt. "Why?" She watched him push himself off his chair then place his mug on the arm of it and saunter towards her. Her heart thudded hard against her chest as she stepped away from the railing while her eyes searched quickly for the door. To give him ample space to pass, she stepped to the side. The back of her shirt brushed against the wall of the house.

Instead of leaving the porch, he stepped directly in front of her. Her heart pumped hard and fast. She took in a deep breath and expelled the air from her mouth in quick little pants.

"Nervous?"

Mandy tilted her chin up and looked him square in the eye. She was not going to give him the satisfaction of knowing that she was nervous. Yet her body trembled with passionate heat. How could she be attracted to this... this, rebel? "No. I'm not." Her chin lifted with confidence. Confidence she didn't feel she had.

"You sure," he asked, "because your breathing seems a little labored?"

His smile wicked. Wolf-like. He was definitely a hunter. Why was he tormenting her like this? Was this his way of humiliating her? He took a step closer. Mandy quickly stepped sideways, but not fast enough to get to the door. His long arm blocked her way as the palm of his hand hit flat against the log, stopping her from going inside. He slowly, deliberately leaned into her. Pure masculine scent surrounded her. His sweet cool minted breath fanned her hot cheeks.

"You're right." His eyes narrowed. "It's from me."

She watched his eyes cruise over her face and focus on her lips. Was he going to kiss her? How would she respond to that? She backed against the wall as far as she could. "T-thank, y... you."

"I want something in return." His eyes turned hungry. Greedy.

She glanced past him to the large oak tree in the front yard. The sun had set. The daylight was gone and nightfall had set in, casting even more shadows. The first hoot of the night owl made her jump. She hoped it was dark enough to hide the blush of her cheeks. With his face was too close to hers she doubted it. "W... what, do you want?" She hated when she stammered like a school girl. She hated showing weakness of any sort.

"You're obviously needed by my family, but don't get in my way. If you see me coming, move it. I don't like being inconvenienced by missing tools, needing to change clothes because you drenched me with water or milk. And…" he stressed, "…don't touch my laundry. Understand?" His other arm went up. His palm slapped against the log wall, caging her completely. "Another thing. Leave my extra-large, frog-faced, double-walled, coffee to-go- mug, and my chair alone."

For what seemed like eternity, they stood there in silence watching each other. Studying each other's moves. He was so incredibly handsome her body got hot as it tingled in her lower belly. Staring at him this close, her senses returned to normal and she wondered why on earth she ever wanted to win this jerk over. He was not going to intimidate her and tell her what to do. If she wanted to spray him with water, or spill milk on him, she'd do just that. If she wanted to dump his whole tool box in the sand, well then, she would do that, too. To top it off she'd not only take his favorite froggy mug, she'd hide it on him. If she had the nerve.

Her eyes narrowed as she pulled back her shoulders, tightened her fist and straightened. Being trapped by human steel frustrated her and twisted in her lower gut. How dare he speak to her like this. How dare he threaten her. Suddenly, she threw her arms up and shoved him back freeing herself from her cage. The hard mass of his chest jolted her. She had to stay focused as the brick wall actually moved back a few steps.

"You honestly think I did all those things on purpose?" she asked in a low serious voice. "If you think I want your attention, you've got crap for brains, Mister. Then again, maybe I'll iron all your shirts and I'll hide around corners with jugs of milk, just to tick you off. I didn't know that was your favorite to-go-mug at first, but now that I do, maybe, I'll hide your froggy mug on you. You will never find it again." Not wanting his family to hear, she whispered harsh and low

"You're not my boss, so I'll do what I want and when I want." She almost lost it when she saw his mouth curled up at the corners. The deep dimple in his cheek urged her to collapse into his arms. His lips parted slightly. He was the most sensual man she'd ever seen. He wanted her to believe he was the meanest man alive, but he was the kindest, sweetest man she'd ever known and he cared. His actions showed it. *Oh God, I like him. I really like him. More than like him.*

"You're a feisty little thing, aren't you?" Adam took another step back. He wanted her more than ever now. She had spunk. As much as her cheeks colored, she stood up for herself and he believed that she'd take no guff from any man. He took in the sweet scent of her. He wanted those lovely pink lips on his. Wanted to experience the warmth of her touch. Needed to feel her firm breasts against his chest. He turned to go down the steps before he did something stupid like wrestle her to the ground and litter her face with kisses. "Good night, Miss Riley."

"Please, call me Mandy."

At the bottom of the stairs he hesitated and turned. The smile on her face was so angelic, it confused him. He had no right to receive such a smile from anyone much less this incredible beauty. It was obvious that she had forgiven him for the way he had spoken and for trapping her against the house. He nodded. His eyes meandered over her body. "Fair enough." His mouth twitched to a quick smile. "Good night, Mandy." He turned and headed towards the barn. His mouth again turned up at the corners as a warm feeling cloaked him with the thought of the floor pillow he gave her. If she liked the pillow so much, he wondered how much she'd like the chair he was staining. Now two days late.

As he did his checks, his mind wouldn't stop thinking about the spitfire woman in his family's home. A good butt-kicking is what he needed for the things he was thinking about her. Curiosity nagged him so he peered out the small window of the tack room to see her still standing right where he had left her. He groaned heavily as she lifted her long hair, sweeping it back then letting it fall down around her shoulders. Her head tilted back as she gazed at the stars and moon above. No one had ever looked so damn beautiful.

He couldn't help but chuckle at all the things that had happened to him since her arrival. He knew there would be changes, but he didn't think they would affect him so severely. He didn't want to think of her, but he couldn't forget her and neither could his aroused body. He rubbed his face a second time. He had to get back to his work and concentrate on his chores.

As if he had willed her away, Mandy turned and went into the house. Finally, she was gone. Gone in a blink of an eye. If it was only that easy to get her out of his mind. If he could tell his hormones that she'd gone.

Needing to check on his friend, Adam left the tack room and briskly walked to the first bunk-house which served as the foremen's home. He entered by the back door and peered into the office where there were two desks, two filing cabinets, two chairs. He shook his head at the sight of Hank's desk and was thankful Hank wasn't doing the scheduling, or the payroll for that matter. Chuck's desk was neat, tidy and organized, then again Chuck had never been through what Hank was going through now.

Adam entered the kitchen where strong coffee sat on the

stove. "Hey, Hank," he said as he entered the living room and watched his friend put down a self-help book and place it on a coffee table beside his rocker recliner.

"Adam." Hank nodded slowly.

"Doing okay?"

"No." Hank put his head down. "I need a drink."

Adam studied his friend. He looked pale under his tanned face and his eyes were moist with tears. His dark hair prematurely turning gray at the temples gave him a much older look than his twenty-nine years. "Come for a walk." Adam jerked his head towards the doorway. He watched Hank slowly get up with his head down, both hands in his front pockets and his shoulders drooped. "Fresh air will do you good," Adam said as they walked through the door and towards the corral. As the silence stretched, Adam could only imagine how much his friend was hurting.

"I don't know if I can do this," Hank said as he stopped at the corral gate. "Those people at the self-help meetings don't understand. Most of them got screwed-up lives, messed up marriages and come from abusive homes. I don't fit. I had a good home life and good parents. I have good friends and people who love me. I had a good marriage. You're just wasting your time bringing me to the meetings."

"Give them a chance, Hank. You'll find out you're not alone. You'll find someone who will understand or at least they can relate to a loss. Everyone's story will be different. Their lives are messed up for a reason. You've got to try, Hank. Do you think Nancy would want you to continue along this path?"

Hank shrugged. "It would have been ten years next month." He toyed with the thick gold band still on his left ring finger. "I miss her. I miss her terribly."

"We all do, Hank. She was a special woman who brought joy to everyone." Adam put his hand on Hank's shoulder. "I'm not going to tell you I understand your loss. I don't understand. That's why you need to go to these meetings. I'm your friend, Hank, but I've never been through what you've been through and neither has anyone else been on this ranch. All I know is that you have to carry on. You've been grieving for almost two years and drinking for more than half of that. I don't believe Nancy would want you to drown yourself in a bottle. She'd want you to carry on with life, Hank. A good life."

"Drinking helps."

"No, Hank. It doesn't. You drink to mask your pain. Pain you have to work through. You get ornery and it tears you apart."

"It makes me forget how lonely and unhappy I am. It makes me happy."

"You just think you're happy. A few drinks make you laugh, tell jokes then a few more sets you into a deep depression. You say things you don't mean and you hurt others. Another drink, you get ugly and hurtful, not to mention it's affecting not only you, but everyone who relies on you. Hank, you're a good friend, a sincere friend, a caring friend when you don't drink. I for one need you. My family needs you."

Hank rubbed his face hard with his hands. "I'll keep trying, Adam. You and I go back a long way. I value our friendship, but I won't promise anything."

"That's all I ask." Adam walked quietly beside his friend as they headed slowly back to the log cabin. Halfway there he heard the front door open and shut. He looked at his watch then towards the main house. With the children in bed Mandy would have her final cup of tea out in the porch before retiring to her room. With the porch light on, he could see her watching them as they walked back to Hank's bunkhouse and he wondered what she was thinking? He had to admit he was pretty rough on her this evening. Rough wasn't the word, he had been darned right rude. "Jeez, she must think I acted like a class A jerk."

"What?" Hank turned and asked.

"Oh, nothing, just talking to myself."

"I understand. I've been doing a lot of that lately."

Adam looked back at the house and noticed Mandy still standing there. His mind went a little wild at how close he had gotten to her on the porch. He had her trapped. Had her where he wanted her. Instead of telling her to move out of his way and demand she leave his chair and mug alone, he should have taken her sincere thank you for the pillow and given her a warm smile.

"I can get back to my place by myself, Adam. You carry on and I'll see you tomorrow."

Adam turned to his friend. "Okay, you have a good night. Oh, and say a prayer. It will help."

"Yeah, I used to pray. I kind of got away from it after I lost Nancy." Hank walked away with his head hung low. "I'll try again, Adam."

"God loves you, my friend." Adam watched Hank walk away slowly. He hurt for his buddy and knew he had a long haul yet to go.

Not tired in the least, Adam headed towards the workshop. He had a chair to finish.

THE NEXT MORNING Adam had already been in the kitchen and left by the time Mandy got there at five-thirty. She took a deep breath of his wonderful all-masculine aftershave that surrounded her. A smell that was only his. With her tea cup in her hand, she glanced into the living room on her way to the front door. The velvet cushion called out to her, so she went and sat down for a moment. Her fingers touched the soft fabric. Her body felt warm all over at the thoughtful gift he had given to her. The man was so confusing yet a man she wanted all to herself.

Fresh morning air blew in from the long living room window begging her to go outside to greet the glorious day. She opened and shut the door quietly and turned towards his chair. Her mouth opened and gasped. "Ohh. Oh… my." Sitting before her was a beautiful wooden lawn chair with her initials, A.R., carved on the back of it. It was so… so… Descriptive words escaped her as she placed her tea cup down on the railing and stared at the flawless lawn chair. She sat in it. A smile crossed her lips as she began to understand that Adam's bark was worse than his bite. She sat back and closed her eyes as she ran both her hands along the smooth finished surface. It was perfect. Now she could sit for a few moments every day and dream of her own porch overlooking her own land.

Booted footsteps crunched on the gravel, causing her to let go of her wonderful daydream. She opened her eyes and watched Adam come up onto the porch steps. His face appeared more relaxed and his stance was not as stiff. Their eyes met briefly and she thought how truly remarkable his were. They held secrets, but also warmth. There was a kindness there, a gentleness that longed to be released. What had happened to make this man so contradicting, so… for the lack of another word right now, angry at times? Cole had said he was out of sorts lately, but why. "Adam, thank you. This chair is so beautiful. You made this?"

"Yeah, it was the only way I could get you to stay out of mine."

There was a trace of a smile on his lips before he strolled over to his chair and sat down to join her. "Thank you. It's very comfortable and just my size." She stood up and ran her hand along the back of it. "I never thought I would ever see a chair that would equal my uncle and brother's furniture but I was wrong." She graced him with a smile. "This one does and believe me that's the absolute ultimate compliment. Fine woodworking, cabinetmaking and finishing has been passed down in my family for generations. All the men in my family are wonderful finishing carpenters and designers." She turned back to admire the chair. "Thank you, Adam."

CHAPTER 9

*A*dam shrugged at the compliment, sending her a message that he didn't care, but her radiant smile pierced his heart opening it a little more. Her eyes sparkled like a fresh pool of blue mineral water from the mountains causing his pulse to accelerate. The sudden urge to touch her and bring her close to him caught him off guard. Again. He stared at her beauty, listened to her voice and allowed her graceful movements to seep into his blood. "You always this cheerful in the mornings?"

"Yes. Why wouldn't I be?" Mandy swept her arm gracefully in a half-circle in front of herself. Her fingers pointed over the property and beyond. "Surrounded by such absolute beauty that God has bestowed on us, one would have to be daft not to be cheerful."

"I can't argue with that," Adam agreed. "He's definitely surrounded us with a beauty no words can express," he added as he watched the natural blush on her angelic face, which pleased him. Maybe he should give her a chance. Would she be like the others? The other women in his life had told him the same thing about the beauty of this land, but with Mandy it wasn't just words. It was the conviction in her voice. Her actions. She truly loved country life. Loved the sweet songbirds. Loved the fresh morning air and the evening sunsets. Here was a gentle, kind, warm and wonderful woman who was great with the children and forgave easily.

Was this the woman of his dreams?

Was she the woman he'd dreamed of while he stared at the ceiling when he couldn't sleep? Would a woman like Mandy be happy with a man like him? Rough, independent, but also a family man that could be a loving husband? And he would be a loving husband to a woman who could love him back. He wanted what every McBride man in history wanted. To be loved for the rest of his life by a woman who could return his love with just as much passion. Shy or not, Mandy was stunning and had to have a man in her life. He wasn't aware of any calls for her except from her family, but maybe she had a cell phone which would be more private.

Suddenly he had a headache. What the hell was he thinking about? He needed a kick in the pants before he needed another woman in his life. He turned towards her and watched her stroke the armrests of the chair and wished she was stroking his arm. She leaned back and smiled. *Yup, I definitely need that kick in the pants.*

"I could sit here all day…" her head turned slightly towards him, "…but I must get the children up." She stood up. "Thank you again for the lovely chair," she said sincerely.

"Welcome," he said sincerely as he watched her gracefully walk away from him and into the house. Maybe, just maybe his thoughts were right.

The long hard, busy day finally came to an end and Adam found himself again stretched out in his favorite chair on the porch. It had been a day from Hell. A ranch hand had to go to the city to help his sister which was fine, but then a second one wasn't paying attention and actually walked right into the barn door splitting his lip so bad it required stitches. A third one, had to drive him to a hospital in Calgary. Adam couldn't pull any of the other hands from their chores and Cole was busy, so he was on his own. Of course, Hank needing a ride back and forth into town for his A.A. group meeting, took up a good part of his day.

To top it off, he tried to avoid being doused with water as Mandy watered the garden again. He recalled her telling him when he held her captive that if she wanted to spray him with water she would. If she wanted to hide around corners and douse him with milk she'd do just that. He cracked a smile remembering her telling him she'd hide his favorite froggy mug and that he'd never find it again. And that she just might iron all of his shirts. Adam knew he had brought it upon himself, so every time he needed to go to the house, he checked to see if she was in the front or the back, and then he used the opposite door. Was he dodging her? *Hell ya.*

He leaned his head back and waited for Mandy to come out for a few minutes to sit in her chair. He missed the story hour because of the never-ending chores, but he damn well wasn't going to miss a few moments with her before she left for home. When the front door opened, his pulse quickened with excitement. He followed her movements as she walked over to the chair and sat down. She leaned back with her duffel bag clutched in her hand on her lap.

"I'm going to miss this chair tomorrow morning." She smiled. "Well..." she sighed loudly and stood, "...good-night, Adam, I'll see you Monday morning.

"Night, drive carefully," he said when he really wanted to say, I'll miss you, I wish you could stay. He rubbed his chin in deep thought as he watched her walk down the porch steps to her truck. "Aha, she's probably nothing but a major pain in the butt," he told himself, but not quite believing it.

He stood, yet as if frozen to the porch floor, he watched her drive away until he couldn't see her red truck any longer. Thinking about the truck again, he continued to wonder how she could afford such an extravagance on a part-time salary.

Adam draped his arms over the railing as he recalled the other day when she was with the children in the corral with the horses. Most city gals would be at least a little leery, but not Mandy. She wasn't the least bit nervous here. In fact, she was comfortable everywhere on the ranch as if she was a part of it. Even when the children brought her little mice, snakes and the other creatures, she wasn't frazzled. She held them and taught the kids to be gentle. He recalled when she walked calmly up to Ryan's half-grown calf he was brushing, she hadn't flinched. Hell, she was right in there practically taking over his chore. He rubbed the mixed-up thoughts from his head and moved towards the steps.

MANDY RETURNED home before midnight and like the Saturday before, her family was anxious to know how her week had turned out. Her Aunt Maggie had saved her a plate of her favorite Chinese food, and her brother made her a cup of her favorite tea, and placed it on the end table beside the love seat she usually sat in.

"Squeak, how's it going with the rebel?" Jason said with a concerned frown, then took a sip of his coffee.

She cringed. If her twin knew how Adam spoke to her, he'd be at the McBride ranch before she could explain that all Adam wanted was to be left alone. Every mishap over the past week had been her fault. She shrugged nonchalantly and took a sip of tea and hoped Jason would drop any more questions.

Recalling the first week, she waved her hands to get her

family's attention. "Oh, I forgot to tell you all about my very first morning on the ranch. Well, I got up, made my tea like I do here, then I had found this totally awesome extra-large, to-go-mug, with a happy green frog on it. Anyway, it was absolutely perfect, not to mention that I wouldn't have to make a second cup. Or even a third." She clapped her hands together. "Well, I went outside and spotted this super amazing comfy chair, so of course I sat in it." She smiled. "As it was, he found me in his thinking chair with his favorite extra-large coffee mug." She laughed as she watched her uncle's shoulders shake as if he knew exactly how Adam felt.

Jason roared with laughter. "One way to tick off a man is to take his favorite coffee mug."

"Are you serious?"

"Sure am." Jason stood up. "Don't you remember Pa having a favorite mug? In fact, he wouldn't even let Ma wash it and often told her it was only black coffee in it anyway."

"I'd totally forgotten about that. I should take my big blue travel mug back with me so I don't have to use small cups. I like a larger mug myself so I guess I can't blame him for being ticked."

Richard chuckled. "I like my large mug, too."

Mandy stood and stretched. "I'm tired, and since I have to be back at the ranch by six a.m., I'm going to hit the hay." She yawned then gave everyone a big hug. "Night, everyone."

"Night, Squeak. By the way, we need both trucks this week so I'll drive ya tomorrow morning."

"I got to be there by six," she reminded him.

"I can get you there by five if you want me to." Jason laughed.

Early Monday morning, Mandy was in the kitchen filling up her mug with green tea and Jason's with black coffee then screwed on the lids.

"Morning, Squeak, ya ready?"

"You bet and I even made your morning coffee." Mandy smiled. "I didn't even wash you mug out." She laughed. "However, I did give it a quick rinse."

"Perfect, I wouldn't want any soap residue in my mug." Jason winked. "Let's head out."

As they drove along the highway, she smiled at the image of Adam relaxing in his favorite chair using his favorite mug.

Arriving back at the McBride ranch made Mandy anxious, so she held her breath and focused on Adam who was on the porch just as she imagined. Maybe Jason wouldn't notice as they pulled up. She got out of the truck as Jason jumped out and retrieved her duffel bag then came around to her side. Lucky for her, Jason didn't question anything, or seem to notice Adam sitting on the porch.

"See you, Jas. Have a good week." She gave him a quick hug and with her duffel bag in hand turned away.

"Hold on there. Not so fast." Jason gave a quick tug on the duffel bag straps. "If you need me anytime, call me. And, Squeak don't let Rebel man bother you. Ya stay away from him, ya hear?" He released the duffel bag strap and leaned forward and kissed her on the forehead.

"Yes, Jas. Don't worry and thanks again."

"Okay." Jason brushed the side of her hair and fluffed up her bangs for her. "Have a good week and see ya Saturday night."

She waved goodbye and watched him drive away. Knowing Adam was sitting watching, she took in a deep breath before she turned to face another week of him making her feel self-conscious. With jelly-like knees, she managed to reach the porch steps. "Good morning, Adam." She lifted her new, large, blue travel mug and smiled. "You have no more worries about me using yours now."

"Let me see." Adam reached over, took it, and examined it.

"That's a nice one." He handed it back to her and nodded with a slight smile.

Mandy took it back quickly and stepped back to put a safe distance between them. Not because she was afraid of him physically, but if he accidentally touched her, she'd spin into another orbit. She'd be dizzy with passion, just like the night he caged her with his body against the house. He had no idea what he did to her. "I should go in and get ready for the day."

"It's only six ten, you have a few more minutes. Have a seat for a while."

Their eyes met briefly, but they spoke volumes. Melanie broke contact first and turned away. "I'll make myself a cup of tea first," she said then opened the door and headed straight for her bedroom.

ADAM BRUSHED his hair back at the recollection of her having to stretch her arm out to show him her new mug. Had he frightened her that much? Knowing full well he'd been damn well rude and uncivilized, he doubted she was going to return to join him. Disappointed, he placed his mug on the arm of his chair and walked to the barn. He wondered about the man who drove Mandy back in the plain-jane 4x4 which was the same one she had driven to the interview. Where was her fancy red truck she had for the past two weeks?

Adam frowned at the thought of the man kissing her on the forehead and wondered what that was all about? If she had been his girlfriend, he wouldn't have cared if anyone was watching or not, he would have grabbed her in his arms and given her, a goodbye kiss like she had never been kissed before. Especially if he wasn't going to see her for a whole week. *I'm in trouble.* His stomach turned sour at the thought of the other man touching her, stroking her beautiful shiny hair, and how comfortable she looked accepting his kiss, even though it was only on the forehead.

He pounded on the bunkhouse door, where six ranch hands lived. "Okay men, rise and shine." He pounded a second time then walked towards the barn.

"Morning, Dee, Stacey and baby." He chuckled. "I'll have to pick a name for you." He unlatched the stall gates. "Come on you three, time for your morning exercises." He laughed when he saw the foal race ahead. Stacey was next. He patted Dee on the rump. "You'll be a mama soon again, Dee." He watched her amble slowly into the small holding corral then closed the gate and went back to the barn. Since his truck was still loaded with feed bags, he decided to stock the loft himself instead of going out with the men.

"Hey, morning, Adam." Chuck, the head foreman, sauntered over with his big dark gray horse following. He wrapped the reins around the corral rail and adjusted his black leather gloves. "You want me to leave a man behind to help you?" He adjusted his chaps.

"Mornin', Chuck. No, I'm fine, thanks." Adam threw a bag of feed over his shoulder and walked into the feed shed then back again for another bag. By ten-thirty he was done when he suddenly heard the filly scream out a whinny. He raced out of the barn to the corral. Before he knew it, he was flat on his backside. "Ooffff." He picked himself up and looked down. "Shit." He glanced at the little filly as it kicked up her heels, while exercising her vocal cords. His eyes narrowed at one of the young ranch hands with a bull in tow. "Jeez, thanks, Ralph." He twisted at the waist, brushed his jeans off and looked at his hand which was caked in… he groaned.

"Sorry, boss, the bull had to go." The young cowboy roared with laughter.

"What the hell are you doing so close to this barn?"

"Wanted a peek at the new foal."

"Peek later." Adam gave his hand a quick shake. "Yuck."

MANDY HAD PICKED up a prescription for Dianne in town and was back at the ranch just as the littlest cowboy woke up. She helped him get his overalls on and played peek-a-boo for a while. "Come on, Bobby, we have to get your laundry done." She took his hand and went downstairs to the laundry room where she found Adam's clothes in the dryer. Again. She chuckled. It was always Adam's clothing. With extra care, she folded his clothes and hung up his shirts. This time no ironing. "Come on, Bobby, you're going to the toy room for a minute while I take these to your uncle's room."

"K, me p'ay cars."

Mandy knew he'd stay at least until he totally messed up the room which wasn't going to give her much time. She raced upstairs and put a few bath towels into the cupboard, then walked into Adam's room with his folded clothes. She froze as she heard movement in the attached bathroom. Her jaw dropped. The neatly folded clothes fell into a heap on the floor as Adam walked out of his bathroom naked as he was drying his hair. "Ah... ah...a h," she stuttered and stammered.

Adam whipped the towel off his head. "Mandy?" he questioned in surprise. "What are you doing in here?" His mouth twitched into a slight grin.

Mandy stared. Her mouth hung open as Adam stood there, butt naked. "I... ah... ah." She bent down to pick up the clothes hoping her hair would cover her red face.

"Leave them." He waved one hand through the air. "Can't a man have some privacy and get dressed in his own room?" he asked shaking his head as he picked up his clean jeans. "Turn around."

"I... I... thought you w... were out," she stammered. Her gaze travelled the length of him. His body rippled with muscle. Her stare fixed on his perfect body as he put on his jeans one muscled leg at a time and hiked them over his perfect butt and groin. Heat boiled under her skin as her whole body flooded with desire as he did up the zipper.

"Mandy..." He stepped towards her, "...do you mind?" He let out a deep groaned chuckle. "Or do you want to keep my shirt?" He took a clean shirt from her trembling hands.

"Oh, y... yes, I mean no..." She remembered to breathe, turned and dashed down the stairs, through the living room, past the den, crossed over the dining room, and into the toy room then plunked herself on the floor. Picking up a book, she fanned her hot flushed face with it. She laughed nervously at the surprised look on his face when he came out of his bathroom with only a heavy gold chain around his neck. He had been a little shocked to see her in his room, but he wasn't the least bit embarrassed. Not that he had anything to be embarrassed about. Nothing at all. In all her born days, she had never even thought such a perfect specimen ever existed.

CHAPTER 10

*A*dam buttoned up his clean shirt as he grumbled. "A guy can't even shower in the middle of the morning. First my cup, then my chair, now she wants my bedroom. What next, the shirt off my back?" He rolled up his sleeves. "Serves me right for landing into bull shit." He laughed as he picked up his dirty rolled up jeans and chucked them into the hamper, then put his clean clothes away. *Crap, now she's got me talking to myself.*

He stood in front of his dresser for a moment, still wondering why she would even consider folding up his laundry and bringing it to his room. He couldn't help but wonder what she thought seeing him butt naked. He took in a breath. She wasn't the first woman to see him undressed and he doubted she'd be the last, but he had to admit, he felt a little embarrassed for her. She was a lady and judging by her flushed cheeks, he questioned how she was going to look him in the face when he got home tonight. Yes, she was definitely a lady and a very beautiful one at that, especially with those flushed cheeks.

"You weed dis." Bobby hiked up his pj bottoms and handed her a large story book.

"Okay, since it's your turn tonight to pick a story, which one do you want?" She named off several titles and showed him the picture in front of each story. His fat little finger pointed to a happy little water beetle sitting on a lily pad. It was from one of her children book collections she had brought from home. Like every other evening, everyone listened quietly until the very end.

"Well, Amanda." John placed his hands on the arms of the chair and braced himself to get up. "Like I've said before, you read beautifully." John nodded with admiration.

"Is that story true, Miss Riley? Do water beetles really like to sun themselves on lily pads?" Crystal asked as she stood up and stood beside her.

Mandy laughed softly. "Well, I'm sure they do. The sun's warm and God made the warmth for every living thing." She closed the book. "Tomorrow I'll read the next two stories, which are about more little bugs that our Creator made. By the end of the week we will have finished a quarter of this book. Then..." she looked at Crystal, "...it will be your turn to choose whether you want to continue with these bug stories or get another." She stood up. "I'll be back in a few minutes." She noticed Adam head towards the door. Slowly she followed, walked outside, and down the porch steps to do her leg exercises.

"Leg still sore?" Adam asked in a deep comforting tone.

Unable to meet his gaze, she shook her head. "No, the pillow is comfortable and I haven't had a sore leg since you gave it to me."

"Care to share with me why it bothers you?"

She turned abruptly. His voice was so close. She hadn't realized he had come down the steps and stood beside her. His chest was inches from her face so she stepped back, to put a safe distance between them. Especially now that she knew what he looked like underneath his clothes. Powerful. Strong. Lethal.

"I didn't mean to startle you."

"No, no, you didn't," she said softly, hoping her voice didn't sound as shaky as she felt. He was in her space and instantly she became aware of his physical size. He was much the same size as Jason, but he wasn't her brother. He was a man who excited her. A man she wanted to touch, and to have him touch her. Heat sizzled through her veins. Warmth radiated to her cheeks.

"Mandy." Adam took a step forward. "I owe you an apology."

"No, you don't." She took another step back for fear of being caged in his arms, yet that was exactly what she wanted. "I... umm... I have to go and check on the children. Good night, Adam." She flew into the house. Mandy questioned why he was trying to apologize to her when she was the one who owed him one for being in his bedroom. Why was he looking at her with such gentleness?

After getting the children to bed, she made her usual way to the kitchen to make her tea, then headed for the living room to see Dianne and Cole. Entering, she froze. What was Adam doing here? "Good night all." She turned and left in haste.

COLE LOOKED at his brother in total surprise. "What was that all about? Are you bothering Mandy?"

"No," Adam said hastily. "What gave you that idea?"

"She usually sits with us for a while so it's strange that she ran when she saw you here. Any thoughts as to why?"

"Look, Cole, I admit when she first came here, I wasn't exactly myself and far from pleasant. I was trying to apologize tonight, but she took off."

"Sounds weird to me. What did you do?"

"I told you, nothing. Like I said, I just wanted to talk to her. I was working up to apologize for my rudeness for the last couple of weeks," Adam snapped.

"Adam, please, don't scare her off," Cole pleaded. "We need her. You know how busy we are and it's even busier now than ever. The ranch is growing in leaps and bounds. All the new calves and colts... I'm glad we don't have goats." Cole chuckled ruefully at his silly little rhyme, then became serious. "Please, just don't scare her." He placed his hands on his hips.

Adam clenched his jaw then put down his coffee mug and stood up. "I'll leave her alone if that makes you happy." He turned. "You can be damned sure of that." He stomped out without looking back.

Cole shook his head and brushed his face hard with both hands. "Damn, I think I just complicated things." He took his seat beside Dianne. "Di, I just wanted to know what's going on."

"You have been hard on Adam lately, Honey. Every time he turns around you're on his case. I'm sorry, but I can't blame him for getting ticked off at you."

"Come on, I'm not that hard on him."

"Listen to me." Dianne leaned forward and patted her husband's hand. "You're harder on him than you think you are and he's been working like a dog. Yes, he's still taking time out to help Hank, and Hank does seem to be settling somewhat. Just maybe Adam is able to help him more than we thought he could. Cole, even though we have Mandy here, you're still home more than you need to be and Adam's been doing most of your share of the workload."

"Are you saying I'm part of his problem?" He frowned. "You saw what happened." He stretched his arm and pointed to the stairs. "She flew up those stairs when she saw him. What the hell does that tell you?" Cole didn't wait for an answer. "Well?"

"Calm down," she whispered.

Cole gritted his teeth. "I am calm."

Dianne waved her hand. "I don't know what's going on here anymore than you do but I don't believe for one minute, Adam will hurt Mandy in any way."

Cole shook his head. "Believe what you want, but I'll tell you one thing." He shook his index finger towards the front door. "If Adam does anything to make Mandy leave, I'm going to beat the crap out of him."

"Oh, that's real big of you. Real brotherly."

"Stop it, Di." Cole slapped his hand on the table. "We've got enough problems around here already without you criticizing how I feel about this whole situation."

"I'm going to bed." Dianne wheeled herself towards the downstairs bedroom. "Good night."

"Yeah, you too. I'm going for a walk." He walked out the front door and slammed it behind him. "Damn." Cole rubbed his face hard then looked into the darkness.

"Cole."

He turned to see his brother in the dark corner of the porch. "Adam." Cole stepped into the darkness to join him. "Why didn't you put the yard light on?"

"I felt like being in the dark. You got a problem with that, too?" Adam said sarcastically.

"Dammit, Adam, don't start with me."

"Hey, how does it feel?"

Cole watched Adam get up. His brother was angry and it was his fault. He should be there for his brother, not against him. He sighed deeply. "I don't want to argue with you, Adam. You're my brother and I respect you. I need you."

Adam laughed and walked to the front door. "Get real, Cole. You've got the problem, not me. Dammit all, lately you only see what you want."

Cole tightened his fist and raised his index finger and cut Adam off from getting to the front door. "Then you tell me what happened in there." He pointed to the living room from outside the window. "Why the hell would Mandy run upstairs when she saw you in the living room? Tell me, because I sure as hell don't have an answer."

"I don't know why." Adam brushed past his brother. "Ask her." He put his hand on the door knob. "I already told you, all I did was try to apologize to her. She fled. Not me."

Cole watched his brother disappear into the house. He shook his head. "What the hell's going on here?" He sighed, went in, shut the lights off then went straight to the bedroom where his wife had managed to get into bed herself.

"You all right, Cole?"

"I'm fine."

Dianne turned her head towards him. "I've been thinking. Maybe they're attracted to each other. I think Mandy's shy and Adam's confused."

Cole stood and stared at his wife who he was so worried about. She was so beautiful with her pretty dark brown, silky, hair fanned over the pillow. The turquoise nightgown she had on excited him. He stripped off his clothes and crawled slowly onto the bed. "Honey, I'm sorry I yelled. I love you." He kissed her cheek. "You're so beautiful." His mouth brushed over her moist lush lips. "I don't like fighting with you, and maybe you're right, I've been too tough on Adam. I'll be there for him more and as far as they're concerned, we'll let them figure it out. Right now, I want to hold you."

"Then snuggle closer, cowboy," she whispered and reached for him.

Cole smiled then switched off the light. "I'll love you forever and ever."

∾

FOR THE REST of the week, Adam was out late on the range with his father, brother and the hands. He ignored Cole as much as he could, even though it was tough, as Cole was true to his word and was around more, to do his share of the workload. As he glared at Cole, his thoughts went to Mandy. As angry as he was with her for running like she did and making him look like a monster, he realized it wasn't her fault. Her shyness and his sudden need to apologize had made her run. It was funny, but he missed her. He missed her stories, her soft voice, her peaches and cream complexion.

He took a second glance at his brother and although Cole was a good man, it still ticked him off that his own brother had asked him what he had said to Mandy to get her so upset. Then again, he couldn't blame Cole, because lately he had been a crabby ass.

Again, his mind shifted to Mandy. He wanted to be with her. Get to know her. Wanted a friendship. Maybe more. But his brain spun back to his past relationships and how he'd been used. He thought he had been in love at one time, but his dreams of having a wife and children of his own were shattered. The women he continued to fall for were users and he couldn't forget that. All they wanted was expensive gifts, presents and money from wealthy ranchers.

Well, no more needy women for him. 'The past is the past,' his brain whispered softly. 'Mandy's different,' his heart squeezed gently. He wiped his forehead with the back of his hand. He needed to talk and apologize to her, but this time he'd make sure she wasn't going to get away from him before he said his piece.

The following evening, Adam and his father were late coming home from the range and had missed dinner and Mandy's story hour. The children were already in bed and

Mandy was now free for the rest of the evening. It was late and the stars were already out. As hungry as he was by now, his dinner could wait. He grabbed a black coffee from the kitchen then headed outside.

As he suspected, she was out in the front yard taking in a few deep breaths of the country air she loved so much. He closed the front door softly and as quietly as possible then silently went to the far end of the porch and leaned on the railing. He watched her while she gazed at the heavenly stars then take in a deep fresh breath of air before she began to exercise her leg, like she often did before she went to bed.

He'd wait patiently until she was done then he'd approach her and she wasn't going back into the house till he was done talking. Knowing that she liked to be in her room by ten thirty, and probably tired from a full day's work, he'd make sure he didn't miss the opportunity to talk to her. And this time he wouldn't mess up.

She was so graceful. So stunning. He couldn't keep his eyes off her. Suddenly when she looked up, her relaxed, calm look turned to surprise. Adam waved to let her know he was there. "Evening, Mandy," he said in a quiet tone of voice. Almost hushed as he watched her go straight to the stairway. If she ran, she'd get there before him so he'd better get moving.

Now.

He took long strides. "Mandy, please, don't go in yet. I need to talk to you for a moment." He got to the front door just in time and blocked her way. "Please, listen to me for a minute." He reached for the side of her face. Her left side. Her hand quickly went up as if to defend herself and backed away. Shocked with her actions, he raised both his hands and backed up. "Hey, I wasn't going to hurt you. Believe me, I wouldn't." He watched her comb the side of her hair with her fingers as she spoke.

"I know, it's just my reflexes." She brought her hand down to her side.

He inched closer, slowly. His left hand rose slowly and this time he reached for her upper arm. A safe place to touch. His curiosity heightened as he watched her eyes shift to his hand and her breathing increased. She stepped away as he inched closer with his hand. "I promise I won't hurt you." He lowered his hand and backed away. "Why are you trembling?"

"I'm not," she denied lowering her head.

"Yes, you are. You're terrified of me and I want to know why. I realize I haven't been the most pleasant man lately, however, I refuse to believe I've given you any cause to tremble at the sight of me." He slapped his thigh with his hand. "Then again, I cornered you last week and I wasn't the friendliest member of the family, so maybe I have given you reason to fear me."

"No, no, you haven't." Her head shook slightly. "I'm sorry you think that."

"I don't think it. I know it. Are you going to tell me why you're afraid?"

"I'm not afraid of you."

He watched her lift her chin and look at him squarely in the eyes. A shy woman with spunk was definitely different. "Can you tell me why my family thinks I've hurt you? Cole's been on my back since the evening you took off to your room. He thinks I've hurt you in some way."

"I'm sorry. I don't want them to think that, so I'll explain it to them."

"Explain," his voice rose more than he wanted it to. "I'm sorry." He stroked his hand through his hair in frustration. "Can you please explain it to me first because I'd like to know what I've done wrong, besides of course being a total jerk for over two weeks. Three," he corrected.

"You haven't done anything wrong, and I'll tell them just that."

"Miss Riley." Ryan came out the door. "Mom said I can stay up later tonight so I can pick out my book for tomorrow. Can you come in to help me before I go to bed?"

Mandy turned. "Yes, of course, Ryan, I'd be happy to." She turned to Adam. "I was late starting tonight and it was an extra-long story. The children take turns in picking out their stories and tomorrow is Ryan's turn." She quickly smiled. "I told him I'd help him pick out a story for tomorrow."

Adam nodded. "I understand." He turned to his nephew. "We'll be just another few minutes." He patted his nephew on the shoulder.

"Okay, Uncle Adam." Ryan looked at his Nanny then darted another quick glance at his uncle. He smiled. "See you inside." He stood for a brief moment and stared at his uncle, then grinned again. He turned and went into the house.

"What was that all about?" Mandy asked with raised eyebrows.

Adam shrugged. "I haven't the foggiest." He gazed into her beautiful blue eyes as he took hold of her hand. He was surprised she didn't pull away as he stepped away from the door. However, he felt her stiffen. Guilt took over his mind, his body tensed with the mere thought of frightening her. Especially one as gentle as Mandy. Her shyness intrigued him. Her spunk turned him on. The soft blush of her cheeks gave her an innocent look and he liked it a lot. He realized he no longer cared if she was from the city or not. "Where were we? Oh yeah." He squeezed her hand gently. "I'm going to get to the bottom of this. Like I said, I don't want you or my family to think I'm a monster. I want to talk, so will you please meet me back out here after you help Ryan pick out a book?"

"I will," she said with a strong voice. "My word of honor."

118

"Thank you." Adam released her hand and watched her go back into the house. His guess was she'd be about an hour the way Ryan enjoyed talking. It was going to be the longest hour of his life.

～

An hour later, Mandy came back outside as she had promised. He was sitting in his favorite chair which was pulled up beside hers. Almost too close. She stepped forward and watched him closely. Underneath the soft yellow porch light, their eyes met and held. Desire, mixed with pain, hidden secrets and need, mirrored her own. What was he up to and why did he want to talk to her all of a sudden?

He stood and held out his hand and with the other he slowly pointed to her chair. "Come and sit down." He stepped forward and cupped her elbow and gently guided her to the chair. "Please."

Mandy allowed him to guide her then sat down. She remembered how excited she was that he had made it for her. That didn't change the fact that she was still curious to why he wanted to talk to her all of a sudden. Well, she was here now, so she may as well listen to what he had to say.

Adam sat down in his chair, moved it slightly, then repositioned it more to face her. He put his elbows on his thighs, clasped his hands then leaned forward. He cleared his throat. "I need to know, why are you afraid of me?" His eyebrows rose with curiosity.

Mandy gave him a half-smile. A smile between being shy about his question, and the inner strength she had that could make a man go away, if she didn't want anything to do with them. Right now, she wanted Adam to stay by her side. She wanted to tell him she wasn't afraid and that she was just baffled by his actions, but the words refused to leave her lips. How could someone so gruff and rude one week, continue to be rude, yet give her a soft floor pillow and a beautiful porch chair the second, disappear for the third and now beg for forgiveness? He wanted her and she knew it. But why?

"Talk to me, Mandy and tell me what you're thinking," he pleaded in a quiet, low and non-threatening voice.

"Why are you wanting to apologize?" She leaned forward towards him. "Why the sudden interest in me after three weeks of…?" She shrugged.

Adam glanced down to the deck flooring for a second, then back at her. "I was rude when you first came and I apologize. As far as being interested, it wasn't exactly sudden. Everything about you from your beautiful face and your shyness, to your love of this way of life, to the spunk you've got intrigues me."

Mandy shook her head. "You hated that I took the Nanny position and you watched every move I made. You wanted me to fail, stumble, and find some sort of weakness. And you found one. Didn't you?" Mandy turned away from him. "There's more to life than physical weakness. You judged me before you knew me." When his large hand covered hers, she turned back to him.

"True. I did judge you. I believed I had enough of women, and they were just a problem for me. I was wrong, but it's not like that anymore. I want to get to know you and I want you to give me a chance."

Mandy looked up at him and removed her hand from his. "Why did you judge me in the first place? I was hired by your brother and his wife."

"It was more like not trusting you and I didn't want you around my family. When you walked up those stairs, I was angry. Mandy, someone as beautiful as you are, turn a man's head and I was afraid, well, you…" he sighed, "…forget it." He stroked his hair back. "I realize these past three weeks, I've been rude, barbaric and unmannerly, and yes I did want you to have the pillow and the chair and yes, I did watch you. I observed you closely and you knew it. You came into my life and I didn't want change. But there is change. I see a side of you that was even more beautiful. Like I said, you're gentle, kind, and loving, and my whole family loves you. You're educated, and I love educated women. Besides, you're a great story teller." He smiled and gave off a low chuckle.

Mandy smiled back. He had the most intriguing smile she had ever seen in a man and his eyes sparkled in the moonlight. "You said you had enough of women. Why?"

"Met up with a couple of liars and cheats." He took in a deep breath. "I vowed the next time I met a woman she was going to be a farm girl, or a rancher. No more city girls who used a man for their own needs and curiosity then leave." He shrugged. "When I asked if you were from Calgary the day you drove up and you said yes, well…" he cringed, "…I judged you wrongly and I feel like a heel. I started to think on how comfortable you are around the animals and the small creatures like the mice and snakes the children bring to you. I took all my distrust out on you and I'm sorry."

Tiny shivers went up her spine. Flutters in her lower belly became uncontrollable. She was surprised that he thought she'd been raised in the city all her life. Surprised that his brother hadn't mentioned it. She debated on telling him she was a rancher's daughter and she hated the city as much as he did, yet he decided not to say anything. It was late, and it was a long story, besides she wanted him to be interested in her no matter where she came from. City, country, small town, or the moon. "I understand."

"Mandy, will you tell me why I frightened you? It has to be more than just my rudeness."

"Adam, I told you the truth, I'm not frightened of you, in

the way you think I am. Maybe you don't believe me because the other women you know lied to you. I didn't lie." She felt her face color. "I was still rather embarrassed from... well... and..." she glanced away then back towards him, "... then when your hand went to the side of my face... I..." She watched him shake his head confirming she had him confused. "The other night?"

His mouth twitched nervously. "Oh, yeah, the bedroom scene." He chuckled low, deep and quick. "Anyway, why don't you like your face touched?" he asked curiously to change the subject so not to embarrass her any more than she was already.

"Adam, I can't tell you right now, so please don't ask. You said you wanted to get to know me and to give you a chance. Well, give me the same chance. I will tell you someday, just not right now, okay." She shrugged. "You want us to start talking, well, there's not enough hours in a day to go over a few years, let alone start to get to know each other at this hour. It's going to take a while." She shrugged. "It's getting late."

Adam raised his hand to her right cheek and stroked it gently then dropped his hand. "I know. I know it takes time. Okay, we start fresh tomorrow."

"I'd like that." Her heart skipped a beat with the chance to get to know him.

"Tell me just one thing." Adam jerked his thumb towards the driveway. "Who was the man who drove you back to the ranch?"

She chuckled softly. "My brother, Jason. My twin." She watched Adam smile for the second time.

"And the pimped-out red truck?" he added. "A boyfriend's?"

"No, I'm not dating. If I was, why would I take on a Nanny position that requires me to live in?"

"I thought about that, but you're a beautiful woman, so I thought maybe you may have been going out with someone who is away during the week, leaving weekends only." He smiled.

"That makes sense." She nodded.

"Anyway, I had better let you go and get some sleep. Saturday tomorrow and the kids will be up early."

Their eyes met and held a second time. His hand touched hers, then he trailed his fingertips up her arms causing tiny electrical currents to charge through her body. She didn't want him to release her, but needed more time, so reluctantly she inched away. It took all her willpower not to give in to the kiss they obviously both wanted.

"Good night, Mandy." He released her.

She walked to the door and placed her hand on the door knob then turned slowly. "By the way, let me ask you a question. Dianne mentioned you went to University. What did you take?"

Adam put his hand into his jeans pocket as he leaned against the wall. "Education. I majored in Geology, then I taught high school for a year, but I missed ranching so much I returned. You know the old saying—'the grass is greener on the other side.' Well, it isn't true."

Mandy smiled. "Interesting. Well, good night, Adam." She opened the door then turned a second time. "Adam."

"Yeah." He stepped towards her.

"One more thing." She cringed inwardly having to ask. "Do you... drink?"

He let out a grunted chuckle. "Well." He shook his head slowly. "I enjoy a beer now and then and have been known to have whisky occasionally. But if you talk to my father or brother lately, I'm sure they'd have a different opinion." He shrugged. "Why?"

"Just wondering." Mandy smiled. "Good night." This time she continued through the doorway.

CHAPTER 11

*a*dam stood in front of his bedroom window and stared out into the darkness. The stars were bright, and the moon full. He opened the window to hear the night sounds, but tonight it was still and quiet. No breeze to rustle the leaves of the trees. No coyotes calling in the hills and the meadowlarks had gone to bed. It was almost eerie. Maybe a storm was brewing?

He turned and looked towards his closed bedroom door. Just on the other side of the hall was the woman who had said she wasn't afraid of him. He pondered why she asked about his drinking and why she didn't comment back when he answered. She was a mystery he couldn't unravel. He walked towards his door and opened it, then stared at her closed one. A light beneath the door suggested she was still awake. Was she thinking of him? He was sure thinking of her.

It felt good telling her the truth regarding his past relationships and that he had a trust issue. He wished he hadn't had so much baggage to carry around and cringed at the thought of what more he had to tell her. He recalled touching her arm. It was a soft simple touch. He would have never thought such a simple touch could stir his emotions to this point. He recalled the look of sheer panic in her face when he reached for the left side of her face. The look unsettled him.

Monica, one of his exes who was a real user, had a long sad story about her father's illness that had cost him the price of a stallion he wanted to use for stud. They had been going out for three months when he gave her his credit card so she could go to him before he passed on. He never saw her again, or his card. Embarrassed, he never told the family about the debt or situation. It was an expensive lesson to learn and to this day Monica was the root of his problems. He had fallen in love with her and they had planned to have a family and live on the ranch. Adam hung his head. He had wanted, needed her so much, but she had tossed him away like an old boot.

He looked at the bottom of the door again. Mandy was different. He'd prayed so hard about it. She had to be the one.

He closed his door and went back to bed. His body ached with frustration. His blood on fire to have her in his arms, but he would have to wait another day, maybe another week. It was only a matter of time. How much time?

MANDY LAY on her bed thinking of Adam as she traced the scar from just above her temple all the way down to the beginning of her jaw, close to her hairline. Would he think about the horrible scars on her body? Would he overlook her imperfections? Not that he loved her, but she wondered if he did, would they disappear?

Whipping the blankets away, Mandy got out of bed and stood in front of the dresser mirror and pulled her long hair back, then closed her eyes for a moment to make the ugliness go away. At one time her skin was smooth to the touch and she had been able to hold her head up and pull her hair back into a ponytail and let her entire face show. Not now. As she slowly opened her eyes, the finger-width long scar came back along with the return of the horrible memories of how it happened.

Backing away from the mirror, Mandy picked up her comb, parted her hair on the right then combed it to the left side and feathered her bangs like she always did. This way her hair was thicker on the left, helping to cover most of the left side of her face, yet not covering her left eye. Actually, she liked the fuller look on one side.

Her hand went to her upper left leg and traced the long, jagged, raised scar there. Underneath was the muscle damage that caused her to limp when she overdid it, or she became tired. She had lost a lot because of a drunk driver and wondered where the man who had taken so much from her and Jason was now. Was he still driving? Had he destroyed other people's lives, or had he killed anyone else? These questions plagued her and she guessed they always would.

Eventually Adam would see them and she couldn't help but wonder what his thoughts would be. Would he look at her with disgust and run like other men had in her past? Last year she had dated a young man from payroll and because of his attention and loving words, she felt confident with herself and showed him the scar. The intimate moment abruptly ended when he commented how ugly it was.

Just after that, an old acquaintance from her college days called her up to take her out for a dinner. It was going well until he drank himself stupid and ended up in a hydro pole. Good riddance to him. Several months ago, she went out with a man from radiology. He told her that the scar on her leg was disgusting and she should have a plastic surgeon look at it. Last month, she met a man through a friend from work who didn't know her problems. The man told her she'd never meet anyone who would accept her because of her scars.

On top of that, the jerk asked her not to say anything to her friend that introduced them. Thankfully she hadn't given into any of them, in fact she would never give herself to a man unless he accepted her the way she was, scars and all. The scars were going to be with her all her life, and he would have to look at them, just as she looks at them every day of her life. Would Adam be prepared to accept her with his perfect body and flawless complexion?

No man would ever have her completely, unless he accepted her totally.

EARLY THE NEXT morning Adam watched Mandy come out of the house with her mug of tea in her hand. Her smile more radiant as they greeted each other with a simple good morning. "Sleep well?" he asked as he recalled his own sleepless night. He had tossed and turned with thoughts of her on his mind. His gaze slowly cruised over her. The cotton sleeveless shorty top she wore ended just above her belly button causing a fierce reaction below his belt. He wanted to touch her flat firm stomach and caress her soft skin and trace his fingers to her breasts. He bit back a groan as he perused long slender legs shielded in a pair of light cotton pants.

She grinned. "Yes, I slept like an ol' bear." She grinned.

He watched the soft blush of her cheeks as she stepped towards the chair he had made for her and sat down. Her eyes hadn't quite met his, giving him reason to believe she wasn't telling him the truth. A small lie, he grinned, but he could handle it as long as she was thinking of him. Those types of sweet lies in his mind were okay.

"Well, it's the kid's first day of summer vacation so now they'll be home 'til the end of August." He chuckled as he watched her place her mug down on the chair's arm. "Your job begins today."

"You got that right. There's going to be more laundry, more chores, more everything." She laughed. "I'm looking forward to spending a fun summer with the children."

He liked the soft glow of her cheeks when she spoke of the kids. She loved them. Her voice and eyes expressed it.

"You're watching me again. What are you thinking of?" Her eyebrows lifted.

"You, of course. I haven't been able to take my eyes off you since the day you walked up those steps. Like I told you last night, I want to know everything about you."

Mandy squirmed in her chair. "There may be things you might dislike about me and that's putting it mildly."

He frowned. He couldn't imagine why she would think that. "There's nothing I could dislike about you," he answered staring at her.

"Nobody's perfect." Mandy shrugged avoiding his gaze.

"Fine, okay, we all have flaws. Nobody's perfect, so we all need to overlook our imperfections and look at the positive. Look at what's inside ourselves." Adam pointed to his heart. "That's what's important." He couldn't believe he was talking to her like this. The things coming out of his mouth surprised the hell out of him. He was encouraging her and couldn't help himself. This attraction he felt for her was strong. It was chemistry. He knew that, but could it be more?

"I know," she said gazing into her mug. "But one has to be strong to overlook the imperfections of another," she added softly.

"Tell me about your imperfections, Mandy and I'll show how I can overlook them." He reached over and took her hand and stroked her slender fingers.

MANDY WANTED to give in and tell him about her imperfections but it was too soon. "I need time," she said as she tried to move her hand from his, but his grip was firm. She looked into his eyes as she took an uneven breath. Need and desire flashed, causing flutters in her lower belly as they continued to stare at each other. He surrendered her hand as his other hand moved slowly up to her right cheek. The strong scent of him and the light touch of his fingertips on the side of her face sent her pulse racing. She was in another world. A world she wanted to share with him.

Would he run if she showed him her scars? Recalling the conversation regarding his past relationship, having lied to him amongst other things, guilt of holding back the truth set in. In a sense, she thought holding back the truth was in a way being deceitful, but she wasn't near ready to expose her scars to him. Besides, she'd been honest enough to tell him she needed more time.

He leaned towards her. His mouth just inches from hers. His warm breath fanned her cheeks. Hot urges swept through her as she parted her mouth for him. When his mouth covered hers, her inner thighs pulsated with heat. Her heart pumped hard and fast in her chest. Wanting more, she opened wider letting him explore. Not leaving his mouth, she allowed him to pick her up and bring her onto his lap.

"Mmm," she moaned as his tongue sought out hers to play and tease. His low groan heightened her need to continue as her hands caressed his upper chest to feel hard-packed muscles. The flames of heat exploded inside her when his hand stroked the side of one breast. "Ohh." She broke the kiss and gasped for air.

"You're beautiful, Mandy," he whispered as his hand cupped

the back of her head and brought her close to his chest. "Am I going too fast?" he asked in a breathless voice.

Out of breath and with urgent need surging through her, she couldn't speak. She longed to carry on, but he was right, he was going too fast so she inched away. "I need to go in." Her eyes focused on his broad chest. She wanted his shirt gone. Wanted to feel his muscular chest naked beneath her fingertips.

"Take all the time you need," his voice low, almost soft. "I am a patient man."

She stared into his dark brown eyes. They were heated, but held understanding and knowing, yet a trace of disappointment.

"See you tonight?" he asked.

"Yes." The thought of continuing this conversation after the children went to bed accelerated her breathing. Was this really happening to her? The question still nagged her, could he ever love a woman with a mild disability, yet strong enough to live on a ranch as long as she took a few extra breaks now and then? "I have to go in," she repeated then stepped back. His strong fingers grabbed her hand firmly yet with gentleness.

"Mandy, don't be afraid of me. I'd never hurt you."

She worried her bottom lip. "I believe you. Physically, I have no fear of you." Emotionally she was scared stiff and wasn't sure if he would hurt her feelings. Bruise her emotions.

THAT AFTERNOON it was time to get back into the saddle as they had discussed during her interview. Cole had gone to the barn to saddle a pretty brown mare with white stockings. She was a pretty little mare and Mandy was thrilled, yet as nervous and as shaky as a newborn filly trying to stand for the first time.

"Here's your chance." Dianne took Mandy's hand and gave her a security squeeze. "You can do this. By the way, nice boots."

"Thank you." Mandy glanced down at the new boots she had bought during one of her town trips for Dianne. "I'm a little jittery, but you're right, I can do this. I just wish Jason was here."

"Cole and I would love to meet your brother, so bring him out anytime."

"Thank you." Mandy looked over and realized Ryan and Crystal were ready to go while Cole stood patiently by the little mare. This was her day and Dianne had arranged for Bobby to spend the day at a friend's home, so she could concentrate on riding instead of taking him on his lesson.

"Come on, Mandy." Cole grinned and sauntered towards the two women. "Dianne, Honey, let Mandy's hand go." He separated their hands and gave his wife a kiss. "You've become Mandy's Nanny."

Watching Cole and Dianne and how tender they were to each other, reminded her of her parents. Both sets. Someday, she swore silently, it will be her turn to love and be loved. Someday. Mandy walked over to her horse, stood by it, and took a deep breath. It had been eight long years since she had been on a horse.

"You can do it," Cole encouraged. "Grab the horn, put your foot into the stirrup, and grab the back of the saddle. On three, you swing over. One. Two. Three."

Adrenalin kicked in giving her a boost up. The thrill of being back in the saddle was something she'd been dreaming of since the accident and today was the beginning of a new chapter in her life.

"Great mount," Dianne called over and raised her thumb. "Have a good ride."

"Ready?" Cole asked.

Mandy nodded. "I sure am. What's her name?"

"Daisy," Cole answered.

She patted the mare's neck. "Good girl, Daisy." She followed behind Cole, while Crystal and Ryan followed single file down the driveway until they got to the open field where Cole waved them all forward.

"Take it easy for your first ride but don't worry, Daisy is well-trained and she's very patient."

"Cole, I'm just so anxious."

"I can only imagine. If I had been away from riding that long, I don't know what I'd do."

Mandy knew what he'd do. He would dream like she was doing and he'd work hard, save every penny and plan to make his dream come true. "I'm so happy I'm getting another chance. Thank you. Jason and I are going back to ranching hopefully soon and when we do, I'm never going to leave the ranch."

"Hey, now let me think..." he straightened and looked southward, "...there's a ranch that runs along our south-eastern pasture just across the Little Calf River." He turned back to face Mandy. "Apparently Mrs. Turner, our friend and neighbor, is ready to sell her property. Privately. I don't know for sure, so you'll have to talk to Dianne for more details. Your brother, Jason, should come over for supper one night and the four of us can talk about it."

"A ranch for sale." Her mind went dizzy with excitement. She scanned the vast area. If it was anything like the McBride Ranch, they'd have to forget it. She didn't want to get her hopes up too high, but she couldn't help think about it. She shifted in the saddle. "This is so exciting." She let out a little squeal of delight before turning serious. "Jason and I have been saving up for years now, and with the investments our ma and pa left us, we're just about ready."

"Your ma and pa?" Cole sent her a confused look.

Mandy crunched her face with sadness. "Our parents and older brother were killed over eight years ago in a car accident, while visiting here in Canada. We were only fifteen, so the family ranch had to be sold."

"Aw, jeez, Mandy, I'm sorry." Cole's eyes shifted quickly over his land then back to Mandy. "Well... if... umm..."

Knowing that Cole didn't know what to say, and not wanting him to feel uncomfortable because of the tragedy in her life, or feel sorry for her, she shifted her weight in the saddle in order to face him better. "Jason and I have had a good life with our aunt and uncle who took us in. We're a strong family..." she lifted her chin up, "...and where going to live our dream. Jason and I have been working and saving together and we're going to get our life back, or at least as much of it as we can. We've decided to stay in Canada and buy in Alberta, because of the special relationship we have with our aunt and uncle. We belong here now." She stroked the horse's neck. "And when we get our ranch, like I said, I'm never going to leave it." She laughed.

Cole nodded. "My mother passed away, and I miss her terribly, but at least I still have my father and brother." He gave her an uneasy nervous grin. "Anyway, uh... ready to go a little faster?"

"I'm ready." She clicked her tongue.

ADAM WAS on his way back to the ranch house when he saw four riders crossing the field. He squinted, then pulled his cowboy hat down to shade his eyes from the sun. He recognized his brother and the kids, but who was the young woman with them? He headed into the direction of the four riders and the closer he got the more surprised he was. Mandy, riding like she had been born in the saddle.

Completely puzzled, he wondered how she learned to ride so fast. For a city girl with a bad leg she was absolutely amazing. He got closer, then suddenly brought his horse to a halt. Why hadn't she told him she knew how to ride? His eyes narrowed and his gut twisted as anger sizzled through his veins when he thought she'd held back on him like his past girlfriends. *You didn't ask her, you idiot. And you were rude.* Adam rolled his eyes and shook his head. It had only been last evening that they had started to talk. He promised her time. He flicked the reins. Zircon moved forward. He wondered where she learned to ride, because one just didn't learn to ride like that on weekends. She was a little stiff in the saddle, but otherwise, pretty damn good. Correction, pretty damn amazing. Adam stopped Zircon and watched for a few minutes as he wondered why he hadn't given her a chance from the first day? If he had, he would have known more about her by now. "Hee yeahhh, Zircon, let's go," he hollered. He only had eight weeks left and he wasn't going to waste any more time. This woman wasn't going to get away from him. This woman was going to be his and his alone.

"Hey," he yelled out. "Mandy, Cole, kids."

They all turned and waved at him.

"Mandy." Adam grinned. "Your riding skills are absolutely amazing."

"If you had made an attempt to be part of the family in the last few weeks, Adam, you would have known Mandy rides," Cole scolded. "I hope you're back with us now, little brother."

"You're right, Cole, I haven't been part of the family lately." Adam reined his horse alongside of Cole's. "I was wrong and I took my frustrations out on you and the family including Mandy from the minute she got here. I'm sorry."

"Hey, Adam, you're my brother and I'll always be here for you."

~

MANDY'S EYES watered at Adam's sincerity and she saw a side of him she loved and realized that he was worth going after. The bond between the McBride brothers was strong. Through thick and thin they'd always be there for each other just like the bond she had with her brother. No one would ever come between them.

"I've got to catch up with the kids." Cole looked at Mandy. "You're doing great so just relax and go with the horse. Don't stiffen up."

"Thanks, Cole. I'll see you back at the ranch." She adjusted her Stetson. The Stetson her father had bought her the day they left Utah. Two weeks before he was killed.

Adam brought his horse around to hers. "Go riding with me?"

"I'd love to, but Bobby is coming home shortly, so I can't be long."

"Any time I can spend with you is a bonus."

"Okay, just for a while." It was going to be the best ride ever and being with the man she wanted to be with made it even more spectacular. The ride wouldn't be long enough, but it was a beginning and being with a man she'd been dreaming about since the first day she saw him was definitely a plus. Even though he had been an arrogant, crabby jerk at the beginning, Mandy thought with a small smile.

Just before trotting back into the yard, she looked back and scanned the vastness of the area. The strong scent of the wild grass tickled her nose as she took in a deep breath. The sound of the cattle bawling in the distance was music to her ears. Life was good in the rolling foothills. She glanced at Adam who was doing the same and she knew how much his love for the land matched hers. She wanted to love this man, but emotionally she needed time. More time to prepare herself and show him what she had to live with and pray he'd accept her for who she was.

Arriving in time to meet Bobby, Mandy dismounted the gentle mare. Her leg was sore, but not like she thought it would be. It was much worse.

"You see to Bobby and I'll see to Daisy." Adam took the mare's reins.

"Thank you." The pain in her leg was now excruciating. Hiding it was going to be next to impossible, but she had to give it her best. Putting on her best happy face, she hurried to get the little cowboy and greet the mother of his little friend.

"Hi, Bobby." Mandy smiled at Bobby as he raced over towards her and gave her a big hug.

"Hi, Miss 'Iley."

"You must be Bobby's Nanny." A dark-haired lady, who looked about Dianne's age, put out her hand." I'm Karen, Michael's mother. We live in Longview, and this is my son, Michael."

"It's a pleasure to meet you, Karen." Releasing Bobby, Mandy took Karen's outreached hand, shook it then turned to Bobby's friend. "It's a pleasure to meet you too, Michael. I'm Mandy and I'm from Calgary." She patted the little boy's shoulder, then looked back at Karen. "I'm here for as long as Dianne and Cole need me." Mandy smiled.

"Well, it was a pleasure and I hope to see you again, Mandy." Karen turned to Bobby. "We'll see you again soon."

After waving goodbye, Mandy took Bobby upstairs and washed him up. She could see that he was tired. At three in the afternoon it was touch and go putting Bobby to bed. Especially when he usually got up at three thirty. But watching him rub his eyes, she tucked him and figured a late afternoon nap wouldn't hurt him. And it would give her a chance to have a warm bath to soothe the pain in her leg.

The warm bath helped a bit, but not enough, so Mandy took

two extra strength pain relievers then slowly made her way downstairs into the kitchen for a quick cup of tea.

"Hey there, Dianne." Mandy took a mug down from the cupboard and poured herself a cup of tea and sat down with Dianne. "Bobby's down for a nap."

"I'm sure he needs it. He and Michael play hard." She laughed. "Now, how was your ride?"

"It was wonderful. Getting back to riding is like a dream, so thank you for arranging it all for me." She leaned over and gave Dianne a big hug.

"You're most welcome." Dianne returned the embrace.

Although the pain in her leg was still there, Mandy organized the kitchen so Dianne could prepare supper. "Cole and I were talking about a ranch that might be coming up for sale. He suggested Jason come over for dinner so the four of us can talk." She took down the cutting board and placed it on the table for Dianne to use later for the ham.

"Cole's right, our neighbor, Mrs. Turner, told me she's definitely ready to sell. Her husband passed away last year and now her daughter wants her to move in with her in Calgary. I'll get more information and you tell Jason to come over." Dianne turned her chair and inched it over beside the stove sideways to open the oven to check the scallops. "Mmm." She closed the oven. "Can you send Cole in for a few minutes?"

"Oh, Cole's not back yet," Mandy answered. "Umm... I came back with Adam." She blushed and got up, went to the cupboard, took out the plates for dinner, put them on the counter then reached for the glasses.

Dianne grinned. "You two talking?"

"Yes, we are," she said softly.

CHAPTER 12

*a*dam caught himself humming as he removed Zircon's saddle and blanket and put them on the stall gate. As he brushed his horse to a high shine he realized how good it felt to laugh again. He enjoyed talking with her. It was good just to be together with a woman who enjoyed the same things he did. He closed his eyes to recapture the memory of the day so he could remember it forever. He wanted to remember the expression of her face as she gazed over the beauty of the land.

After Adam finished brushing his horse and securing the stall gate he grabbed hold of the saddle and blanket and put them away in the tack room. He returned and entered Daisy's stall. "Hey girl, your turn next," he cooed to the young mare as he stripped her of her saddle and blanket and began brushing her.

"Adam."

As her soft voice called out to him, his heart lifted. He liked the sound of his name coming from her lips. "I'm in Daisy's stall."

"I'm sorry I took so long. I needed a quick bath after I put Bobby down for a nap, then I talked and helped Dianne for a bit." Mandy unlatched the gate and entered. "Your nephew is having a nap and Dianne is making supper which by the way is mouth-watering."

Adam gazed at her natural beauty. Even though there was a hit of pain in her face, her cheeks glowed from the afternoon ride and her eyes sparkled with excitement and she was without a doubt the most incredible woman he had ever seen. Knowing how sensitive she was about talking about her leg, he didn't ask questions, instead he gathered her into his arms hoping she could forget about her pain for a while. He slowly lowered his head and found her mouth. Her lips soft and pliable against his own. His tongue found hers and beckoned it to mate with his. Every muscle and fiber in his body found a new life as she played with him. Teased him with her tongue. Reluctantly, he released her. "What do you say we head up to the hayloft?" He winked.

"You're kidding. I hope."

He shrugged. "Wishing and hoping is more like it."

"Wish all you want." She giggled softly. "A roll in the hay is not my idea of fun." She blushed.

"Not fun. How do you know it's not?" he asked teasingly. "Ever done it?"

"No. Not the way you're thinking." She picked up a handful of hay from Daisy's bin. "Here, feel it."

Adam touched it and smiled. "Okay." He watched curiously as Mandy crunched it in her delicate hands then laughed. Surprised and shocked as she grabbed the front of his shirt, pushed him up against the stall's half wall, and stuffed the handful of hay down his shirt then patted his chest. He couldn't believe how bold she was. She definitely turned him on.

"Itchy?" she asked with a grin. "Those Hollywood movie producers, and those silly romance writers don't know what they're talking about when they describe or show someone making love in the hay. Not only that, the editors are just as bad because they are supposed to catch things like that." She laughed. "Sounds romantic, but it's awful itchy and really uncomfortable," she stressed. "Of course, that's just my opinion."

"You definitely have a point." He grinned. "Especially for the person who's on the bottom," he said as he untucked his shirt from his jeans, took the hem of it, and tore it open. All the snaps released at once exposing his massive chest. As he took it off and shook it, he watched her cheeks go pink. He loved her cheeks. "One thing a romance writer is right about, it's romantic to kiss in the barn." He put on his shirt and brought her close to him. He felt her palm on his bare chest. The jolt from her hand rubbing his chest stunned him, yet his body hardened instantly to her touch. His heart thumped hard against the inner walls of his chest.

She was some woman.

MANDY'S BODY soared with absolute delight as butterflies swarmed in the very pit of her stomach. Her heart beat like it had never beat before. Similar to the pounding of horses' hooves racing along the hard prairie ground. She needed rest, but she'd deal with the pain and rest later.

She stroked the nape of his neck and slowly drew her hands down his bare chest. Hard firm muscles flinched at her touch, making her wish he hadn't put his shirt back on. Although totally unbuttoned, she wanted to touch and gaze at all of him. The need and desire to have him, made her bold and urged her on. It was a whole new experience and she enjoyed it. Savored and welcomed it. His large hands stroked the sides of her slender neck while she continued to caress his hard chest muscles. Slowly, deliberately, his hands lowered to roam over the sides of her breasts. They began to tingle. Throb with every beat of her heart. Her knees felt like cooked noodles. If his words were true, she'd give herself to him.

Thoughts of her ugly scars pulled her back from temptation. "Oh, Adam." Her eyes closed as she leaned up against him, stopping his hands from fully covering her breasts, yet allowing him to surround her whole body with his solid arms. Warmth cloaked her. No other man had ever made her feel so alive. So good about herself.

Suddenly she became aware of his hard arousal and inched back away from him. Her eyes toured down his chest past his belt buckle. She swallowed hard. Feeling unsure, she backed farther away. "Adam." Her eyes widened.

"I'm sorry." He shrugged. "It's you. You're extraordinary."

Mandy couldn't help but cruise over his body a second time. Her mouth opened wider as heat rose to her cheeks. She glanced up into his eyes that reflected her own desire. He was ready to take her right then and there. The thought was frightening yet electrifying at the same time. "I... I'll see y... you back at the house." She left quickly, hearing Adam groan. As she walked slowly back, she knew she was in trouble. Her heart was being filled by him.

Instead of joining the family at the dinner table, Mandy entered the living room and chose to sit down on Adam's favorite rocker recliner, by the window. Needing a little time to herself, she took her boots off and put her feet up onto the ottoman. She knew she had overdone it and wished she had worn her support brace. Her upper left leg throbbed, her muscles tightened and her knee was swollen and hot to the touch. Massaging it, she regretted not being more careful. The evening had only begun and Adam was sure to witness her limp. She was falling in love with him, yet she didn't want him to see her physical weakness.

Adam left the table, entered the living room and stood by the chair where Mandy was and watched her sleep. Her sweet face was flushed more than usual giving him reason to believe she'd overworked herself. He'd witnessed her pain from time to time and it disturbed him. If only he could pick her up and cuddle her. Gather all of her in his arms to comfort her and take the pain away.

A slight twitch of a smile reached his lips as he thought about the changes in his own life. He was falling in love with her hard and fast. Mandy had opened his heart and it was like fresh mountain air being pumped into his entire body. A first spring rainfall after a long harsh winter. He felt alive with a whole new meaning to the word love. Aware that his brother had come into the living room, he turned and spoke in a hushed voice. "She's quite a woman."

"Yup," Cole agreed quietly. "She's special and I don't think you'll ever find anyone else like her." He patted Adam on the back then sat down in one of the two leather recliners.

Adam turned to study his brother for a moment and wondered if he and Mandy could ever have that close special relationship his brother had with Dianne. He watched the rest of his family come into the living room quietly, except for his little nephew who was loud and boisterous at the best of times.

"Mommy, we genning a stooie." Bobby pointed. "Miss Iley, seeping," he pouted.

"Let Miss Riley sleep, son she's had a busy day. Her brother's coming to pick her up so she can go home early tonight," Dianne explained.

"What time is Jason coming?" Adam asked Dianne keeping his voice quiet.

"He called just after you and Cole came in. I told him she could go home anytime so he's on his way."

"Well, kids." Adam winked at his niece and nephews. "I guess you got me to read to you tonight." Silence took over as the children looked up at him with pouty faces.

"Hey." Cole looked at his children with a slight frown. "Your Uncle Adam reads exceptionally well."

"You're right, Pa. We're sorry, Uncle Adam," Ryan said quietly and Crystal agreed.

"No problem, kids, as I totally understand and I'd rather hear Miss Riley read, too."

MANDY WOKE from her nap with a stiff leg. She glanced at Adam who was sitting cross-legged on her big floor pillow reading. His baritone voice pleased her ears, but her problem right now was, how could she position her leg so the pain wouldn't show on her face? Mandy shifted her weight in the big chair.

"Miss Riley's awake," Ryan said as he jumped up, dashed across the room to where Mandy was sitting. "Uncle Adam is taking your place tonight."

"Yes, I see." She smiled. "Nice to know you've got a back-up reader when I fall asleep."

"Don't worry, you've had three full weeks of work and reading every night," Dianne said, picking up the hand cream by the coffee table. "Oh, and Jason called and he's coming early to pick you up."

"Okay," Mandy said with a straight face, managing to hide her disappointment. There would be no time for Adam. When he stopped reading, their eyes locked, sending each other silent signals of desire. For the first time in her life, she didn't want to go home after her job was done. She had found something here. Something intriguing.

When the doorbell rang with an old-fashioned ding dong, Mandy watched Cole get up to answer it. Voices of introduction verified her brother had already arrived.

"My sister has spoken highly of y'all 'n' your kin," Jason said as he stepped into the living room with Cole. Seeing his sister, he bee-lined it straight over to her side, bent down and gave her a kiss on her forehead. "Hey, Squeak." He frowned when he got a good look at her. "Oh crap, Mandy, what have ya been doin'?" He straightened.

"Everyone, this is Jason, Mandy's brother." Cole did the introductions. "Jason, my wife Dianne, my father, John, brother Adam, and my children, Ryan, Crystal and Bobby."

Jason turned to the family. "Pleased to meet y'all." He stepped forward and shook hands with Dianne. "Real pleasure, ma'am. Mandy speaks very fondly of ya." Jason shook John's hand and nodded. "Pleasure, sir." He nodded to all the children and smiled. "You young'uns sure won my sister's heart. She told me y'all are real special."

"I like the way you talk," Crystal said.

"Me, too," Ryan agreed. "I wish I could talk like you."

"Well, I like the way y'all talk." Jason smiled.

"But you have an accent," Ryan said.

Jason ruffled Ryan's hair. "Well, Ryan, I don't hear it. I think it's y'all that have the accent." He thickened his drawl for the children, then chuckled. He turned to Adam, nodded and extended his hand. "Adam."

Mandy noticed Jason's solemn face while he sized Adam up as they shook hands.

"Jason, glad to meet you."

Mandy watched Adam. There was no animosity, just a pleasant smile towards her brother. Adam didn't have a clue what

Jason thought of him and prayed her brother remembered his manners.

Jason turned back to Mandy and bent down. "How ya doin', Squeak?" he said quietly, but didn't give her a chance to answer. "Dianne told me ya been ridin'." He placed his hand on her left knee then the right and back to the left. "Ya ain't been wearin' your brace?"

"Jason." She glared. "Give me a lecture later, not now." She lowered her head and turned away from the McBrides.

"Where your things?" Jason asked. "I'll fetch them fer ya."

Mandy glanced around the room. Cole had taken the two youngest upstairs and John had left the room leaving Dianne and Ryan quietly talking. Adam sat leaning forward in the large leather chair with his arms resting on his knees, his hands clasped together as his eyes focused on them. Had he heard her conversation with her brother? Mandy knew he wanted a few minutes with her as much as she wanted with him. But if he stayed, he'd notice her limp which would be more pronounced than usual.

She moved the ottoman slowly with her right leg. "I can bend it," she whispered to Jason. "I'll relax it for a minute while you get my things. I'll try to make it out by the time you come down stairs," she whispered, hoping Adam couldn't hear.

ADAM WATCHED Jason stroke Mandy's left temple with his thumb pad as they had a private conversation. The strain on Mandy's face as she whispered to her brother concerned him. As Jason continued with the treatment, her pain seemed to diminish, at least somewhat. Twins? He'd seen documents about twins and how they just seemed to know about each other's feelings. What they needed. They had this sixth sense about each other and they seemed to have some sort of mental telepathy or something. To Adam, it looked as simple as if he'd massaged his own temple for an oncoming headache. Yet Jason seemed to have a special way to do it to relieve her pain. Whatever Jason was doing, it seemed to relax her before his eyes. Adam wanted to know how to help her, but of course her brother would know best.

"I didn't think I would be hurting this bad after riding," she told her brother.

"Relax a moment." Jason stopped his treatment and slowly left his sister's side and turned to Dianne. "Ma'am could ya direct me to Amanda's room? She'd be needin' her overnight bag."

"It's just at the top of the stairs, first door to your right."

Jason nodded and left.

Like a flash of lightning, Adam was out of his seat and across the room to kneel down beside her. "Why didn't you come to me if you're in that much pain?" he questioned.

"I'm sorry, Adam, but Jason knows how to take care of me and you need to give me more time."

Adam stroked his forehead. He'd promised her he'd be patient, on the other hand he sensed she was holding something back. Whatever it was, it was important and she didn't want him to know about it. He gazed into her eyes and prayed he wasn't making another mistake because his heart was exposed wide open. She had to be different than the other women; if she wasn't he'd never be able to cope. "Don't hide anything from me. Please."

"Adam, you don't understand."

"Then talk to me," he pleaded.

She shook her head slowly. "I can't. Not yet. Give me a little more time, we just started talking." She turned her head away. "You promised to be patient."

"Yes, I did and I'll keep that promise." He took her hand and squeezed it gently then leaned over and kissed her soft cheek. He watched her eyes shift nervously from the stairs going to the second floor back to him. She bit her bottom lip. "Honey, what's wrong?" He touched her warm cheek.

"I complimented every one of your family but you. I'm sorry." She sighed. "I told Jason you were a rebel."

He chuckled short and quick then shrugged. "I felt his disapproval in his handshake." He heard Jason's footsteps as he began to descend. "I'm not a rebel. A rebel's different. I've been a crabby son of a bitch lately." He shrugged a second time then reluctantly backed away. "I'll give him some space, but not for long," he whispered then returned to his chair.

"Ya ready, Squeak?"

Adam noticed the warning in Jason's face as he approached his sister.

"I am."

Adam watched her take in a deep breath and shift forward. She lowered her head, but not before he saw tears glisten on her long lashes. It took every ounce of his strength not to rush over to her. Instead his hands clenched the chair's arms.

Jason put his arms around her shoulders and under her knees.

"No, Jason, I can walk. Just help me up."

Jason whispered into her ear. "Ya can't walk and ya know it. Let's just git."

"Please, don't embarrass me any more than I am." She stiffened on her brother.

"Fine." Jason stepped back and held out his hand. "Take it." He helped her up. "Ya think you're embarrassed now, wait 'til they see ya try ta walk." He turned to the McBride family. "Again, it's a pleasure to meet ya'll." Much to Mandy's embarrassment, he quickly picked her up. "Sorry, but we're goin'."

~

ADAM'S HEART ached just seeing the intense pain on her face. He had seen it before but not to this extreme and he hadn't realized it was this bad. In fact, so bad it was unbearable to watch and it crushed his heart. He turned to Dianne. "Did you see the pain in her face?"

"I did. She overdid it this afternoon, but she'll be fine, Adam, because she's stronger than you think. She goes for acupuncture when it gets too much to handle so I'll arrange for her to have some time off."

Adam nodded thoughtfully. "I heard Jason say something about wearing a support brace." He picked up Mandy's boots and sat down in the chair she had just vacated. "Did you know about that?" He traced the boot pattern with his finger.

"No. Mandy and I have got real close in the past three weeks and we've been talking a fair amount, but she doesn't tell me everything." Dianne shrugged. "I don't know if I should be telling you this because I think she'll want to tell you herself when she gets to know you better, but I think you should know, so here goes the short version." Dianne leaned forward. "Eight years ago, they were in a motor vehicle accident which killed both their parents and older brother. Jason and Mandy were hurt bad. In fact, hospitalized."

Adam closed his eyes and stroked his forehead. "Oh, my, God... both parents... and a brother... I can't imagine the loss." Adam slowly looked at Dianne. "She spoke about God surrounding us with so much beauty the other day, I think she has a lot of faith if she can still speak of the gifts God gives us." Adam shook his head slowly. "If they were both hurt and the loss they suffered it would bring them very close to each other." He groaned nervously. "He's pretty protective of her."

"You're right." Dianne nodded.

Adam stood up. "Anyway, I have to do the nightly checks." He put her boots on the mat beside the front closet in the foyer then turned to Dianne. "Did you notice Jason's American accent?"

"Sure did. They're originally from Utah."

"Explains it. Much thicker than Mandy's. Maybe a bit too thick, if you ask me. I mean come on, Dianne, we got American ranch hands here working for us and they're from farther south and their accent isn't near as thick as Jason's." He rolled his eyes and stepped away from the foyer.

"Well to be fair, I think he was doing it more for the kid's sake. Ryan and Crystal enjoyed listening to him and they did comment on how cool it was." Dianne smiled.

"You're kidding me, right? You actually believe that? Come on, Dianne." Adam shook his head. "I'm...a gonna... git... my... chores... done... then... hit... the... hay." He smiled as he drawled out the short sentence. "Is that thick enough fer ya?" He laughed loud and hard.

Dianne let out a hardy laugh. "Good night, Adam."

Adam continued to laugh as he went back into the foyer. "I'll work on my accent." He laughed louder as he opened the door. "Good night, Dianne."

THE WARM WESTERN winds coming through the truck window would normally have calmed Mandy's frazzled nerves but sitting next to Jason and waiting for him to begin his lecture, was causing her more tension. "I know you're going to say something, so you may as well get it over with and quit the Utah drawl. It's a little much, don't you think? And you talk about Adam being a rebel."

"Fine, I'll quit the drawl. As far as your pain goes, Amanda, your pain tonight is your lecture." Jason glanced at her. "But I'll tell you again. When you go through this pain, I feel it and you know it, that's why I called early. Remember Ma telling us the story of how bonded she was with her family and was so connected, they could feel each other's discomfort, along with each other's joy. I don't understand it but it happens within families that have a special connection. We have that bonding, Amanda, and being twins gives us that added connection. It's a special gift we have and we have to learn not to abuse it."

"Jason, I'm so sorry. I was so thrilled about riding that my mind was elsewhere."

Jason glanced at his sister. "I know and believe me I understand." He focused back to the road. "Well, you may as well tell me about this rebel friend of yours."

She jerked her head towards him. "What do you mean?" she asked nervously.

"I'm not blind and I could see how you two were watching each other. I could practically feel the vibrations in the room when he came to you. So are you going to tell me, or do I call the Neanderthal and give him a piece of my mind for not looking after you properly."

"Jason, first of all he's not a Neanderthal or a rebel for that matter." Although she had to admit she liked the Neanderthal type. "Oh, fine, I'll tell you." She told Jason everything she knew about Adam then added that he had apologized for being rude, and how nice he'd been to her since. She admitted that she cared about him and that her feelings were growing, but she hadn't told him about her scars or about their parents and older brother. She left out that he was enabling a ranch hand who was drinking, and of course kissing him in the barn. That was not any of Jason's business.

Jason groaned. "I hope he's a patient man, because you've been hiding behind your hair for years and I'm the only one so far who can touch and massage that scar. I know that's a comfort to you and it helps you to relax and sleep better when you've had a tough day. But if there's a future for you and… this… cowboy, you'll have to trust him to help you." He gave her a quick look. "Please tell me you're not in love with him?" He glanced at her. "I don't like him or trust him."

"Stop treating me like a child, Jason. If I make a mistake then so be it. Just be there for me. Okay?"

Jason parked the truck, turned in his seat to face his sister and stared at her for a moment then nodded. "Okay, Squeak."

She stared back. For the first time in her life, she didn't trust him. He was up to something.

CHAPTER 13

*I*t was a weekend Adam never wanted to repeat. In the wee hours of Sunday morning, just as he got into bed he heard Hank crying in the middle of the yard. He didn't know how much more he could take from his friend with another setback and he was back to square one. Then after everyone left for church on Sunday, the foreman from the neighboring ranch called to tell him that one of their bulls was headed down the road towards town.

When Adam headed towards the barn to saddle up Zircon, he passed his truck with its hood up. He had taken a second glance and could have cried when he noticed his beautiful engine. The carb job Hank was supposed to do on the old tractor was done to his beautiful treasured truck. What the hell was Hank thinking? "Crap, shit, damn it all, Hank, my truck doesn't have a carburetor. Its fuel injected," Adam yelled then cursed some more. He stared at his beautiful truck. He could feel moisture forming in his eyes. He had to turn away. His poor, poor beautiful truck was a friggin' mess. If he had time to spare, he would have sat down right then and there beside his precious, gorgeous truck and cried like a baby.

The one good thing that happened, even though it was one in the morning, Dee had a sturdy healthy colt.

It was two o'clock Monday morning, when Adam finally flopped into bed with his arms spread out. He'd been too exhausted to strip off his clothes before he hit the bed, but managed to toe off his boots. The heavy thud on the floor told him he'd succeeded and his feet were free. Taking in a deep breath, he unbuckled his belt, lifted his hips, pushed his jeans down and wiggled out of them then pushed them onto the floor. By the time he loosened the top button of his shirt his eyes were closed.

By five-thirty, Adam was leaning forward on the deck railing with his hands clutched around his second cup of coffee. "Where is she?" he whispered to himself in frustration. He looked down the graveled driveway and wondered if she was ever going to share with him her past? Tell him her problems? He wanted her to trust him. Fully.

Just as he moved away from the railing to get a third cup of coffee, Jason's blue 4x4 drove up. He stood watching as Jason got out and went around to Mandy's side, handed her a small suitcase and stood in front of her. He watched Jason glance over towards him and wondered what he was saying to her. He could only imagine. The threats in his eyes and the insincere handshake on Saturday night, hadn't gone unnoticed. He'd be watching his sister closer and would most likely call her more, or even show up unannounced. He huffed. He couldn't blame him, but he didn't like it. Not one bit.

≈

"CALL ME LATER." Jason pushed her hair back on both sides like he did so often. "Relax." He shook his head. "Hey, you've had a good couple nights' sleep, now ya haven't been here five minutes and you're already uptight. I don't think this is the job for ya, sis. Or is it that cowboy friend of yours makin' ya tense? The one who's standing on the porch waiting to get his hands on ya?"

"Jason, please, we've been through all this over and over again. I told you to stop treating me like a child. I'm not going into a relationship I can't handle. Besides…" she glanced at her brother's scar on his upper arm to the top of his wrist, "…he's been having coffee out on the porch for years just like I used to do when we lived on our ranch." Getting ready to leave, she took her purse out of the truck.

"I remember. I worry about ya, is all." Jason stepped forward and pulled her hair forward on the left side, then flicked up her bangs. That done, he leaned against the truck and crossed his arms. "I don't want him to hurt ya. I think ya, c'n do better. Vic Moor is interested in ya, and he knows our history and he's seen them scars. He's a good man, Amanda."

"You're right. Vic's wonderful, but…" she leaned closer to him, "…I ain't interested and ya talkin' with that drawl 'gain." She stepped back. "Stop it. It's way too thick, even for you."

"Okay fine, I'll talk proper like." He raised his hands and shook his head. "I have to get back an' help Uncle Richard. We have several deliveries to do and he wants to start on a dining suite. You have a good week, Squeak, and thanks 'gain, for lettin' me have the truck."

"It's half yours." She grinned. "I'll call you midweek, and don't worry." She gave her brother a hug.

Mandy paused halfway to the porch and turned to watch Jason disappear. It had been two long nights away from Adam. Long enough she felt she had to start all over. Again. He had seen her in pain on Saturday night and she wondered if he would accept her weakness? She'd find out soon enough, she thought and squared her shoulders.

~

"Morning, Mandy." Adam moved slowly towards her. "How was your weekend?"

"Relaxing, thank you," she said moving up onto the porch, but keeping her distance.

He stepped closer. Cole and Dianne were right, she was shy, or was it because Jason's truck hadn't completely disappeared yet? It was obvious to him he'd have to make the first move, so he took another step forward and took her hand. Her smile encouraged him to wrap his arms around her. "It's been a long weekend without you." He lowered his head then paused. When she didn't move, he brushed his mouth against her hair. The exotic fragrance of her shampoo that smelled of wildflowers in the mountains was causing a reaction. His arms tightened around her bringing her closer. "I've never missed anyone like I've missed you." He hugged her tightly; his mouth slowly searched for hers. His body ached with his need of her. Her pure feminine purr of pleasure caused a burst of joy inside him.

"Oh, Adam." She sighed heavily.

Their mouths fused together. Their bodies tight and hot. Both were oblivious to the early morning sounds or the fresh mountain air that kissed their cheeks. To the rising sun that was giving its blessing on two people who were so responsive to each other. Totally unaware of a truck that had pulled up. Unaware of the slam of a heavy metal door. Nor had they heard booted footsteps crunching on the driveway. A thud of work boots on wooden steps.

"Ya doin' your job, Amanda?" Jason said loud and clear.

Mandy jerked out of Adam's arms and twisted around. "Jason?" she gasped in total surprise. "Why are you back?"

"Ya forgot your manuscript in the truck. Ya know, the one you're workin' on. I c'n see how much you're goin' git done."

155

Jason threw the wrapped manuscript down on the porch floor then glared at them both.

"Jason, please," Mandy pleaded and stepped forward.

He turned to leave, then stopped and looked straight at Adam. "Ya hurt her, Mister…" with clenched fist and his index finger pointed stiff and straight he growled a warning, "…ya gonna find out what pain's all about." His eyes shifted to his sister. "And if ya don't think I won't know, ya better think again."

Adam watched Mandy stiffen. Her breathing heavy. "Hey, hold on, Jason, I'm not going to hurt your sister." Adam stepped forward. "I'll give you my word."

"Ya'd better not." Jason turned, walked down the steps and headed straight for his truck.

"Jason, wait," Adam called out, but to no avail he continued to walk away. Adam watched Mandy's brother get in the truck, slam the door, shift into gear, and take off leaving gravel flying in every direction.

"I'm sorry, Adam." Her face flushed.

Adam let her go into the house then glanced at the driveway. He didn't like Jason's threats, but he understood how much he loved his sister, because he loved his own family just as much. He also thought Jason was carrying this protection bit a little too far.

He glanced at the large brown envelope on the porch floor, picked it up, turned it over to see elegant handwriting. The Little Painted Pony, by Amanda Joy Riley. He sat down in his chair and pulled the manuscript out. On the front page, a drawing of a little painted pony. Curious, he flipped through the pages and noticed other drawings of the same pony with a young girl and boy. *Twins.* Drawings of a ranch house, a barn and other animals. The story itself seemed to be how to care for your horses, and other farm animals and appeared to be quite lengthy. He figured, a book for older kids, possibly ages eight to thirteen or so. Flipping through it a second time, he noticed notes in the margins about what chores to do first and priorities on a ranch. He smiled. 'A good cowboy takes care of his horse before his own needs,' was written in the margin. Drawings that weren't completed and the last page ended in mid-sentence. He put the manuscript back into the brown envelope and wondered if she would try to get it published.

Adam stood up and brought the envelope into the house where he found Mandy in the kitchen with the children planning out their week with Dianne. He handed her the package and admitted with a chuckle. "I peeked." He smiled at her soft pink cheeks.

"You're the first one to see a glimpse of this book. I don't let anyone read my work until it's finished."

"You have others?" His eyebrows shot up.

"Yes." She nodded. "I have ten published so far. All pertaining to farming and ranch life for seven-to thirteen-year-olds and two are being released in a month or so." She crunched up her nose. "This one has to be completed A.S.A.P."

"You write stories, Miss Riley?" Crystal piped up with her big brown eyes wide open.

"Yes, Crystal, I do."

"Can you read them to us some day?" Ryan asked anxiously.

"I'll bring the published ones with me next Monday so we can add them to your library."

"Oh, that would be wonderful and we'll pay you for them," Dianne said. "We strongly believe in supporting our local artists." She smiled. "Are they based on true stories?"

"Yes, these stories help city children learn how farm and ranch kids care for their animals and how they have to make good choices on a ranch, so they're safe. Or, if a farm or ranch child reads them, they learn how chores can be fun."

Adam pulled up a chair. Never again was he going to miss

conversations that happened in the kitchen, den, living room, or on the porch. Or anywhere else his family gathered.

IF JASON HADN'T COME BACK to drop off Mandy's manuscript, she wouldn't have been sitting at the breakfast nook with Adam, the children and Dianne. She would have been much happier being back on the porch steps locking lips with Adam instead of answering so many questions about her books. In the five years she had been writing, she hadn't talked so much to anyone about her stories other than with her family and of course her editor. Her books were becoming extremely popular with the pre-and early teens and their parents. With it being the end of June, she'd have to seriously buckle down. With the kids out of school, her time was limited. And even more limited now that her and Adam were involved.

"Jason and I grew up on a cattle ranch in Northern Utah." Mandy watched Adam lower his head. "When I was fifteen, I was in a car accident and both my parents and older brother, Martin, were killed while we were visiting here in Canada. Just like your family, we all stick together so my Uncle Richard and his wife, Aunt Maggie, adopted us legally so we could get our Canadian citizenship." She glanced at Adam. His eyes glued to her.

"Mandy, I told Adam the short version of you losing your parents, but not about your life history," Dianne admitted.

"I needed to know after Jason picked you up." He shrugged. "So, I asked Dianne a few questions. Losing my mother at twenty-six, was bad enough," Adam said as he shook his head in disbelief.

Mandy nodded. "Jason and I..."

"You don't have a mother or father?" Ryan interrupted.

She smiled tightly. "My parents and brother Martin, are in heaven now, so I live with my twin brother, Jason and..."

"Who looks after you now?" Crystal asked curiously.

She glanced at Adam and gave him a slight smile then looked back to the children. "I look after myself." She could feel her face grow hot. "Well, Jason looks after me when I need help and I still have my Aunt Maggie and Uncle Richard who we've lived with since the accident. They're my family."

"Just like when Jason helped you out on Saturday?" Ryan questioned.

"Yes, Ryan, I needed Jason then."

"Why did he help you out, Miss Riley?" Ryan asked.

"Well." She pulled her hair forward.

"Are you okay?" Adam leaned over, touched her hand and gave it a gentle squeeze.

She nodded and carried on. "Ryan, the accident. Umm... Jason and I were both hurt in the family van when it was hit." She nervously glanced over to Adam and figured he may as well know her weakness. If for any reason he didn't like a gimp, he may as well know now. She looked back at Ryan. "When the windows in our van were broken, a large piece of glass fell on my knee and upper leg. It damaged some of my muscles and when the van rolled over, it twisted my knee and damaged the ligaments and cartilage."

After swallowing hard, she continued. "Some of the damage to my leg muscles never healed completely so there are times when it still bothers me. Like when I went riding on Saturday with you and your dad. It wasn't just the riding that bothered me, it was because I did too much all in one day. I should have..." she paused and thought about mentioning the brace, but decided not to, "...I should have taken it slower. I exercise daily, but it's been eight years since I've been on a horse and I got over-anxious."

"You sure do ride good for being away from horses for that long," Ryan said quickly.

"Thank you. I started riding when I was three when my dad gave each of us a pony and by the time we were ten, we were out looking after the herd with him and Martin. He taught us to rope, look after new calves if they needed extra feedings, and of course muck out stalls. Every year our father would give us more responsibilities and by the time we were fifteen we were getting pretty independent and often went out with the foreman. Both Jason and I could take over certain chores for him when he had to leave the ranch for any number of reasons."

"My friend in school is in a wheelchair because of a car accident," Ryan blurted out. "He told me his doctor said he shouldn't be in a chair too long and he'd have to do a lot of exercises."

"Ryan, hopefully your friend will be okay, but he has to listen to his doctor. After the accident, I was in a wheelchair for almost five months. I could have been out of it in three." She swallowed the lump in her throat and wondered if she should tell them about her head injury which had given her severe headaches for months. She decided to leave that part out too. For now. "I had a hard time coping with the loss of my family, so I wouldn't speak to anyone for the first two months. Except to Jason and even then, very little. I fought everyone who tried to help me, the more I fought, the weaker I got. One day, ohh, about three months after I got out of the hospital, Jason got real mad."

"How long were you in the hospital for?" Ryan asked.

"Almost eight weeks."

"That was a long time, Miss Riley," Crystal said. "Why?"

Mandy sighed. She thought about how she was going to answer another question without telling everyone about her head injury. Everything led to the injury she didn't want to discuss and she couldn't go there. Yet. "Well, I had another injury that had to be tended to. Maybe I'll tell you about that another time."

"Okay, tell us why Jason was mad?" Ryan asked.

"Well, I had a class 'A' bad attitude. One day at breakfast I got mad at Jason and I went to my room and slammed the door. Jason followed me and hauled me back out of bed and plunked me back in my wheelchair then wheeled me outside." She chuckled. "I was still in my nightgown and he took me to the end of the yard and told me to stay there and think about what I was doing to him and the rest of the people who loved me. He put an apple down on the ground and a bottle of water then told me to get it myself and walked away."

"That was mean," Crystal spoke up.

"At first, I thought so too, but then I started to think. I had no right to hurt the people who loved me. My parents and brother, Martin, were gone and there wasn't a thing I could do about it. I still had Jason, my aunt and uncle and all my beautiful memories. And, they were also going through sad times because my parents and brother were their family, too. I wasn't alone. I had a family. My self-pity was destroying me and everyone who loved me and I had no right to do that. My attitude was hurting others."

"Did you get the apple?" Ryan chuckled.

Mandy smiled, thinking back all those years. "Yes, I did. Jason came back a couple hours later and asked me if I needed more time to think. He told me my pain was his and he couldn't stand any more of it. You see…" she leaned on the table with her arms crossed, "…Jason and I can feel each other's pain, and also our joy. He knows when I'm hurting and I know when he is. It's rare, but it happens in families. Especially with twins. The bonding is so incredible; you can actually feel what the other person is feeling. It sounds strange and it's hard to explain, but like I said, it happens. It's strong in our family. Jason and I have a gift and I had to learn not to abuse it."

"Can he still feel your pain?" Dianne asked.

"Yes, he can, and I feel his. We can also feel each other's joy, happiness and the positive in our lives. I spoke about the pain more because it was a lesson I had to learn. Saturday was an example. I thought of only myself and I overdid it. The excitement of getting back on a horse was so thrilling I didn't think of the consequences." She sighed. "I was selfish."

Mandy stroked the side of her temple. For the past eight years she'd told the same story over and over again, but this time in much more detail. This time with much more depth. At least now she was telling it to people who had come to care for her. Adam and his family were the first to hear of her and Jason's gift. "Jason knew I was hurting and that's why he helped me," she continued as she stroked the left side of her temple.

"Mandy, you're looking tired," Adam said. "I'll take the kids so you can go and rest for a while."

"Thank you, Adam, but I'll be fine." She lied. Telling her story in such detail mentally exhausted her. "I think we had better go out for a while and get some fresh air, besides there's chores to be done and today it's the tack room."

"Can't you tell us more about your ranch in Utah?" Ryan said.

"Yeah, tell us. We love the way you talk," Crystal said leaning forward.

"Crystal, remember how Jason talked. He's got a real accent," Ryan said enthusiastically.

Mandy smiled. She never thought about herself having an accent and as far as Jason was concerned, he could really put it on, thick. "I'll tell you something. Jason can be quite an entertainer." She laughed. "Anyway, I'll tell you more about our ranch life later. Right now, we have to get our chores done."

CHAPTER 14

*G*oing to the corral to see Stacey, Dee, and the two babies, who were now running and kicking up their little hooves and playing was such a pleasure. Everyone laughed at how the little ones seemed to show off.

"I love watching the babies," Ryan said.

"Me too," Crystal chirped.

After watching the horses for a few more minutes, Mandy turned to the kids. "Okay, let's get our chores done so we can come back later." She herded the three children into the tack room which definitely needed work. By the time they had finished listening to her life story, there was only an hour left before lunch, so Mandy decided to concentrate on getting things organized to work after their meal.

Mandy lined up three pails of hot water, took out the rags and dropped one into each bucket, then instructed the children to take out the dust pans, brooms, and whisks from the storage locker. They sorted what needed to be cleaned and repaired in different piles then tossed all the dirty rags into the washing machine, that needed a serious wipe down itself, added detergent, and pushed start. At least one chore would be half-done for when they returned. "Okay, we're all organized so let's go eat."

During lunch, Crystal and Ryan told their mother how Miss Riley really knew how to organize. They lost their manners, gobbled up their lunch, excused themselves and headed back to the tack room.

"I'm never going to let you go," Dianne said.

"Fine with me." Mandy grinned. "I'm enjoying it here, but right now I'd better go see if Crystal and Ryan made it to the tack room or are they out playing." She took Bobby out of his chair. "Come on, Sweetie, I'll see if I can find you a job."

Mandy found the children sitting on the corral railing watching the babies. She cleared her throat and watched both children jump down. "Having a nice time?" She tried to be stern but failed terribly, as her mouth went up at the corners. "You two haven't done a thing while your mom and I finished our lunch and you know this tack room has to be done. Come on, I'll help you finish."

Bobby got the job of sweeping the lower shelf where he fit nicely. His chubby fingers wrapped around the dust broom as he diligently cleaned. A job she'd have to redo, but she didn't mind one bit. Ryan polished the saddles, cleaned the bits and hardware, while Crystal cleaned and organized the various brushes, combs, and hoof picks. While the children placed everything back in their appropriate places, Mandy organized the reins, leads, ropes, and halters, then picked up a horse blanket that needed mending. She hugged it to her chest and took in a deep breath of the tack room smells that she had missed so much.

She glanced at Bobby who had fallen asleep on the bottom shelf with the mini-broom clutched in his hand. She placed her hand on the littlest helper's back. "Awe… little man, this isn't such a bad place for a little cowboy to have his nap." She laughed softly, gently stroked his hair then found some clean soft rags to use as a pillow for him.

As she untangled leads, she thought about all the good people in her life. She touched the pencil-width, jagged, raised scar on her temple. Was it really that bad? Jason and her family never thought so. Neither did Jason's friend, Vic Moor, who kept asking her out. But Vic, who was extremely persistent, was only a friend and she didn't feel for him the way he obviously felt for her. She wanted Adam McBride.

Finished with her chore, she put away towels, sheepskins and blankets while Ryan and Crystal finished their tasks. Moments later, big brown eyes opened. The littlest cowboy was awake and ready for action. His mischievous gaze went straight for the pail of warm soapy water. He scurried out of his resting place and in a flash, he was down on his knees with soap bubbles in his chubby hands and his cheeks puffed out.

"Hey, Bobby, stop that," Ryan hollered as soap bubbles flew everywhere.

As much as the soap would eliminate most of the dirt on the little boy's face and hands, Mandy had to scoop him up before the whole pail got dumped. She laughed. There would be a ring around the bath tub tonight. Maybe someday she'd have her own little boy, who would make a ring around her tub after a day of chores on her own ranch. Another hour later, she stepped back with Ryan and Crystal and inspected the tack room. It smelled clean and looked great.

"Hey, you guys, it's suppertime," Cole hollered out as he walked in then stopped abruptly. "Wow, this is amazing." He glanced around at the impressive job. "I've never seen the tack room so clean and organized. This is totally awesome." He nodded as he gazed around the room.

"It was fun," Crystal said.

"Yeah, Pa, we had a good time," Ryan piped up.

"Me elped too, Pa," Bobby squealed as he ran up to Cole and hugged his knee. "I elped, Wyan ceen."

"I see you helped Ryan and it's a super dooper bang-up job." He bent down and hugged Bobby, ruffled Crystal's hair and patted Ryan on the back. "You all deserve a surprise."

"What, Pa, what?" Crystal and Ryan clapped their hands in excitement.

Cole picked up Bobby and yelled out. "Roast beef dinner." He swung the little boy up in the air and down again.

"Ahh, Pa," Ryan complained.

"Hey, don't complain, that's a great surprise. Monday's usually leftovers, but no leftovers left." He laughed and put Bobby on his shoulders. "Come on, Mandy, kids, let's go, its chow time."

"Yahoo, Pa," Ryan yelled and raced ahead.

ADAM GLANCED AT HIS WATCH. In ten more minutes he was going to be home for supper. Ten more minutes he'd look upon Mandy's beautiful face, listen to her sweet voice and kiss her soft pink lips. Just thinking about her turned his body hot and hard with desire.

"Boss, you'd better come quick," lead foreman, Chuck Larson, called out. "Dean and I found a dead calf."

With disappointment that he couldn't keep his thoughts of Mandy going, he turned Zircon around and followed Chuck. The foreman was right, there was a dead calf and it had been dragged into the thicket. The tracks were definitely cat.

"Cougar tracks all over the place, Boss," Dean said. "I trailed 'em the saf'noon and got a glimpse of it. I'm a figurin' it's a mighty big male."

"We haven't had a cougar here for some time now," Adam

said then turned to another young cowboy who came along. "Ben, get word to Cole and tell him we need every available man." He turned to Chuck. "Organize the men to bring the cattle in closer." He turned to young Dean who was tugging at his sleeve as he continued to talk to Chuck. "We'll have to get old Charlie to bring out his hounds in the morning." He nodded. "What, Dean?"

"Ya want me to bury the carcass deep, then go a huntin'?" Dean asked.

Adam looked at the young cowboy. As much as he liked the hard-working, good-natured, kid, he couldn't stand his American accent. He sounded so much like Jason. That wasn't fair to judge, as most of his friends were American, either from the States themselves, or they were born there and moved up to Canada. And there was Mandy. He'd have to remember not to judge all Americans by Jason. "You can bury it with another man watching your back. And don't think about going hunting by yourself." Adam reminded them that cougars were particularly fond of horse flesh, so they were to buddy up and keep their eyes and ears open.

"Chuck, where's Hank?" Adam hollered as he scanned the area.

"Sorry, Adam, but when I went to wake him up this morning, he was just getting into bed. He told me he can't handle it any longer." Chuck shrugged. "I don't know how to help him anymore."

Adam turned to Chuck and sighed heavily. He didn't have time to babysit Hank. "After you get the men..." he shifted his weight in the saddle, "...will you take over... completely... I'll..."

"Adam, you'll have to let Hank be. We'll deal with him later."

Adam hesitated then glanced towards home. Chuck right, but Hank needed him.

"Adam, we have enough problems right now and we're short of men and I can't ask the night boys to do double. They've already done a lot of extra hours and they're exhausted. Besides, Hank's probably still in bed passed out so at least he's safe."

Adam turned to Chuck's low, warning tone. Chuck was their number one foreman, he risked losing him if he didn't heed his warning.

Chuck nodded. "We'll get Hank back on track together. Adam, he's my friend, too."

$\sim$

"I WONDER what's keeping the men?" Dianne said with worry. "It's not usually like them to be out so late." She sighed. "Ohh, I wish cell phones worked out here."

"There could be a number of reasons, but I'm sure they're all right, Dianne," Mandy said ignoring her own uneasiness.

"I know, but I worry lately, especially since I've been in this blasted chair."

To change the subject, Mandy asked, "Dianne, tell me how you fell off your horse."

Dianne nodded. "I was out with Chuck herding strays and for some reason my horse spooked and reared. It's not like her to do that and I wasn't prepared. If I hadn't twisted my other knee I could have at least had a walking cast and a pair of crutches."

"I've fallen off a few times in my life," Mandy added. "I remember once I was racing my brothers back to the barn and didn't stop soon enough. I tried to get off." She laughed out loud. "I ended up being part of the barn door for a few minutes. Talk about embarrassing."

Dianne covered her mouth and inhaled deeply. "Ouch. That must have hurt."

"My pride, more than anything." Mandy twisted her face.

The evening was beautiful. The breeze calming, allowing Mandy to soak in the magnificent beauty of the western sunsets even though the sunset never lasted very long. The sun went behind the mountains almost before you could blink. Not like the real prairie sunsets, where they were absolutely breath-taking and one could soak up the intense beauty of the big prairie skies.

"It's extraordinary out here. I can't get enough of this wide-open countryside." She glanced at Dianne. "We're so fortunate to live in this part of the country. I'll always love Utah, it's a part of me and it will always be in my heart. But, now, I can't think of anywhere I would rather live than Western Canada. We have everything. Vast golden prairies and pasture land. Rolling hills and the majestic mountains to the west. Rich forests, fresh mountain lakes and streams." She slowly got out of her chair and walked to the railing. "Just think, Dianne." She spread her arms out. "People come from all over the world just to see our national parks and places like the Continental Divide. There's so much here, and it's all in our own back yard."

"You're right and I count my blessings every night."

Mandy looked up to the open sky and wished upon the first star of the evening. "Yeah... me... too. God has given us so much..." Her voice trailed off into a soft whisper.

"Yes... He has..." Dianne agreed.

The two women listened to the late evening sounds as peace came over the valley. The crickets, the evening songbirds singing to their young. The distant sound of the cattle settling for the night. A stillness that brought warmth and tranquility over the land.

As beautiful as the evening was, the chill of the late evening air sent them into the house for a cup of tea. By the time the clock chimed eleven thirty the men still hadn't returned. "Where do you think they'd be?" Mandy asked with worry as she rubbed her temple to relieve the tension.

"Southwest pasture, I think. I'll call over to the bunkhouse and ask one of the hands who may know what's going on."

Just then John McBride walked in. "You ladies still up?"

"We were… sort of worried." Dianne's voice cracked.

John walked over and gave her a kiss on the forehead then knelt down beside her. He took her hand. "Cole, Adam, Chuck and all the hands are fine. Everything is okay. I'm sorry, Honey, we should have sent word." John stood and sat in the chair beside his daughter-in-law. "We found cougar tracks and another dead calf." He glanced at Mandy. "So, we're doubling up on the men and everything is going to be okay," he assured both women.

Both ladies heaved a sigh of relief.

"Thanks, Dad."

John stood and stepped over towards Mandy. "How are you doing tonight, Amanda?" He patted her shoulder.

"Fine thank you, Sir."

"I hear you and the kids did a remarkable job in the tack room today. Cole told me he hasn't seen it that clean in years."

"It needed to be done." She shrugged and smiled.

"After you're finished your nanny job, you can be tack room foreman."

"You're on. I'm tough, though." She giggled.

"Tough marshmallow." John laughed as he poured himself a cup of coffee.

"John, have you ever been hit in the head with a tough marshmallow? You know, the kind that's been in the pantry for a year or so. Unwrapped."

John laughed. "Can't say I have." He took a sip of coffee. "Aha, that's good."

"Well I have, and it hurts," she said softly.

John laughed low and deep then winked.

"Well… I think I'm going to check on the horses,"

Mandy said.

"I'll do that, Amanda," John offered and put down his coffee mug.

"Oh, no that's fine, I'd like to. Besides, I enjoy the quiet of the evening." She left quickly hoping to see Adam soon. Kissing in the barn had been fun and very exciting. She'd even roll in the hay with him knowing that his body, hands, and kisses would make her forget the itch it can cause. She walked slowly along the brightly moonlit path towards the barn. The warm summer breeze felt good as she lifted her hair up then let it fall well past her shoulders.

She entered the large barn doors which were still open waiting for Adam and his men to return. Flipping one of three light switches, she headed towards the stalled mares. In the first stall there was a pretty little chestnut with two white socks who came to her and sniffed her shirt. "You're a lovely girl and I'm sure you're going to have your baby tonight?" She laughed. "Yeah, probably two in the morning." She gave her one last pat. "I'll see you later." Mandy gave her a quick kiss on her soft nose.

On the other side, Dee was waiting for her pat. Dee nuzzled her baby as if she wanted to introduce him to her. Mandy unlatched the gate and stepped in. "You've got a nice little boy there, Dee." She smiled and stroked Dee's neck and let the baby sniff her hand. "You're a darling. Well, I got to go and see your friend, so I'll see you tomorrow." She re-latched the gate.

Stacey was waiting for her good night pat. "How are you doing, Mama?" She opened the gate and walked in. The gentle mare sniffed her shirt and nuzzled her hand. The baby copied her mother for some attention. "Adam won't be back for a while," she spoke softly and stroked the baby's forehead and the mother's neck. "So, I thought I'd say good night to you. Tell me, who brought you in for the night?" Stacey whinnied then gave off a short snort. "Oh, he did, did he." She laughed. She didn't know who had brought the horses in and it didn't matter, as they were safe and comfortable.

Suddenly, a rustling at the back of the barn caught her attention. "Hello," she called out. "Who's there?" She leaned over the stall gate to see a dark shadow move. Her gut twisted. Icy chills raced up her spine as the feeling of being watched grew. "Who's there?" she hollered. This time with a stronger voice. Still no answer.

Perspiration dotted her forehead as the dark figure moved again. Her heart pumped painfully as she stared at the dark corner. Her fingers clutched the top of the stall gate as she wished she had put all the lights on. Her head turned right. Her eyes gazed at the open barn door at the opposite end. Could she make a run for it and get to the house and report a prowler? Frozen in Stacey's stall, she tried to calculate the distance to the open barn door. She didn't know if she could run fast enough past all those stalls with weak, rubbery knees. The rustling sound grabbed her attention again as she jerked her head back towards the dark corner. Her heart pumped faster and harder.

She jumped when a horse whinnied at the far end. The darkest part of the barn. The part of the barn where the shadow was. *Cougar.* "No. Can't be. The horses would be unsettled." She leaned over the stall gate. "Who's there?" she screamed out a demand.

"I... it's m..me," a voice came back to her. A man's voice, and it wasn't a McBride.

"Come out from there," she demanded.

"I c..can't. 'Elp me."

She swallowed hard and rubbed her sweaty palms on the back of her jeans as she slowly opened the stall gate. "You come out from behind there now. There's nothing in this barn that will hurt you." She demanded as she took a tiny step towards the rustling. Her eyes adjusted to the dim light. "Mister."

"H..elp... h..elp...me... p..please." The voice weak and strained.

Mandy took another step forward. Hearing a deep groan, she took another, then another. With a quick glance behind her, she realized the distance to the open barn door was becoming farther and farther away. Taking risks was a part of life, yet was this risk a safe one, or was it just plain stupid? A deep groan again caught her attention. "Who are you?" She heard the tremble of her own voice. The shadow on the floor moved. She leaned forward and squinted as she focused on a curled-up body of a man in pain. "Oh my." She knelt down. "Are you hurt?"

"Y..yeah," he groaned deeply.

There was just enough light she could tell the man was in trouble. Suddenly, the overwhelming stench of beer and strong dirty hands were on her. "You blundering idiot. Get your hands off of me," she screamed.

"Ahhh... sssorry, s..sorry."

Mandy jerked her head to the side and fell backwards. A heavy weight fell over her. "Get off me," she screamed again and pushed the drunken man away. He staggered and fell back.

"Ohhhh, sss..sorry." He stumbled and fell again.

Mandy realized it was Hank. Her anger grew as she reminded herself that not all drinkers were killers. The stench of him brought back the memory of that fatal day as she watched him stagger to his feet. Her stomach churned at the sight of him.

"I... d-didn't m-m...mean to s..s.s.scare you, l..lady," he said as he slurred his words and stumbled again. This time his bottle of beer went flying and smashed against the large metal hinge of the tack room door.

"Oh, damn you," Mandy cursed and brushed her clothes off. She smelled her hands. "You clumsy ox." She turned to walk away but his painful groan made her turn back. The disgusting creature was bleeding from the forehead. He could bleed to death as far as she was concerned. *He deserves help like any other human being.* A deep voice spoke from deep within her soul. Mandy took in a deep breath and straightened her shoulders. The voice from within was right, so she took a quick step forward and helped the man up.

"M..mme... head 'urts," Hank groaned.

"It should for all that poison you're putting into your body," she scolded.

"I... I miss m..me Nancy," he slurred.

"If I were Nancy, I'd throw you out," she hissed at him. "Here, put your arm around my neck and I'll get you back to your bunkhouse."

"I'll help him." A strong deep male voice came from the center of the barn.

Mandy jerked her head up and toward the light at the end of the barn. "Adam, you're back." Relief set in as she watched him walk towards them. Jaw tight. His eyes narrowed. His fists clenched.

"Umm... he's drunk," she said as she shifted her weight.

"Ahh, Aaaadem." Hank leaned into her.

She turned her face. The stench of his breath took hers away. "He's cut himself."

"I'll take care of him." He nodded and pulled Hank towards him, freeing Mandy. "Are you all right, Mandy?" he asked with deep concern.

Mandy ignored his question and said, "I'll get the first aid kit." She watched Adam stare at her for a moment as he held Hank up. His face full of confusion.

"Thank you." He turned and walked towards the foremen's cabin with Hank glued to his hip.

Mandy hurried to the tack room, grabbed the first aid kit and raced out of the barn where a couple of cowboys pointed to where Adam had taken Hank.

"The foremen's cabin," a young cowboy hollered out. "We'll get coffee."

Mandy entered the cabin where both Chuck and Hank lived. The living room was well-lit with masculine furniture and a shelf with family pictures, a bronze horse figure and several silver buckles lined up on a shelf.

On one recliner, a pile of dirty clothes. Tiny bits of paper from a beer bottle label were in a heap on a wooden side table beside a half-eaten sandwich. She headed towards Adam's voice and entered Hank's bedroom. The bed surprisingly enough looked clean, but the smell of puke turned her stomach.

"This is it, Hank, the meetings with A.A. aren't helping so you're going in for treatment."

Mandy rolled her eyes believing Hank would never listen to anyone and that he was too far gone. She stepped towards the entrance to the private bathroom leading off of his bedroom. "Chuck's lucky he doesn't have to share this bedroom or bathroom," she murmured as she listened to Adam.

"You're not coming back to this ranch, Hank, until you get help with this drinking."

"Oh, boss, I's s..sorry. I is s..sorry."

"No, you're not. Now get this stinking shirt off."

Mandy heard the shower being turned on.

"Strip and get washed up."

"Need help?" she called from behind the door.

"No, thanks. Are you okay, Mandy?" Adam hollered back.

"I'm fine," she said stiffly. "He startled me when I was checking on Stacey and Dee."

"He's harmless," Adam said.

She opened the bathroom door a crack. "Yeah, until he gets keys to a truck," she said sharply then shoved the first aid kit into Adam's outreached hand. "One of the ranch hands is getting black coffee." She glared at Adam and left.

CHAPTER 15

*A*dam placed his frog mug on the kitchen table. He'd seen her new blue to-go mug, but he knew she enjoyed drinking her tea from his. It was the ultimate best, so he pushed it in front of her, sat down and let out a hefty sigh. His eyes focused on her trembling fingers that accepted the mug filled with her favorite green tea and brought it up to her pale lips and blew gently on the hot liquid. Her hair, still damp from her shower, smelled of fresh strawberries. Her baby blue cotton housecoat with matching pajamas underneath was buttoned almost to the top, which was fine with him, as this was not the time to fantasize about her soft warm skin. The look she had given him earlier when he was helping Hank was enough to stop a raging bull in his tracks. If he lost any chance with her, Hank wouldn't need counseling, he'd need a surgeon.

"Thank you." She took a sip.

"You're welcome." He moved his chair closer and leaned forward to face her directly and looked at her pale face. He raised his arm and slipped his hand underneath her damp hair and gently massaged her neck. "I'm sorry you had to see that. He'll be gone tomorrow and won't be back." He watched her raise her eyes over the mug towards him, sending him a silent message that he was on very thin ice.

She lowered the mug. "He smelled like the man that killed my parents and brother," she said as her voice cracked with emotions. "People like him should be locked up and the key thrown away." She put the mug on the table and rubbed her temple. "I'm sorry, I know that sounds cruel, but I can't help the way I feel."

Adam couldn't help release the throaty nervous chuckle at her comment about his friend. "Why did you help him, then?" He noticed a bruise forming on her upper arm. He touched it gently. "What's this?"

"To answer your first question, I had to." She huffed. "He's still a human being and well… God nudged me."

"Yes, he is. However, I think you're also a very kind and compassionate woman." He glanced at the forming bruise again and jerked his chin towards it.

Mandy put the mug down and looked at her upper arm, then gently touched it. "I didn't have that one before, so I guess that's when he fell on me." She rolled her eyes.

Adam cringed at the thought of his friend so out of control with drunkenness that he had hurt Mandy.

"I'm very angry right now." She moved her chair over to put a safe distance between them.

Adam took a deep breath. She may be angry, but he saw much more. She had a heart of an angel. Her eyes glistened with tears. He now knew why she had asked him if he drank or not and he couldn't blame her. He shifted his chair closer as his hand slowly touched hers. "Hank is never going to hurt you, Mandy. Trust me." His thumb pad brushed away the teardrop as it escaped from one of her blue eyes. "Finish your tea and I'll walk you to your room so you can get some sleep." They sat quietly as he watched her sip the tea until it was finished. Her face pale, underneath hot flushed cheeks.

"What makes people want to drink so much? What makes them want to destroy themselves and others?"

"He lost his wife, Nancy, two years ago when she fell off a horse and broke her neck. Hank blames himself, even though it wasn't his fault."

"Ohh dear... I'm so sorry. I told him..."

"I know, I heard. You didn't know, so don't beat yourself up over it. The fact is, Hank needs help and, well, I finally realized I can't help him. My family's right, I'm not an Addictions Counsellor." Adam shrugged. "Anyway, Nancy and Hank met when they were both nineteen and were married for eight years. Even after his wife died he never touched the stuff. He worked hard, but the pain of losing her wouldn't go away. Even after a year and a half, he kept it together, but then he broke down. He started drinking about six months ago. The Hank you see now isn't the same man."

"Adam, I'm sorry, so sorry for his loss. No one needs to live with the guilt of thinking they've hurt, or in his case killed someone they love deeply. But, he's still a danger to society and someone else is going to get hurt. Even killed," she stressed with concern.

"I know," Adam said slowly. "He's going into treatment tomorrow." He pushed his chair away from the table. "Come on, it's late." He held out his hand and was pleased that she trusted him enough to accept it.

He walked slowly upstairs and led her to the bedroom and entered. When he let go of her hand, cold replaced the warmth of it. His breathing increased. He had to get out of her room, or he was going to have major consequences. He folded back the covers. "Here, crawl in and I'll tuck you in." He covered her and as promised, tucked her in. "If you need me call. I'll leave the door open a crack." He was tempted to take her mouth. But not tonight. She had gone through enough. "Good night, Mandy," he said gently and kissed her on the forehead before leaving.

IN THE WEE hours of the morning, Mandy turned towards the door creaking open. Without a doubt Adam was the most incredible man alive and he was standing in her doorway covered in his dark burgundy knee-length robe and pajama bottoms. His unmistakably broad chest with partially exposed rich dark chest hair, caused her body to react. A reaction that was still new to her. A feeling that pleased her. As he opened it wider she noticed a worried look cross his brow.

"Can't sleep?" he asked in a low, soothing voice.

She sat up in bed and studied his movements as he stepped closer. "No." Her heart rate accelerated a hundred-fold as he sat down on the edge of her bed.

"Neither could I. I was worried about you," he said with concern.

With both hands Mandy brought the covers up to her chin. Her eyes concentrated on his large bronzed hand that had come to rest beside her upper leg. Warmth radiated through the blanket. If his hand got any closer, she was going to go out of her mind with what she wanted him to do to her with those hands. She didn't need this new feeling right now.

She didn't want to think about the hand that was gentle towards her, yet strong enough to hold up and help his drunken friend. The hand that helped deliver a foal and worked hard. She believed Adam was an honorable man and Hank should be proud to have a friend in him. What bothered her, was even though he now understood his friend needed help, he still didn't realize how much a drunk could hurt someone. He thought

Hank was harmless, but she knew better. "I'm glad you came back when you did," she spoke softly as her eyes lingered on his.

"So am I."

She watched him reach for her hand and entwine his fingers with hers. A strange sense of belonging set in, yet she couldn't understand why his eyes were filled with hurt, or pain. What had life thrown at him? How could she feel this strange sense of belonging when they were worlds apart?

"Tell me. Are you frightened of Hank?"

"No, not in the way you think. He startled me at first because I didn't know who or what was in the barn. I tripped, then he fell on top of me." She went silent for a moment then took in a deep breath. "I got scared, because he was drunk and I didn't know what his intentions were. He brought back some terrible memories with the smell of him and how he slurred his words and he staggered. But for some reason, I sensed he wouldn't hurt me physically." She shivered. "Adam, what scares me is, well... like I said downstairs, his drinking is going to seriously hurt someone someday." She took in a deep breath. "I'm glad you came back to take care of him. Even though I would have." She rolled her eyes.

He tugged gently on her hand.

The urge to allow him to support her gave way, as he pulled her towards him. His support turned to yearning as his fingers traced up and down her arm leaving little trails of shivers along their wake. Warm shivers. Pleasant shivers as he moved closer up the bed and wrapped his arm around her shoulders, bringing her closer to him.

He hugged her tight. "Like I said, he'll be in treatment tomorrow. I promise."

Mandy laid her head on his shoulder. His hand brushed her hair back then he stroked her right cheek with his fingertips. His strong fingers tilted up her chin. His mouth brushed gently over her soft lips, then parted them. His exploring mouth made her mouth soft and eager for its moist warm touch.

Knowing full well she should stop him, but her body wasn't allowing her to. Hearing herself moan with delight, she moved her mouth away to take in a breath. He smelled good as she began to caress his neck with her mouth. The warmth of his body began to melt with hers, as she found his mouth again. She could hardly breathe for the want of him.

BEING BUNDLED up like a mummy with her pajamas and robe on, and the covers up to her chin, Adam diligently searched for soft warm skin. When he felt her stiffen, yet hadn't stopped him, he continued. He moved closer to her. His eyes cruised her mouth, her eyes, her whole face. How far would she allow him to go? Should he push this to the limit? *Careful. She needs rest. She's vulnerable.* He knew that the trauma had sent her searching for security.

His eyes searched hers as he inched his fingers to the left side of her face. He watched her mouth open slightly. Her eyes widened. Her body in the first stage of trembling. "Relax, I won't hurt you," he whispered and watched her swallow, hard. He didn't know why she was beginning to panic, but he could see it in her eyes. He was going to lose her if he went any further. His hand continued to slowly, cautiously, reach for her left temple. The side of her face she kept hidden from him. From everyone.

"Please... don't." Her eyes glistened with moisture.

"Hey," he whispered. "I'm not going to hurt you." He paused. "Your hair is beautiful. You're beautiful. But why do you hide behind it?"

She ignored his question and gently pushed on his chest as she inched away from him. "I'm going to show you something, before our relationship gets any deeper. You may not like what you see or want me after. You won't be the first man who has rejected me because of it."

He cringed as she told him of her past boyfriends and their comments. They were hurtful remarks and cruel criticisms of how ugly her scars were and how she'd never find anyone who would love her because of them. Adam listened as she told him that one man suggested plastic surgery. He kissed her gently on the forehead then leaned back. "I want you, no matter what your scars look like," he whispered.

"We'll see." Her small words were direct and stiff. In a few short moments she'd be able to tell if he was repulsed by her or not. She shifted over to the middle of the bed and slowly, pushed her night shirt up to her hip then took his hand and placed it on her leg while she searched his eyes. She guided his hand up and down the long, white, raised, jagged scar.

She watched his face for any sign of pity or disgust. To her surprise, there was a look of compassion, warmth and acceptance. There was no look of repulsion. He wasn't sickened by it. His hands gently continued to stroke it.

"Does it hurt?" he whispered.

She nodded then shrugged. "There's permanent muscle damage and some pain at times." Mandy continued to watch his face. Still no contempt or repulsion. She didn't mind the curiosity and didn't mind the questions, in fact she expected it. "You're not repulsed by it?" she asked curiously.

Adam shook his head slowly and looked into her eyes. "No, of course not," he said sincerely.

Mandy listened very carefully to the tone of his voice. He appeared to be telling her the truth, but maybe he was a good liar. How could he not be repulsed by the ugliness of her leg? All the other men were, so why would Adam be any different? She shook her head.

"Mandy, please believe me. Trust me."

"I want to, but…"

"No, no buts…"

He had accepted her for who she was? His eyes, his voice, his tender touch told her so. The joy of acceptance stirred her very soul.

ADAM FELT her eagerness as she squirmed beneath him. Her warm soft body aroused and wanting. Impatient. Her soft moans increased causing his body to harden. He wanted her, his body ready and she wasn't stopping him. He was sure he could convince her to continue with love making. Suddenly he felt a slight tremor and his heart called out to him to be careful. You may hurt her, you need to be gentle. His heart begged him not to frighten her or take her for his own selfish reasons. If you love her like you say, then back off and give her time; what happened tonight was a traumatic experience.

He remembered what he wanted in a woman and the life-long dream he had and how much he wanted to share it with someone special. He slowly inched away. "Mandy." He kissed her soft cheeks. "I'm falling in love with you." He kissed her moist full lips tenderly. "I promised you more time." He rolled away from her, adjusting his robe to hide the evidence of his desire and need. With a quick turn, he was in the rocker recliner lounge chair facing the bed. Far enough away so he wouldn't be tempted, but close enough he could see the gentle blush of her cheeks, but not feel the heat of her warm firm body. Cool air from the open window helped calm him.

He watched her watch him as she lay curled up. Her breathing was still heavy. Her cheeks flushed. He noticed her long fingers twisting the blanket. What was she thinking? What was her body telling her? What was her heart saying? When he said he was falling in love with her, she hadn't said anything.

~

MANDY COVERED her face with her arm. Her body hot and aroused. Sensations between her thighs tingled. Why had he stopped? She enjoyed the tiny electrical currents that shot up her spine and the butterflies and the warmth he gave her. He excited her like no other man had. She wanted more from him. She was ready physically. But deep down she knew that until he saw the rest of her, she would always stiffen when they got to a certain point of intense need. She would continue to send out some signal that would tell him she wasn't ready. It was truly remarkable that he was able to read her signs. Fortunately. Or was it unfortunate? She wanted him to teach her the art of love making. "Adam." She moved her arm away from her eyes and looked towards him. He was watching her and she didn't mind this time.

"I'm listening," he said quietly.

"What made you stop?"

"You're not ready." His smile warm and sincere.

"How did you know?" she asked in a whisper. Her eyes fixed on his.

"Are you?"

She closed her eyes. "I don't know." She opened them and smiled ever so slightly. "I have these sensations, a burning desire in my body. I want you, but this is all so new to me."

"Rest, sleep, enough for tonight."

She wanted to keep hearing his voice. "Adam, I love your voice. Tell me a story."

"Okay, but don't be afraid to go to sleep. If you do, I'll finish the story tomorrow."

ADAM NODDED as he made himself comfortable in the large rocker recliner. He leaned forward with his elbows resting on his knees, his hands folded together as he began to speak. "Once upon a time there was this little boy named Adam Scott McBride. He was a feisty little fellow who played rough and worked hard. He had a gentle mother who taught him the beautiful things in life. Taught him to listen to the songbirds in the morning. To play in the gentle summer rain. To listen to the crickets and frogs at night, then look up at the stars and count them as each one was a blessing. His mother showed him and his brother how to hug and how to take someone by the hand and help them. She taught us how to pray and that their faith would lead them to happiness." Noticing her breathing was slow and steady, he ended the story for the night. Wanting her to know about his life, he'd finished his story tomorrow.

Sitting by her side, he was amazed at how his body relaxed and how good it felt to be near her. He realized just being close to this beautiful, sweet woman was enough. Of course, he desired to be one with her someday, but for now, he would be content to be at her side and savor the precious time by just being in her room. Guarding her throughout the night.

Adam quietly got up from the lounge chair and tucked her in, then reached for the extra quilt at the bottom of the bed, sat back down and covered himself. As quietly as he could, he adjusted the lounge to a recline position. He'd watch over her for a while to make sure she'd sleep peacefully.

Sunbeams streamed through the window, finding Adam still asleep in the recliner. Mandy smiled as she focused on his rugged handsome face as he slept. Her thoughts turned to last night and how patient and gentle he had been with her. Being an emotional wreck and extremely vulnerable after the encounter with Hank, he could have taken her. But he hadn't. Even though she had encouraged him, because she wanted him herself. The promise to herself not to allow any man to take her unless he accepted her as she was, was almost broken. He had seen one scar, but not the one she felt was the center of her soul.

As she watched him, his head move slightly, causing her to still. Her eyes never wavered when his body twisted in the chair. His long pajama-clad leg moved, shifting the quilt and his robe to expose his magnificent muscle-rippled chest totally. Rich dark hair tapered evenly down to his waist band, making her forget to breathe. The greatest urge to touch his solid body flowed through her like hot lava. She wasn't experienced by a long shot, but she'd seen her share of men in gyms, on beaches and yes even years ago when she was in the physiotherapy department herself. Not one of them had a body like Adam. Not one.

A thunder of horses' hooves came racing into the yard before noon with several men hoopin' 'n' holler'n. "We got it," one young cowboy yelled to John who was standing on the porch in his chaps ready to go out on his second time around. Mandy turned to watch Dianne and the kids come around from the side of the house and come up the ramp.

"Got what?" Dianne hollered out.

"The cougar," the young cowboy repeated as his horse

continued to prance in front of the deck. He dismounted and headed towards a pick-up truck where another young cowboy had opened a cooler filled with beer.

Mandy watched Adam and Cole ride up to the porch.

"An old male. Looks like he's had his day, but still got another one of our calves," Adam announced quietly as he watched a few more of the cowboys ride up and dismount. "I gotta settle these boys down a little. Some of these young bucks haven't seen a cougar let alone go hunting for one and they're still worked up." Adam nodded then clicked his tongue as the horse moved around the wheelchair ramp and towards the truck.

Mandy watched as one of the young men began handing out beer. They gathered around to laugh and joke and guzzle. Cole took a beer, followed by Adam. As they tilted their heads back she focused on Dianne's facial expression. There was no concern on her face, so she focused back on Adam as he dismounted with his beer still in his hand. While Adam chatted with a couple of the cowboys, other men went and got a second beer. She watched Adam laugh and take another swig.

"One problem solved," John said as he walked down the steps and took a beer from Adam's outreached hand. "Thanks, son. Now I'm going to give you two another job," he said and took a gulp. "The new kid quit this morning just after you two left. Guess he couldn't keep up with the men, so you'll have to re-assign another hand for his duties and we'll hire a couple more full-time hands."

Mandy watched the three McBride men finish off their beer then watched Adam give a young cowboy a friendly slap on the back and praised him. Her breathing ceased as he headed towards the cooler. Was he going for another? When he put his empty back, and walked away from the cooler, she breathed a great sigh of relief. Her eyes glanced at Cole and his father as they did the same. Her heart rate returned to normal.

John turned. "Let's get coffee and something to eat." He motioned to one of the young hands. "Kid, you're the youngest, and you've had your share of beer, so take these three horses to the barn, and take care of them." He handed him three sets of reins. "Can you do it?" He put his arm around the kid's shoulder and gave him an encouraging manly hug.

"Yes, Sir," the lanky boy said eagerly as he handed over his empty bottle to John. "Thank you, sir."

"You're welcome, Kid."

Leaving the rest of the cowboys to finish celebrating and to clean up, the McBride men walked up the steps. They all looked impressive with their Stetsons, boots and chaps. She watched Adam take out a red and white mint from his pocket, unwrap it and pop it into his mouth.

"Hi." Adam bent over and kissed her on the mouth. "Hungry?"

"You bet." The sweet mint hadn't yet completely disguised the beer on his breath as a strange feeling of acceptance washed over her.

Cole took his place at the table and took a sip of coffee. "I have a couple of experienced hands interested so I'll call them in for an interview as soon as I'm finished lunch."

"Who are these hands? Local boys?" Adam asked Cole as he grabbed a sandwich from the plate closest to him that was piled high with man-sized sandwiches. He took a big bite. "Mmm, these are great Dianne," he said taking a mouthful.

"Both from Calgary. A Dave Henderson and a J. Mackenzie. Both have experience."

Mandy suddenly choked on her milk. She grabbed a napkin to wipe up the dribbles on her chin then excused herself from the table.

"You all right, Mandy?" Adam got up right away to help her. She giggled nervously and nodded her head between coughs. Her hand waved him away as she went into the living room. "I'm fine. I just swallowed the wrong way." Her mind turned to her brother, Jason Mackenzie Riley. "Go have your lunch, Adam, I'm fine. Really." Her mind went back to Jason and what was he doing applying for the job when he had a job as a fine finishing carpenter. He not only designed beautiful wood furniture, but with his Business Management Degree, he had a good future with their uncle until they got their own ranch. Even then, he could continue working in the family business part-time. She knew why, he was her protector and he wasn't going to let up. She pressed down hard on the phone buttons.

"Hello, Riley Fine Furniture."

"Jason."

"Yo, Squeak, nice to hear from ya. How's it goin' this fine afta'noon?"

"Fine, Mr. Mackenzie," she said sarcastically. "And drop that silly thick drawl." After a short snicker from Jason, the few seconds of silence was long enough to tell her what he had done and she didn't like it one bit. "Please, don't."

"Why not, you know I miss ranch life as much as you. This way I can pick up a few pointers I've forgotten."

"Oh, and keep an eye on me, too?"

"No, that's not it. But not a bad idea."

"Jason please, I'm finally coping with my fears, emotions and everything else. I don't need my brother watching me."

"Aah, Squeak. If they run the ranch like they should, I won't be near you. Ranch hands don't hang around the main house. The foremen maybe, and if there's an older hand who has been there for years, fine, but the regular hands, no. I'll be out working and when I'm not, I'll be at the bunk-house with the other men."

"Can't you wait until we have our own place? I talked to my

publisher the other day and there's another check coming for me. You know what to do with it."

"Be reasonable, Amanda."

"No, Jason I don't need you interfering. And using your second name was sneaky."

"First of all, I promise I won't interfere. I don't know if I even have the job yet. Huh, I'm sure you can fix it so I won't be hired, that's why I used my middle name. I figured you'd connect me, but I was hoping I'd get the interview before you knew. Or did you tell them? Eh." Jason laughed. "Like my new Canadian word. It only took eight years to catch on. Can't drawl that word out." Jason howled with laughter.

"Oh, stop it, Jason, not everyone in Canada uses, eh. In fact, truth be told, very few people do. Actually, I hear them say, 'you know,' more than I hear, eh, so get your Canadian words straight. Now good-bye, Jason see you later."

"Bye, Squeak. Wish me luck, eh." Jason laughed and hung up.

For a moment Mandy wished Jason and his accent, would go back to Utah.

CHAPTER 16

*A*dam watched Mandy as she sat back down at the table and he wondered who she had called to make her so pale. Whoever it was had upset her to the point of silence. Was Dave Henderson or J. Mackenzie a former boyfriend?

"You, all right?" he asked in a hushed voice.

"Yes, fine, thank you." She sighed nervously.

Adam watched her eyes shift from him to his brother. Trouble was brewing and from the look on her face, it was mighty upsetting.

"Do you both do the interviewing?"

"Yes," Cole answered. "Why, Mandy?"

"Well... uh... I know J. Mackenzie." She turned to Adam. "He's my brother and Mackenzie, is his middle name."

Adam heard Cole chuckle. This was not a laughing matter.

"This will be an interesting interview," Cole said as he turned to his brother and grinned.

"Yeah, it will be." Adam groaned.

"He'll have a fair interview and the respect like everyone else," John demanded as he glanced around the table. "If he's qualified and can do the work and has good references, then he has a right to the job. It's that simple and I don't give a damn what name he chooses to go by. First, middle, last, or a pet name. Do you three understand me?" John's voice of authority rang loud and clear.

"Yes, sir," Mandy said.

"Yes, Pa," Cole and Adam answered in unison.

Adam knew that was the end of the J. Mackenzie discussion, at least for now. His father was right, no one had the right to pre-judge Jason's ability and if he worked as hard as his sister he'd get the job. His eyes met Mandy's. Through her silence, he figured she definitely did not want Jason here anymore than he did. "I've got to run into town."

"You going to take Hank to treatment?" Dianne asked.

"Yes."

"Wish him all the best from all of us," Cole said, stood up and faced Adam.

Adam made a fist and hit his brother in the shoulder lightly. "I'll tell him. See you later." He turned to Mandy. "I'll be back by dinner."

"Mandy." John nodded to her. "In my den. Please," he said with a firm voice as he dropped his napkin on the table, turned and left the dining room.

"Yes, Sir, right away." She placed her napkin on the table and looked at Dianne nervously.

"You'll be fine. Dad is the nicest, sweetest person you will ever know. Relax," Dianne whispered.

Mandy nodded then turned to Crystal. "Help your mother for a few minutes while I talk to your grandfather?"

Mandy twitched a nervous smile as she entered the den and sat down in the leather chair opposite the large oak desk. "Mr. McBride."

He nodded to her. "I'll get straight to the point." He moved his leather chair and leaned back. "I don't like to interfere in people's lives, decisions or choices they make, never made a habit of it and I don't intend to start now. However, Amanda, I just want to give you a heads up. If working hard runs in your family, then your brother will be working for us. This will not have anything to do with your job. Okay?"

"Yes, Sir. I understand. Thanks for the heads up." She stood and turned towards the door, then suddenly stopped and turned back. "John, I was wondering where you got your dining room suite including the hutch and corner curio cabinet?" She noticed his stare went right to her face.

John studied her eyes, nose, mouth and chin then nodded slowly as if in deep thought. "Amanda... Riley." His mouth turned to grin. "By... chance... are you... Ivan Riley's granddaughter?" He stood up slowly as he continued to study her features. "You've got the Riley smile and your grandfather's eyes and his stubborn chin." His grin turned into a big friendly ear to ear smile.

"Yes, I am." She gave him a radiant smile.

"Well, well, well." He shook his head slowly in thought. "Your grandfather was a good friend of my father's." John stepped towards her. "They were friends from grade school and I remember him well. He was a wonderful man, your grandfather and a damn good carpenter." He nodded his head, shoved his hands into his jeans pockets and thought for a moment. "I remember my father taking me to your grandfather's shop once in a while. I was fascinated by what he could create out of a piece of wood." He smiled. "What made you notice?"

"Well, my Uncle Richard carried on with the business and I recognized the design. The design changed a little two years before my grandfather passed away, but it's still pretty distinct."

"Richard Riley." He nodded his head slowly in thought. "I don't remember your uncle, but I remember a Steven Riley. He was about, ohh, six maybe seven years younger than myself and was always in the shop with your grandfather. He married an American girl and built up a ranch in Utah."

"My mother, Joy. Her maiden name was Carlson." Mandy smiled. "Steven was my father. Uncle Richard is my father's youngest brother." She wanted to tell him the whole story about how she came to live with Richard and Maggie and how they adopted them, but she had to get back to Dianne.

"Well, if your uncle is as talented as your grandfather, he'll have quite a business."

"He does and he is extremely talented. His workmanship is exquisite and very refined. He owns the Riley Fine Furniture Company."

"I'll be darned." John brushed his graying hair back with one hand. "But I'm not surprised. It's the finest furniture in all of Canada and just to let you know, not only the dining room furniture but my whole bedroom suite is your grandfather's, and so is Cole's and Dianne's and Adam's, too. We gave your grandfather a special design we wanted and he built it. But his stamp, his brand as I call it, is on the back." John gave her a hardy pat on her back. "Well, it sure is a pleasure to meet Ivan's granddaughter. My father would have loved to meet you. By the way, did your brother take on any of the talent?"

"Absolutely. He's a beautiful finishing carpenter and works for our uncle, but his first love is ranching. He's more like our pa. Even though our pa was pretty good himself." She smiled and shrugged. "That's another story."

John gave her a quick big hug. "Right…" he released her, "…I guess we'd better get to our chores." He followed her out. "It was an absolute honor to talk to you, Amanda. We must sit and talk again some evening." His smile was sincere. "Soon, very soon."

"It will be my pleasure, John."

∽

Adam rode along the fence line by himself for a while after he had brought Hank into a treatment center in Calgary. He hated leaving his friend with strangers, but even though Hank looked lost and almost fragile, it was for the best. He'd have professional people looking after him. People who knew how to help. He gave Hank as much encouragement as he could and left his home number at the Addictions Center. Hank didn't have family, so he put his name down as next of kin. He wished Hank well and told him to call when he could and he'd visit during visiting hours.

After some time alone and feeling a little better that his friend would get the help he needed, Adam turned his horse around and went back to the house. He had to get back for the interviews for the new ranch hands, which included J. Mackenzie. He wasn't at all happy Jason was applying, let alone he'd no doubt he'd get the job. What ticked him off was that Jason didn't use his last name. It was downright sneaky. He sighed deeply, knowing that there was no fifty-fifty chance as Cole would override him if it came to it.

For three years now, his father had given the responsibility to him and Cole to do the hiring so he would have to have a pretty good excuse to reject Jason. Adam wondered what Mandy thought of the situation, especially with the look on her face when she found out her brother had applied. She didn't look pleased. With Jason's physical size, and willingness to work, Adam knew he'd be able to manage the ranch chores all right. If Mandy was able to ride a horse after eight years and do pretty damn good, he would lay odds Jason was even better.

Adam entered the barn with his horse behind him wondering how truly close Mandy was to her brother. Would he influence her? Would he interfere? His questions made him dizzy as he continued to unsaddle his horse. He recalled telling Mandy he can be patient, but his patience was going to be mighty thin when it came to her brother.

~

BACK FROM SHOPPING, Mandy noticed there was no sign of Jason's truck. It had been over two hours and she wondered if his interview was over and if he had got the job. She pulled out her cell phone and scrolled for his number.

"Yo, Squeak, how are ya?"

"Hi, Jas, I just wanted to know how your interview went." She swallowed hard as she waited for him to answer.

"Hey, Sis, I called Cole and told him I changed my mind. You were right. I was only wantin' the job to watch over ya." He huffed. "That wouldn't have been fair to ya."

"Thank you, Jas. I appreciate it."

"You're welcome, Amanda. Well, I gotta go, I'm doin' the company books. See ya later."

"Love you, Jason."

"Love ya too, Squeak. Bye."

Mandy gathered up her parcels and headed towards the front door. Her brother was a good man and she loved him dearly, but she was sure glad he was finally letting her live her own life. Walking up the porch steps, she turned to see Adam and Cole laughing with a new man. She guessed it was the new hired hand.

In the living room, Mandy found Dianne polishing the end tables. A green plastic milk crate on wheels beside the couch was filled with small toys, coffee cups and side plates. "Cleaning day, Dianne?" She laughed.

"It's taking me awhile." Dianne puffed out her cheeks then threw the rag on the table. Dianne pointed to the makeshift cart.

"This is Cole's idea of helping me." She laughed. "He put wheels and a long handle on this silly milk crate, so I can push it around." She laughed again. "He should patent the design."

Mandy looked over the contraption. "That's a pretty good idea." She took the handle, tipped the crate onto two wheels and pushed it back and forth. "It runs pretty smooth." Mandy set it back on its four wheels and let go of the handle. "Yeah, pretty good idea." She looked at Dianne and smiled.

"What can I say, it helps me do the job." She reached over and took the handle with one hand, tipped it and pushed it back and forth a couple of times on its two wheels. "Yupper, Cole did a fine job of making this." She laughed and parked the crate to the side and continued to dust.

"Here, let me help." Mandy picked out the dishes from the milk crate. "I'll go make tea. Where are the kids?"

"Good idea," Dianne said as she tossed the rags into the crate and followed Mandy to the kitchen. "In the playroom. They're fine."

Mandy stacked the dishes into the dishwasher as they chatted then sat down to enjoy a cup of tea in peace and quiet. Then suddenly the three McBride men walked in the back door. Their quiet time was over.

"Ladies." Cole nodded and went straight for the fridge, opened it, took out three bottles of iced tea, handed one to his father and one to Adam.

John and Cole had smiles on their faces. Adam was silent and serious as usual. The three men went straight through the dining room to the den.

Dianne turned to Mandy. "What do you think?"

"I don't know. I called Jason and he's not going to take the job. He told me he called Cole and told him he had changed his mind." She shrugged. "So why is Adam so quiet and serious?"

"Adam has always been the more serious one."

"Di," Cole called out from the den. "Telephone."

"While you take that call, I'll check on the children." Mandy stood up, gulped the last of her tea then went to the toy room and groaned. "Oh, no, you two, what a mess."

"Bobby made it. I was trying to read him my new book, but he wouldn't listen," Crystal said.

"That's okay." Mandy picked up some stuffies. "It won't take long." She tossed them into the toy box. "Will you help me, Crystal?" She continued to gather toy trucks and cars.

"Okay." Crystal picked up some books and the pencil crayons.

Halfway through clean-up, John entered the toy room. "Amanda, would you come into the living room? Kids, come with me."

Both children fought over who was going to take Mandy's hand as she got up from the floor and headed towards the door. She smiled.

"The children have become very attached to you." John smiled and touched both of the children's cheeks. "We're lucky to have Miss Riley here with us."

"We love her, Papa," Crystal rang out.

"Yea, we not gonna let er go, right Ciny?" Bobby screamed out and hugged Mandy's arm tightly.

John winked, then led the way into the living room where Cole was sitting beside Dianne. He took the big leather armchair then told the kids to go and see their uncle. Mandy sat on the couch.

"That was my physiotherapist," Dianne spoke up. "She wants me to start therapy on my good leg. I need a couple of hours with the therapist tomorrow and, Mandy, I want you to come with me?"

"Of course, I'll go with you," she said.

"I'll need someone to help me with the exercises." Dianne smiled. "I think it will be more fun doing leg exercises together."

"Yeah, two gimps in one house." Mandy laughed with Dianne.

Cole grunted. "You two won't be laughing when therapy starts," he said seriously and with concern.

"Laughter is the best medicine." Mandy smiled. "Dianne will be out of her chair in no time flat. Cole, I know my injuries were different, but if I had been as happy as Dianne when I was in my chair, I wouldn't have been in it for so long."

"You were in a wheelchair?" Cole raised his brows.

"Yes, that's why I can laugh about it."

Both John and Cole glanced at her with puzzled expressions. Realizing Dianne hadn't said anything to the family, Mandy gave them both a quick account of the horrible accident and how she and Jason came to live permanently in Canada with Richard and Maggie.

"Oh, jeez, Amanda." John rubbed his forehead hard. "I understand the terrible loss you feel, but the pure agony of losing so many loved ones at one time." He hung his head shaking it in disbelief.

"John, I have many happy memories and I cling to them. Jason and I help each other out when we need support. Uncle Richard and Aunt Maggie love us unconditionally and have given us a good life. It was their family, too." She glanced at Dianne then Cole. "Back to Dianne's problem. Cartilage and ligament damage is painful and it's not going to be easy. Dianne, it's going to be tough, but you're young, strong and determined. You'll be back on your horse in no time." She nodded.

"I'll do whatever I can to get out of this chair."

"We'll start working tomorrow, together."

"You're quite the young lady, Amanda." John nodded. "You're right, we all have to carry on. And, you are tougher than

I thought, so maybe you will get that foreman's job later," John said with a short laugh.

"I just might take you up on that." Mandy giggled.

Booted footsteps came through the door. Everyone turned towards Adam.

"I just ran some cash over to Buddy's for putting my beautiful truck back together after Hank…" Adam shook his head as he scowled. "Let's… oh, crap… let's not go there. I got my truck back and I'm happy. And Hank, is never, ever, going to touch my truck again," Adam said then gave everyone a half smile. "What's up?"

"Son." John pointed to a chair. "We're making arrangements for Dianne to go to Calgary tomorrow for her first therapy session. Amanda's going with her to help."

Adam sat down on the couch beside Mandy. He twitched a smile. "Hi," he said quietly then nodded at Dianne. "If there's anything I can do to help, let me know," he said sincerely.

"So, you're saying… your truck's fixed?" Cole asked.

"Yeah, I did. I picked it up before the interview. Runs like a top." He groaned. "Hank's a lucky man."

Cole grunted out a short chuckle. "Jeez, Adam, I think I would have cried like a big baby if it had been my truck."

"Believe me, I almost did. If I hadn't had so many other things to do." He shrugged. "Anyway, how can I help?"

"Oh, yeah, I need your truck tomorrow," Cole said. "All the other vehicles are being used for whatever the reason and I'm taking the 4x4 to take the kids over to Dianne's parents and get them settled for a few days."

"No problem. The keys are in the visor. Ryan going?"

"No, he's staying to help with the chores."

"Good. The new fencing is ready to be put in the south pasture."

"I had better check on the younger two," Mandy said and got up and went to the door.

"They're in the flower garden," Adam informed her with a quick nod.

Melanie turned to him. Their eyes met, yet she noticed a blank stare. He was emotionless and it upset her.

～

ADAM GRUMBLED THE SECOND MANDY, Dianne, and his father left the room. "Cole, did you hire Jason while I went to Buddy's to pick up my truck?"

"Jeez, Adam, no I didn't. I haven't had a chance to talk to you with the interview and all. Jason called just after you left and changed his mind. He's not taking the job. Which in my opinion is too bad, because I believe he'd be a damn good worker and we need more hands that we don't have to constantly babysit."

"I agree he'd be a damn hard worker but thank goodness he's not working for us. I told you how I feel about Mandy and I don't want him meddling."

"Well, he's not taking the job, so there won't be a problem for you."

"Good," Adam groaned.

"Stop being so uptight. Jeez, man, if I had known you were so bothered about Jason getting the job I would have text you, or even called you right away." Cole touched his forehead, spread out his fingers, then dropped his hand to his side. "You know Mandy loves you, Adam. She may not have told you in so many words, but we see the love in her eyes when she looks at you."

"Yeah, but her brother might have changed that," Adam grunted.

"Come on, Adam, you don't believe that."

Adam ignored his brother. "To be realistic, we really haven't known Mandy that long. What if she's just using us like all the others?" He hated the words he'd just spoken. Hated himself for speaking them, but his old fears of being rejected were strong and it frazzled his brain.

"What?" Cole raised his brows. "How can you mistrust or even think that about her?" He stood up. "Oh, sure we haven't known her very long. I don't have to because I've always been a good judge of character. Besides, what on earth would she be using us for?"

"Cole, you don't understand." He felt his voice shake. "For some reason women don't want to share their life with me. They don't want to be a part of my life. All they want is money and sex. They want a good time then leave." Adam brushed his hair back from his forehead with his hand. "They take, take and take some more. Then take off." He paced back and forth in front of his brother. He stopped and glanced at Cole's shocked facial expression. He hung his head and took a deep breath then rubbed his face hard with both hands.

Everything he had said wasn't true about Mandy and he felt sick to his stomach for thinking of such impure thoughts about the woman he was falling in love with. "Mandy's different," he whispered. "She's not like the others is she, Cole?" He looked at his brother. He needed reassurance from someone who truly loved him. His fear of rejection was so great he needed his brother's help. He needed his older brother to guide him, because he was the only one beside his father and Dianne he could trust.

Adam looked away and sat down on the leather couch. "Don't look at me like that. I don't need your criticism, or doubt of who I am. You're my brother and I need your support. You told me I could come to you. Count on you." Fear of rejection continued to chill his blood and twist his gut.

"You're my brother and I love you." Cole sat down beside

him, folded his hands then turned his head to face him. "You can't go there with Mandy and don't lower yourself like those women who used you. You're a good man, Adam. You just happened to get involved with a couple bad apples. They saw, a kind, caring, compassionate man, and they used you. They were the bad ones. Don't let them change who you are. You told me many times that you want what Dianne and I have. You've always confided in me and told me what you want in life. Adam, let those bad apples go. Let that stallion issue go. Let the past go and move on."

Adam jerked his head up. "You know about the stallion?" He worked his jaw. "I've never told anyone."

Cole picked at a few threads from his old rolled up shirt cuff. "Yeah, I knew. Sullivan came by and he felt really bad for you and wished he could have helped you out somehow, but he desperately needed the money, so he had to sell it to someone else." Cole sighed. "You were hurting enough as it was, so I kept it to myself. Anyway, Adam, back to your present problem here." Cole folded his hands in front of him and looked at his brother. "You want your own dream to come true. You've got it with Mandy." Cole got up from the couch and slapped Adam on the shoulder. "Grab hold of love and don't let go."

Adam really didn't need to hear all this from Cole, he already knew Mandy was special and wasn't like any other woman. He could no more mistrust or use Mandy for selfish reasons, than ride butt naked in an open field in front of his hired hands. But it was nice to have it confirmed from his older brother. Adam nodded in agreement then slowly got up off the couch. "You're right." He gave his brother a quick crooked grin, then headed towards the door then turned. "Thanks, Cole."

CHAPTER 17

$\mathcal{A}$dam watched Mandy weed the garden with the children. She made work fun. Fun through song, touch and praise. He loved her soft voice and soft giggles when she played with them. He loved her touch, her graceful movements along with her strength and determination. He just plain loved everything about her. Cole was right, about everything. Especially about Jason having nothing to do with him falling in love with Mandy.

Guilt and shame hit Adam like a lead weight for what he had said to Cole about her. How could he ever think of such thoughts about the woman he was falling in love with? He sauntered over to the garden by the big oak tree. "How are things going on here?" He gave her his best smile and watched her eyes sparkle when she looked up at him. His heart beat hard against his chest.

"Good, we're almost done," she said as she gathered both children and gave them a group hug.

"We done good, Miss Riley. Right, Crysil," Bobby chirped as he clapped his hands.

204

"We sure did," Crystal agreed and ruffled her little brother's hair.

His heart melted as her love for his niece and nephew showed in her face. Even the flowers seemed to smile as they turned their little faces towards her in the gentle warm breeze. Her gentle delicate nature intrigued him. She had an inner strength she didn't even know she had.

"Hey, kids, I need to talk to your Nanny so keep working." He held out his hand and hoped she'd take it.

"My hands are dirty."

He stepped forward. "No matter, I need you for a moment," he said sincerely as she wiped her hands on the grass then on her jeans. To his surprise, she extended her hand and allowed him to help her up. This simple touch of her hand was promising as he led her around to the back of the house then turned to her. Their eyes met. He wiped a spot of mud from the bridge of her nose and chuckled. "You've got some of the flower garden on your face."

"Adam." Her hands went to his chest and pushed him away from her. "What happened back in the house?" She rubbed her forehead. "Your smile towards me wasn't sincere. If you even call it a smile. It was more like a twitch, so tell me what kind of game you're playing, because I don't like games." She crossed her arms. "I've had enough of emotional game playing in my lifetime."

Adam put his hands into his front pockets. He was afraid this might happen and this time, the fault was all his. He took a deep breath. "I'm sorry. I was wrong. I've had so many things to think about." He took in a deep breath. "Honestly, when your brother called, I got angry and took it out on you. I know how he feels about me and I'm not particularly fond of him either."

"He's not taking the job, Adam." Mandy crossed her arms.

Adam nodded. "Yeah Cole told me a few minutes ago and

I'm not sorry, but I'm sorry I took it out on you. That wasn't fair." He watched her carefully. He wanted this to work out so he stepped closer to her.

"My brother has nothing to do with the way I feel about you." She took a step back. "And you're right, Jason doesn't like you and I already told you why. I told him you were a rebel." She shrugged. "He's stubborn, Adam and he's very protective of me. Is your family any different between each other?" She tilted her chin up and turned away.

Adam took a giant step toward her and grabbed her arm. "Stop, please." He turned her around quickly and placed both hands firmly on both of her shoulders. "Please just listen." He gazed into her cool blue eyes. He knew he was on a fine thread here and he'd better make it quick before she made another break for it. "Forgive me. Give me another chance to explain." He watched her nod as he loosened his grip. His hands slowly slid down her arms to her hands then took her hands into his. "I was wrong. I should have talked to you right away when you told me he was applying for the job. You're right, it's got nothing to do with you. Like I told you before, rebel is not the right word. True rebels know who they are, and do not compromise their individuality, or personal opinion for anyone. But, I'll admit that I've definitely been a crabby jerk lately and that's a far cry from being a rebel." He shrugged. "And, I've been rough and not patient at all. So, help me and we can start again and get this right. We'll take it one step at a time." His hand came up to stroke her soft cheeks. She was allowing him to touch her, giving him reason to believe he was forgiven. "Mandy," he whispered quietly. He was thankful for the chance he was going to get with her. A second chance he didn't deserve, but was going to get.

Mandy nodded. "I'll help you understand, because I want both of you to become friends." Her voice was a soft whisper.

He leaned into her until their foreheads touched. "Thank

you," he said sincerely as he gazed in to her pretty blue irises. Flecks of gold and the shimmering lines of blues mesmerized him. "Oh my, God, you have the most remarkable eye color ever."

"And so do you," she whispered back. "I see tiny flecks of gold. Your brown eyes are so dark and rich and so amazing." Her tilted her head back a little to look deeper. "Wow, pools of…"

Adam took his hands and cupped her face. "How about another bedtime story?" he whispered as he continued to stare into her pretty eyes. "I promise no more games. We'll talk and get to know each other," he murmured as he lowered his head and covered her mouth with his. "Mmmm." He lifted his head and looked into her face.

"I'd love a bedtime story," she whispered back.

He took her mouth fully. She accepted his. His body throbbed with anticipation as his kiss deepened. Her soft mouth opened wider for him.

"Kissy, kissy, kissy."

Mandy jerked, pushing Adam away and turned to the mischievous children who were giggling while making kissing sounds with their mouth.

"Kissy, kissy, kissy," the children sang out.

Adam took a giant step towards the children. Crystal squealed and ran. Bobby flapped his hands and took off excitedly after his sister.

"Kids will be kids." Mandy laughed. "Don't you just love them?" Her eyes twinkled as she watched them run. "I'd better get back to work"

"Me, too. If I don't finish, I won't be in for story time with the family."

"Family story time doesn't matter." She wiggled her eyebrows teasingly. "I want a personal story." She blushed.

He groaned as he gently squeezed her hand as they walked

back to the front. He chuckled when he saw his nephew and niece roll over on the ground giggling and laughing. "You two having fun?" he asked as he released her hand. "You shouldn't have been peeking."

"We know, but it's fun," Crystal said with a little giggle of her own.

"Well, the next time I want to talk to Miss Riley for a few minutes, you two keep doing your chores," he scolded gently.

"We don't have to peek next time cause we already know what you want to talk to her about." Crystal rolled over on the grass laughing and kicking her feet in the air. "You don't want to talk about nutin'," she squealed louder as Bobby clapped his hands with pure innocence, then pounced with uncontrolled laughter onto his sister.

Adam shook his head at his niece and nephew as a smile spread across his face. "I'll see you later." He gave her a quick kiss on the cheek. Thank you." He kissed the other cheek and left her with the squealing children.

THAT NIGHT, Adam came to Mandy's room as promised and took her into his arms. "I shouldn't be here." He kissed her long and slow. Reluctantly, he released her. "I told you I'd tell you a story, but I'd rather make love to you." He could see the bewildered look in her face. His thumb pads stroked her soft pink cheeks as he stared into her crystal blue eyes. "You're so... so... Oh God, there's no words to describe your absolute beauty, Mandy." He couldn't take his eyes off her. His heart began to race. He had to cool down. "I'm going to lie on one side of the bed, you on the other, we'll face each other while I tell you stories." He took her hand and led her to the bed then picked her up and laid her gently on top of it. He took a breath, then positioned her arms close beside her sides. "I'm going to tuck you in so snug I won't be tempted." He flipped the blanket that hung over the bed side, and put it over her, then rolled her over and over until she was on the other side of the bed. Her soft laughter warmed his heart. "There."

"I can't move," she complained lightheartedly then laughed softly.

"My point exactly. There's so many blankets and layers between us I won't feel you move an inch." But he knew what was beneath the blankets. Warm soft skin. *How I'd love to touch and feel every inch of you.* His brain told him not to go down that road and to back off as his fingertips stroked her cheek. A hint of fear traced her face, just like the other night. Amazed at his own self-control he inched back. A control over his body that he never dreamed he ever had. Deep inside, he knew she still wasn't ready to make love to him. He backed away to the edge of the bed, propped his head up and stared at her. He watched her eyes follow the length of him. Her curiosity intrigued him. His body screamed for her touch, just as it had last night and every night since he'd first set eyes on her.

"Adam, are you going to tell me a story?" she whispered.

He smiled. "Yes." He opened his mouth to begin the story, but words refused to come out. He licked his dry parched lips as he watched her look away.

"Adam, why are you here?" Her eyes lifted towards him.

"I want to be," he whispered. "You know I've fallen in love with you. Don't you?"

"Yes, but why? Why me?" She wiggled her arms out of her cocoon and undid the tight blankets.

He frowned. He felt uncertain how to answer her question. Why not her? She was perfect. She was everything in a woman he ever wanted.

She shook her head a second time. "I'm having a hard time believing you want me, let alone love me."

"Why?" he asked quietly.

She shrugged. "Well, it's just that you're so... so competent, strong... so... well, I don't understand why you would want..."

He leaned forward and put his index finger lightly to her lips to stop her from speaking. "You've been hurt." He watched her lower her eyes. This was an extremely serious time for them both, so Adam got off the bed, pulled the recliner up to the bedside and sat in it. "Look at me." He leaned forward. His fingertips turned her head towards him. "No need to repeat what you told me last night. Listen. I'm not perfect myself, but I'm not like those men. They aren't worth discussing and they were cruel to say such things." He leaned over and kissed her cheek. "Like I told you before, your scars don't bother me. Trust me."

Adam took in a deep breath. "Story time," he whispered and leaned over her a second time and kissed her forehead. He got up slowly from the recliner and took his place back on the other side of the bed. "Rest now. Go to sleep." He pulled her close.

"Adam?"

"What," he whispered.

"First tell me, what's troubling you? Sometimes I see anger in your face and in your eyes. It's like there's hate eating at you."

Adam sighed deeply and rolled onto his back. His arm covered his eyes. "Jeez, Mandy, you don't need to hear this right now."

"Yes, I do. I've told you most of my issues and why men don't want me. Now it's your turn. All I know is that you don't trust women, so is that why you're angry at times? Will you ever totally trust me?" She touched his arm. "You promised no games."

After a moment of silence, Adam took her hand. If he loved

her she deserved to be told everything about his past. If he wanted her trust, he had better show her she could trust him. If he wanted to know her secrets, he'd better tell his. He took in a deep breath and prayed she wasn't like the others. His heart said this time he was safe, yet he couldn't help but shield his heart from crumbling again. "I've been such a fool when it comes to love. Let's just say... I thought I was in love... more than once. That was before I found out I was being used for my money. There are women out there who want to go out with wealthy ranchers. Use them and leave. Play games. I don't like games any more than you do."

She nodded. "Games with young, handsome ranchers."

Adam nodded with a huff. "Well, they certainly had the words to play with, too. And of course, like a fool, a grown-up fool, I was sucked in." He tightened his jaw. "I've learned a lot since then and I don't need flattery and I don't need false words and mind games. I'm going to be totally honest with you and I'm going to wear my heart on my sleeve." He swallowed hard. "The last woman I dated told me a sob story that would bring anyone to their knees. I believed her when she told me how sick her father was and she needed to go to him before he died. I understood, because I lost my mother and she knew my weakness. I gave her my credit card with a wide-open amount." He grunted. "She didn't bankrupt me by all means, but there went my stallion I wanted for stud."

"I know what a good stallion costs," she said seriously. "So, nobody can find her?"

"I have a friend who's a P.I. and he's aware of the situation. I told him to check in at times and if he finds her fine, but I'm not going to spend any more hard-earned cash on her. It's been reported and documented. Apparently, she's done this before and the authorities are out looking for her, too. Frankly I don't even want to discuss it. If he or anyone finds her, I'll do something, other than that, I have to carry on." He shrugged.

"Maybe you were meant to meet up with me." Her eyes flashed a smile.

"Yep, maybe so and vice-versa." He winked. "Let's get off this depressing topic. You and I have both been hurt and now it's time for a new chapter in both our lives. Now is the time for true love." He smiled sincerely. "Story time," he whispered. "Close your eyes." He straightened the blankets to make her comfortable. "You've had a busy day, so if you fall asleep, I'll repeat the story tomorrow."

He turned on his side and propped up his head. "Chapter two." He took in a deep breath. "My brother Cole and I had a secret hide-a-way that we would often go to so we could dream of the future. What kind of cattle we would raise and what kind of horses we would ride. We would talk about the girls in our class and wonder if we would ever marry. We played and worked hard together and we were always there for each other. We loved our grandparents who lived with us and we often went up to the line cabin in the mountains during slower times on the ranch. Going to the line cabin was fun with just grandfather and my brother alone. Grandfather told so many wild adventure stories on how he used to go hunting with other ranchers to get rid of animals that caused problems in the area. I like his grizzly bear stories the best."

Adam whispered and watched her eyes go heavy with sleep. The last few days for Mandy were tough so he continued just to make sure she was totally in a deep sleep. "Our grandfather would take us on trail-rides and go further into the mountains. Grandpa was the best ever and our grandma was the sweetest, most gentle lady any kid could have for a grandmother. She made the best oatmeal raisin cookies with hot chocolate, when we came home from our adventures and of course on other occasions."

Her breathing soft, gentle and she was more beautiful than yesterday. His heart opened, warmed and softened and his anger diminished. Slowly he got off the bed and sat back down on the recliner, threw a sheet over himself and quietly adjusted the foot rest.

～

BOBBY AND CRYSTAL went over to Dianne's mother's place for a week so Dianne and Mandy could go over the exercises they had to do. They no sooner sat down in the living room with a cup of tea, when the front door flew open and Ryan came barreling in.

"Miss Riley. Miss Riley," Ryan shouted. "Jason came over and he's fighting with Uncle Adam. Come. Come quickly." Ryan waved his hand fast and furious. "Hurry, hurry." He bolted back out the door.

Mandy jumped off the couch and rushed out the door after Ryan. She stood on the top of the porch steps and watched in total disbelief Jason arguing with Adam. "Jason, stop it," she screamed at the top of her lungs as she glared at him. "Stop, please." She watched Adam and Jason freeze and turn towards her. Their faces flushed. She realized as much as she loved Jason and as much as they were bonded, he was taking this protection issue too far. She watched Adam step back and wipe off the blood from his tanned cheek bone. He had been defending himself, yet he had refused to fight back and was trying to calm Jason down. She shook her head at her twin brother.

Cole came around the corner of the house just as Dianne wheeled herself beside Mandy.

She stared at Jason in disbelief. "Go home, Jason, please."

"I was on a delivery this morning with Uncle Richard and I

met up with someone interesting. Why don't you talk to rebel man here and ask your Neanderthal friend how he treats his girl-friends?" Jason took a step towards Adam. "Remember Elaine?"

"Of course, she's a friend. Just calm down, Jason," Adam said in a low-level tone of voice.

"You snake," Jason sneered. "Any other dark secrets you're hiding from my..." Jason pounded on his chest with one strong fist, "...sister."

"Stop it, Jason." In her whole life she couldn't remember screaming at her brother or anyone for that matter. Her knees felt like hot rubber. Her whole body trembled. Jason was trying to take her away from a man she was falling in love with. She understood her brother as they'd been torn away from family once before, but this was different. This time Jason had to realize the family could grow. Maybe he could have another older brother. No one would ever replace Martin, but Adam could be a friend. A true friend to Jason. Why couldn't he see that?

Missing a step, Mandy went down and fell on her left knee. The intense pain rippled through her like hot coals. Both Jason and Adam took a step towards her. "Stop right there," she commanded and glared at the two men she loved the most, while Cole helped her up. "I'm all right, Cole. Thank you. I'll be fine." She released Cole's helpful hand. "Jason why are you doing this? Can't you trust me to make my own choices?"

"Amanda, I don't want you hurt by this... this s... snake." He shook his finger at Adam.

"Jason, listen to me. I believe I love Adam. I don't know what the future is going to be for us, but I want to find out and I don't care about his past relationships. He's good to me. You have to let me go. You're my brother and I love you and I always will, but you have to let me live my own life. The love you and I share is a special love and no one, and I mean no one can ever take that away from us." She turned to Adam as her eyes clouded with moisture. "Adam, I love my brother and I love you. I don't know where our future lies, but I'm willing to give all I've got." She watched him take in a deep breath. He placed his hands on his hips. Her heart flipped. He looked so good. Yet she may lose him because she knew how Adam felt about Jason. He didn't like Jason any better than Jason liked him.

She looked back at Jason. "Someday, Jason, you're going to fall in love with someone. Will that mean I'm out of your life, or will you love me like I love you right now?" Tears clouded her vision. Her voice quivered. "You left me one day for a couple of hours to think about my life and how I was hurting the ones I love." She put her hand up near her throbbing temple. If she didn't sit down soon her head was going to split open. The pain in her knee resembled a hot branding iron. She searched the pain in her brother's eyes and knew he felt it then glanced at Adam and watched the deep concern form in his face.

They stepped towards her. She raised her hand, stepped back, and grabbed firmly onto the hand railing. "Jason, I want you to go home and think about what you're doing right now." Tears streamed down her face. "Adam, you're a good man, but you need to think, too. He's my brother and he's having a tough time right now letting me go. You're going to have to understand that." Unable to control her tears any longer, she released them to spill over her hot flushed cheeks. Her knees so weak, she knew she was going down. "Both of you, go." She watched Adam pick up his Stetson off the ground and Jason turn away, both leaving in opposite directions. Her hand went up to her forehead. Everything went black.

CHAPTER 18

*a*dam sat on a log, on the banks of the Little Calf River, which cut through the McBride land and rinsed his blue bandana with clear cool water to bathe his bruised, bloody, swollen cheek. His thoughts turned to Mandy and how pale she looked while she hollered at them. The pain in her eyes tormented him. He stilled for a moment and realized just how much he truly wanted her in his life. "Damn Jason," he said with clenched teeth as he turned the bandana over to the cooler side.

It baffled him how Jason had found out about his friend, Elaine, whom he had trusted and cared for. A good friend whom he'd known since grade school. A friend who he told how Monica had tossed him away after he pledged his love for her. Elaine told him she'd always be there for him, but one day even she had had enough of his negative attitude and he couldn't blame her one bit. Before she walked away, Elaine reminded him that someday a woman he truly loved would come along, and he'd have to change his attitude if he wanted a life filled with love and tenderness.

Adam's thoughts returned to the present and the disagreement he had with Jason. He figured he had to exaggerate the story, because Elaine was still his friend and someday he was going to introduce Elaine and her husband, Dave, to Mandy. But, then there was Stewart, Elaine's brother, who resented him. Maybe Jason had met up with him and not Elaine at all. He began to realize how much families protected their own, and Stewart was just protecting Elaine and making sure their friendship didn't go any farther. Jason was doing the same with Mandy. Adam chuckled under his breath as he continued to cool his cheek. These men were absolutely no different from him. He would protect his family at any cost himself.

Adam stood and began to pace back and forth on the banks of the river until his pulse and anger levelled off. He rubbed his forehead. This time not to erase his mind of Mandy like he had done before. But to keep her beautiful smile, sparkling eyes and her lovely voice, in his memory. He wanted to keep the tender moments they had shared. His heart ached like it had never ached before. "Oh, Mandy," he whispered. "I need you. I want you. I love you."

He stopped pacing and focused on the sparkling running river. The current steadily passing him. The small river appeared to enjoy the warmth of the summer day and didn't have a care in the world. It carried on, minding its own business as it meandered past the tall wild grasses, curved around gentle bends and past lazy, sleepy cattle resting in the day's heat.

A small branch with several green leaves attached floated slowly by. He watched it for a moment then began to panic, as perspiration dotted his forehead. His heart rate increased. A dark cloud seemed to appear when the branch disappeared around the bend in the river. Disappeared forever. "Mandy." He mouthed her pretty name as he stared in the distance. Was it a personal sign from above that he could lose her? He stuffed the bandana in his pocket, walked towards his horse, grabbed the reins and mounted.

❧

BACK AT THE MCBRIDE RANCH, Cole picked Mandy up and brought her into the house and laid her on the living room couch. "I'll get a cool cloth," he said to Dianne.

Dianne positioned her wheelchair in front of the couch and felt Mandy's forehead. "And some crushed ice," she hollered out as she moved her hand to her knee. "In fact, get a pail of cold water and put ice into it. And a couple of cold cloths and a pair of scissors. I'm going to cut her pant leg."

Cole brought everything then watched Dianne cut her cotton slacks past her knee while he placed a cool compress on her forehead. Dianne stopped abruptly when she saw the wide long jagged white scar. "No wonder she's in pain." Dianne looked up at Cole. "Mandy told me a large piece of glass from the accident cut her leg wide open. Something that goes this deep had to leave some sort of damage."

Cole nodded in agreement as he flipped the cool cloth over. "She's still out cold," he said with concern.

"She'll be okay, Cole, she's totally exhausted," she said as she applied the cold compress to her knee then removed the now warm compress from her forehead and rinsed it. As she reapplied the cool cloth, Dianne looked closer. "Oh look. This is why she keeps her hair down on this side. This is what she's hiding." Dianne pushed her hair back.

Cole stared at the pencil-width, white scar, that went from her temple to her delicate jaw bone. "That's nothing. You can barely see it."

Dianne put her fingertips on Mandy's temple. "You can feel her pulse throbbing. I'd bet my bottom dollar this is where all her stresses, fears and anxiety go." She looked up at her husband. "It's just like when your dad worries, or is stressing about something, he rubs his left forearm and wrist. The forearm and wrist he broke in several places years ago, when he fell off the horse he was breaking. Everyone has a stress point." Her sentence trailed off as she turned over the hot cloth to the cool side.

"Yeah, you're right," Cole said slowly and methodically. "For you, it might be your knee, like mine is the left collar bone, I broke three years ago."

Dianne covered the scar back up with Mandy's long hair and looked at her husband. "Adam told me the day Jason picked her up that he noticed him massaging her temple. It relaxed her, but she won't tell him why?"

"I remember, but why hide them?" he asked. "They're not that bad. I mean, the one on the leg is visible, but it's not as if it's... well... whatever, it's not bad." He shrugged in confusion. "I know Adam wouldn't love her any less because of them."

"I agree, but I don't think it's just a scar she's hiding. It's all her emotions, her feelings, her past, her fears of loss. I don't know how to explain it, but it's going to take time to let Adam into her life."

"If I'm understanding right, the day she shares this with Adam, there will be a new chapter in their lives," Cole said.

"Yes." Dianne smiled back. "I hope so. They'll make a beautiful couple."

"If the two rebel brothers can work things out."

"She's a smart cookie, she'll make it work," Dianne said and took off the hot compress from Mandy's knee, rinsed it out in the cold water and reapplied it. "I feel for Adam, he's got a struggle a-head of him. I think he truly loves her."

Cole laid a sheet over Mandy and put a pillow under her head. He chuckled low and whispered. "I can't help but laugh at Jason's description of Adam. Snake. Neanderthal. Rebel. Was there anything I missed?"

They laughed quietly yet fondly at Adam's expense, then quietly left Mandy to rest.

MANDY WOKE up a few hours later with a major headache from the screaming she had done. Her thoughts went to the incident outside with Adam and Jason. Jason was so angry and he didn't understand that Adam's past didn't matter. He didn't know Adam had already told her about his fears, abandonment issues, and how his exes treated him because of who he was. A rich, young, powerful rancher. Women wanted him and sought him out.

She adored her brother and their past life together bonded them. Forever. But now Jason needed to understand their family would grow and he'd be a part of it. All of this was to be her own personal struggle with herself, her emotions and getting over her own fears. Now the two men she loved the most were fighting. She wiped the tears from her cheeks and glanced at the table and saw her brace. Dianne and Cole had to have seen her scars. Cringing, she reached for it and put it on, then as stiff and sore as she was, she got up, changed her clothes and went outside.

Mandy took in a deep breath as she approached Dianne who was under the oak tree doing her leg exercises. "Hi, Dianne," she said in a light cheery voice to cover the nervousness as she stood in front of the garden. "Lovely day."

"Mandy, you should be resting."

"It's too nice to be indoors and I love the garden at this time of year." Mandy glanced at Dianne's weights for her leg on her lap. "Have you completed your exercises this afternoon?"

"Yes, and I've charted it. So far not too bad."

"Good."

"Are you, all right?" Dianne reached over and pointed to the grass. "Come, sit down and relax."

"I'm sorry, Dianne." Mandy sat under the oak tree on the

grass, stretched out her legs and touched the brace on her knee. "I don't usually get so angry."

"I understand."

Mandy stared at the colorful blooms in the garden. "Did you and Cole help me?"

"Yes, do you want to talk about it?" Dianne encouraged.

Mandy shrugged. "My hair was damp when I woke. I guess you saw..."

Dianne leaned over and put her hand on top of Mandy's. "Yes, we both did."

Mandy didn't want to talk about her scars. She looked away. "I guess you know by now I'm in love with Adam, but I love my brother, too." Her voice cracked and her heart ached.

"I understand. We believe Adam loves you, too and... well... your brother also loves you. You both have been through so much together and he's trying to protect you, but right now he sees Adam as a threat."

Mandy looked at Dianne with a frown. "What do you mean he sees Adam as a threat?"

"Jason has been protecting you for years and now another man comes into your life and where does that leave him?"

"Never thought of it in that way, but Jason isn't going to vanish from my life. He has to know that."

"How about your dreams of owning that ranch together? How about his feelings of being left alone?"

"We can still be partners," she told Dianne. "We've been partners for years with our saving and planning and dreaming. I'm not going to take that away from him. When things get settled, Jason can buy me out, or vice versa. We'll make some sort of arrangements to suit us both if it all works out with Adam and me."

"Mandy, listen to me. Jason isn't thinking like that right now. All he sees and understands is that Adam is taking you away from him. He's frightened. He doesn't realize he's not losing his sister. He doesn't realize, he can have a friend in Adam. That's why he came out to the ranch to see you. He wanted to know if you're okay and he just happened to meet up with Adam first." Dianne patted Mandy's shoulder. "What information he got from town regarding Elaine, I have no idea what that's about."

"Why didn't I think of that?"

"You're too close to it."

Mandy sat quiet for a moment. Dianne was completely right. She and Jason were so close, they couldn't see the problem right in front of their faces, yet there it was, in black and white. She was going into another relationship and wanting Jason to be happy for her. She had it all and Jason had no one, but her. Besides having Uncle Richard and Aunt Maggie, he felt left behind. Abandoned. Alone.

"Mandy, if you're that close to getting a piece of land, then talk to Jason now. That piece of land won't last two minutes when my friend decides to sell. No one knows but me, and of course Cole at this point. I can talk to her so you can make a private deal instead of going through the real estate hassle. Call Jason and talk. Play your cards right and you can have it all."

Mandy nodded slowly. "Okay." She smiled. "Thanks, Dianne."

CHAPTER 19

"You what?" Adam's face distorted as he questioned Dianne. His gaze darted from Dianne to Cole during Sunday evening dinner. "Why. Why?" he asked in total frustration.

"We gave Mandy a few days off because she's not well and she needs some rest," Dianne said calmly, putting a small slice of roast beef into her mouth.

"Is she, all right? How sick is she? I gotta call her." Adam stood up and went to the phone. "Did Jason come back and take her home?" he asked as he picked up the land line receiver.

"I drove her home," Cole answered.

Adam put down the phone. "You?" He frowned. "Why didn't she ask me to take her home? I would have driven her."

"You weren't back yet, Adam." Dianne tapped on the table. "Come and sit down. She's going to be fine, it's just been stressful for her lately."

Adam grunted. "Yeah." He growled. "You know, I can imagine how stressed she is. That damn idiot brother of hers has been upsetting her lately and he won't listen to me." Adam stood back up and tossed the linen napkin on the table. "Now

Mandy's gone and I hope Jason's happy having her home." He pushed the chair up against the table. "I need a break." His voice laced with frustration. He opened the liquor cabinet and picked up a twenty-six of rye. "See you around."

"Adam Scott," John hollered out. "Do you think drinking is going to make your problems go away?"

"Nope, but I can forget them for a while." Adam clenched his jaw as he glanced at the bottle, as if it was a valued prize. "Works for Hank."

"Yeah, by the way, how's Hank doing?" Cole asked.

Adam glared at his brother. "Why don't you call him? He's a friend of yours, too, unless you've forgotten. And don't change the subject." Adam turned his back. "Have a lovely Sunday dinner."

"All this time helping Hank and you're going to start drinking? What's that about, brother?" Cole asked and stood up. "Adam, please sit down."

"Whatever." Adam shook his head and turned towards the door.

John stood up. "Will you two boys drop it so we can have dinner in peace."

"Sorry, Pa." Adam shrugged. His arm stretched out with the neck of the liquor bottle held tight in his left fist.

"Adam," Cole yelled back. "Let's talk."

"I just told you, I need a break." Hurt by Mandy going home without her telling him, he walked out the front door and headed towards his truck, put the whisky bottle in the lock box in the back, got in and drove off to his grandfather's property.

Years ago, Grandfather McBride had bought 100 acres south of Claresholm, west of Willow Creek for a retirement property for him and his wife. A place to go and relax and enjoy each other while the family took over the responsibilities of the ranch. His grandfather had started off building a one-room line cabin while grandmother tilled a place for her garden. Later, grandfather added on a bedroom while grandmother continued to beautify mother nature. They enjoyed their retirement and together built a cozy spot for themselves. They loved when their grandsons came to visit. During the evenings they'd sit around a campfire and tell stories of the good old days and the McBride family history.

Several years ago, when the grandparents had passed on and the will was read, both Cole and Adam had inherited the property. Now it was Adam's turn to use it. Adam's turn to be able to think things through without interruption. A little peace and quiet would help him through his own problems.

By the time he got to the line cabin, it was dark and his frustration level had subsided. He put the bottle of rye on the counter, then grabbed a glass from the cupboard. Using the kitchen sink pump, he poured himself a cold, clear glass of water and gulped it down. "Ahhhh... that's good mountain water." He wiped his mouth off with his shirt sleeve and took another drink of the sweet water. "Ahh, thank you, Grandfather." He raised his glass as a salute, then took a third swallow. Putting the glass on the counter, he again wiped his face off with his shirt sleeve and stood and stared at the water pump for a moment. He remembered the day his grandfather had put the kitchen pump in. His grandmother was so excited.

Taking in a quick sigh and stretching the kinks out of his neck after the drive, Adam reached for the unopened rye bottle. He looked at the label then put it in the cupboard, then stepped outside onto the wooden deck. The stars twinkled, the moon full and bright, lighting up the paths his grandfather had made over the years. He wished Mandy was here with him to see the beauty that God created. It was too dark to see the mountains, but he could smell the fresh crisp mountain air. With Mandy having a few days off, he'd have a few days to think.

Since Dianne broke her leg and with Mandy coming into his life, Adam's emotions had been on an extreme high to an extreme low and as much as he was falling in love with her, he needed time for himself. Mandy would get a few days of rest herself then they'd start over again together.

He placed his hand on the short wooden post and wiggled it, then groaned when the rail that ran the length of the small cabin jiggled. He glanced over the planked deck and smiled at the memory of his grandparents sitting together on the old two-seated swing at the end of it. The creaks and groans of the old swing helped calm his frazzled nerves when he sat down. He wanted Mandy here sitting with him and wondered how she was doing.

He toed the wooden planked floor and made the swing move. "Huh, still in pretty good shape," he told himself as he gazed around his surroundings. He figured that a few new boards, a coat of paint and a new post, the little deck would look like new. He got up, stretched, yawned and went back into the cabin and headed straight for the double bed. Thinking of the day's events, he sighed heavily.

"If only you were beside me now, Mandy, we could share stories together," he whispered then closed his eyes to the dream he'd been thinking about all day long.

By Monday morning, Mandy felt refreshed and woke early. Thanks to Aunt Maggie's special blend of tea, she had the best sleep in a long time. Aunt Maggie had lost her parents when she was only eighteen, so she understood Mandy all too well.

"I called Doctor Ming this morning and he's scheduled you for a series of acupuncture treatments," Maggie said as they sat in the living room with a regular cup of tea. "He had his receptionist move appointments up and wants to see you by nine-thirty."

"Thanks, Auntie."

"I also made hair appointments for today. You and I are going to treat ourselves to a shampoo and trim, and we are also getting a manicure and pedicure. How does that sound?"

"Sounds like fun and I do need a trim." Mandy pulled her hair back and put it up. "Maybe I should get it cut short." She stood up and looked into the brass-framed oval mirror hanging above the sofa. "What do you think?"

"You'll look just as beautiful with a short cut."

Mandy smiled at her aunt. "It'll be easier to keep if Jason and I are going to buy that ranch. I won't have time to fuss with my hair."

"You have a point and speaking of that ranch, don't take too long, you know property goes fast these days."

"Dianne's talked to her friend and told her that Jason and I are interested." She sat back down on the couch. "It might be out of our reach, but I would like to look at it anyway."

"Your uncle and I are very excited for the both of you." Maggie stood, picked up the tea cups and walked into the kitchen. "I'm even more excited it's not far away." She put the dishes into the dishwasher. "You better talk to your uncle, because he's been figuring things out since you and Jason told him about your plans." Maggie grinned.

"What is it?" Mandy questioned.

"Ahaa… it's a surprise. I'll let your uncle tell you."

"Oh, Aunt Maggie, I can't wait, this sounds too exciting," she said as her voice echoed her excitement. "Can you give me a hint?"

Maggie's eyes twinkled. "All I'm going to say is you're going to be very, very pleased. Now, let's go get your treatment over with, have breakfast at Smiths, then off to the beauty parlor."

~

THRILLED with her new haircut and new outfits she bought with her Aunt, Mandy's spirits were riding high. She glanced in the mirror and turned her head back and forth slowly watching her hair gracefully glide over her shoulders. "I love it." She beamed.

"You look stunning," Maggie acknowledged. "I love the way it frames your face and it brings out your pretty blue eyes."

"I wonder if Adam will like it." Mandy turned away from the mirror with a sinking feeling that the problems were still waiting for her. "Ohh, Aunt Maggie, I wish I had talked to Adam and had him drive me home instead of relying on Cole and Dianne. We promised each other no games and here I am at home without telling him first."

"I'm sure he'll understand, dear," Maggie said. "Why don't you go back to work tomorrow and tell him you weren't feeling well? Be honest with him. Then talk to your brother and tell him how you feel about Adam. Tell him you hope he'll be happy for you and that you can still be partners with this ranch deal. If it works out with Adam, then Jason can buy you out. Think about it, Jason hasn't been on a ranch for eight years and when you do get property, he may need Adam's help."

"Yeah." Mandy smiled. "You and Dianne think so much alike. In fact, she's said much the same thing."

"She must be a very wise lady." Maggie smiled then kissed Mandy on the cheek.

"Aunt Maggie, do you mind if I go back this afternoon, I want to see Adam today?"

"Of course not."

"Thanks, Auntie." She threw her arms around her and gave her a squeeze. Her heart felt over-whelmed with the love that flowed between them. "I love you."

"You two back from the hairdressers?" Uncle Richard's deep voice rang out as he walked through the door. He stopped dead in his tracks. "Ohh, my goodness. I don't know if I want my little girl going back to that ranch. I can certainly understand Jason's concern."

"Oh, Uncle Richard, please don't start." She crunched up her face.

"Aw, Sweetheart, I'm just teasing. I trust your judgement. It's the young men I don't trust." He gave her a wink.

"Uncle Richard, can you drive me back to the McBride Ranch?"

"Sure, but first I'd like to talk to you and Jason. He's in the shop."

Mandy smiled when she saw her aunt wink. A burst of excitement flipped in her stomach. What surprise did her uncle have for her and Jason?

MANDY RAN outside and raced to the shop, opened the door and raced towards the finishing room and called out for her brother. The door opened.

"Hi, Squeak," Jason said with a solemn face. His lips barely moved as he turned back towards the hutch he was finishing off.

Mandy quickly glanced around to see if there were any of the drivers or employees around. With no one in the shop she took a step towards him. Her heart ached for her brother and the loneliness he must have felt for the couple days they hadn't talked. But, it was time to talk now and straighten things out. "Uncle Richard wants to talk to us both."

"I ain't surprised. Ya got everyone sidin' with ya. Ya even sided with Adam and told me to git on home. Anyway, I'm glad I ain't workin' there, cause I don't hav' ta look at the snake."

"Oh, quit whining, Jason, it's about our investments. Now, are we going to look at that ranch Dianne told me about or not?" She watched Jason perk up. "I trust Dianne's judgement. But we still have to go over and look at it. We've got to talk."

"Ya still gonna buy a ranch with me?" Jason asked eagerly. "Ya still gonna be my partner?"

"Of course, we're still going to be partners. I don't know what my future holds, so let's get started. Listen, you may end up buying me out, but for now I want that ranch. Dianne's talked to her friend and we have first refusal. And please, Jason, drop the drawl."

Jason nodded then gave her a quick quirky grin. He put down his tools, escorted her out of the finishing room and out of the building and walked up to the house. In the kitchen, Uncle Richard was sorting out papers over a cup of coffee.

"Hi, son, take a break and have a seat here." Richard pointed to a chair.

"Howdy, Uncle Richard." Jason took a chair then glanced at his sister. "I aint changin' the word howdy," he told her straight. "I like your hair cut, Squeak."

"Thanks, Jas," Mandy said as she watched him reach for the sugar bowl and dump two heaping spoons full of sugar into his black coffee.

Richard pulled out a folder and a pen. "So, you're both interested in buying a ranch close by."

"Yes, we are," Mandy answered as she flicked on the burner and placed the kettle on top. "It's the ranch just across the river from the McBride's' and Dianne's friend is giving us first refusal." She took her cup from the shelf and tossed in a tea bag. "I want to talk to you both about it."

"We've saved up some money, Uncle Richard," Jason added as he pulled out a small booklet from his shirt pocket. He gave Mandy a reassuring smile as he passed it to Richard.

Mandy recognized the savings account pass book. Her eyes widened. "You actually carry around a savings account pass book?" She watched Jason blush.

"Well... ya can still get them ya know." He shrugged and twitched a smile. "I open it now 'n' then 'n' dream." He laughed then put up his hand palm out. "Cut the drawl. Got it." He rolled his eyes. "I get it updated every month. The bank tellers are... well they're quite supportive." He blushed harder as he glanced back at the passbook.

"And I thought I was the dreamer." Mandy chuckled and took her brothers hand. "I understand."

Richard smiled lovingly at his niece and nephew then took the pass book from Jason's outreached hand. He glanced at it while he listened to what they had been doing for the past eight years. He knew they had saved their allowance when they were teenagers. He knew of the published book money Mandy received from her publisher. A percentage of their paychecks from their jobs. All put into what they called a ranch fund. They had a joint checking account for their necessities such as car insurance, clothing, gas and other daily expenses. "You two have done extremely well." Extremely pleased with them, he passed the booklet back to Jason. "Especially since you were also deter-mined to pay rent to us when you started working."

"It was only right to contribute," Mandy said.

"Well, I'm proud of you both and I guess I won't have to worry about you two being foolish."

"We've been listenin' to ya more than ya think, Uncle Richard," Jason informed.

Richard smiled. "If your parents are watching right now, I know they'd be happy and very proud of both of you."

Mandy could see moisture in her uncle's eyes. He loved his older brother very much and it had been just as hard on him after the accident. "Speaking of our parents," Mandy said. "You always told us that when the time came and we wanted something so bad we could taste it, we were to come to you for advice." She smiled. "Well, as you've known for years, we want to start our own ranch."

"That I have." Richard nodded. "And I'm very surprised you haven't come to me sooner."

Jason grinned. "Mandy and I are wantin' to see this ranch and maybe make an offer. With what Dianne's said 'bout it, we're definitely interested. With the money we've saved up, Mandy 'n' I are hopin' we can git some help with the investments you've been talkin' 'bout from Dad and Mom's estate." Jason gave his sister a real sassy grin. "Okay, okay, Squeak, no more drawl." He chuckled then turned his head towards Richard. "I just can't help it. I get on a roll." He muttered as he quickly glanced at his sister again.

"That drawl has become a habit."

"Listen up you two." Uncle Richard waved a couple of papers in the air. "Your parents were financially comfortable and as you know, they gave me power of attorney. In your parent's will, they've asked me to look after your investments until you were at least twenty-five." Richard smiled. "Or until I felt you were responsible enough to manage on your own. It was your parents' wish that you both were mature enough to manage the finances and the investments. In my opinion, even with what life has thrown at all of us, you two have been mature enough for years. However, since you hadn't brought it up I just continued investing your portion."

Richard nodded. "Anyway, I've made several investments

from your parents' ranch and it comes to a very comfortable sum. You both have a very healthy portfolio and you will definitely have enough to buy that ranch outright, with any livestock they have left."

Richard took a sip of his coffee. "There's plenty left over and if you two work as hard and invest wisely, just as your parents did and as your aunt and I've done you can be set for life. Your children will be comfortable as well." Richard smiled. "First thing I want to say is, how proud I am of you both. To this day, I miss my brother, Steven, very much and we miss your mother, Joy, who was a warm and loving woman and a true friend. When they died, they gave us the most precious gift on earth. You two. I love you both more than you'll ever know. And not to forget Martin, I loved him also." Richard reached over the table and grasped both his children's hands and squeezed with deep sincerity. "You both have made your Aunt Maggie and I very happy and proud."

"Oh, Uncle Richard." Mandy took her hand away from his, got up from her chair and wrapped her arms around his neck. "I love you, too. You've been wonderful parents to us." She kissed his cheek then released him. As she pulled her chair closer she watched Jason give him a big bear hug as tears welled up in his eyes.

Uncle Richard wiped the moisture from his. "Let's get to some serious talking here." He took in a deep slow breath then swallowed hard. He nodded slowly. "Some of your stocks and bonds and shares are tied up and it will take time to collect. Some of them I'm hoping you'll leave as is. Jason, with your business management degree, you'll be able to understand everything I've done." He smiled lovingly.

"Now, between you both, your share of the inheritance, has grown to over eight million dollars. And some change." Richard chuckled.

Mandy stared unbelievingly at her uncle. "What?" She blinked.

"You have between you two, exactly…" he grinned broadly, "…eight million, nine hundred and seventy-five thousand dollars. And some change." His eyes sparkled with the delightful news.

"Oh, oh, my lord, Uncle Richard." Too excited to sit, Jason jumped up. "We had no idea. We knew you were investing for us, but we had no idea it would be so much." Jason picked up his sister and whooped with joy.

"I know you didn't," Richard said watching them with delight.

Jason put his sister down and yelled out another whoopee.

"Are you sure?" Mandy's voice high-pitched with excitement.

"I'm sure." Richard opened up the folder, moved it so it faced them and handed Jason several pieces of paper. "Of course, the certificates, bonds, stocks and financial papers are all in the safety deposit box. These written records just show you what I've done."

Once Jason settled and sat down, Mandy half stood and leaned on the table and turned her head so she could read what her uncle had spread out. She glanced at Jason as he shook his head in disbelief. Too stunned to speak, she sat back down.

"I can't believe this." Jason shook his head a second time. "I know you told us you were investing Dad and Mom's money throughout the years, Uncle Richard. But… I still can't believe it." Jason brushed his hair back with both his hands. "I can't believe this," he yelled glancing at his sister with ecstasy.

"Me either. I… I uhh, I'm stunned." She laughed uncontrollably to believe their unbelievingly good future. "This is overwhelming."

Richard beamed at their reactions then became serious again. "Now remember, a fool and his money are soon parted. Always think of the future and don't let money rule your life. Don't let it spoil you. And, whatever you do, don't let it come between you and your family. We've given you kids a good home and we've all been more than comfortable and have worked hard. The difference is, with having money, you can work at a job you love. You can have employees, people working for you and you can hire good bookkeepers, accountants and lawyers." Richard tapped the paper with his pen.

"My example is The Riley Fine Furniture Company. I'm very proud of it, and it's grown to be the finest wood furniture company in Canada and in the Western U.S.A. We've got furniture stores all through the country, but, I still love the original shop behind the house. That little shop has kept me close to home. Close to my wife and the two of you. I'm sure I don't have to explain to either of you how grateful I am to have had the opportunity to stay home as much as I could. Your parents made a lot of this possible. I was able to hire reliable, honest hard-working staff to manage and look after all the stores in both Canada and the United States."

Richard smiled. "Now, just one more thing. Both of you have worked in my shop. Jason, you're a wonderful finishing carpenter and you've earned every penny you made with the company. Amanda, your bedroom suite designs you made a couple years ago have become extremely popular with teenage girls. The youth furniture designs from a few years ago, you thought were just doodles, brought in so much revenue, we now have a youth furniture department attached to each store. Plus, all the years you've helped keep the shop organized."

Richard took in another deep breath. "I never told you this, but you both have investments in the Riley Fine Furniture Company. You're my children, that's part of your inheritance. We'll discuss that later." He glanced at Jason. "You and I will have to sit down and go over everything." He then glanced at his niece. "I know you'd rather be mucking out a stall or cleaning a tack room than talking finances, but I'd like you to come with Jason. You have to know this, Amanda."

She nodded. "You're right." She grinned. "But like you just said, just give me a horse, and a little barn and I'll be happy." She chuckled.

Uncle Richard lovingly squeezed her hand. "Now, Sweetheart, go call Dianne and maybe you can talk to her friend today. You two can start to make a deal right now."

"Now?" Mandy said with enthusiasm.

"You bet, Honey. Your future is set. If this woman is as organized as I am, trust me, you'll get the ranch sooner than you think."

ADAM PUTTERED around the line cabin, pulled the weeds which had grown up along the side of it, and clipped the bush out back which had been his grandmother's favorite. His grandfather loved the wilderness look, but he had always kept that one bush shaped nicely for grandma. He didn't know the name of it, but it came from a nursery in Calgary. His grandparents, Alex and Josie McBride, savored every day, every hour they had together.

Adam stood back and looked at the job he had done on the pretty leafed bush. A smile crossed his face at the memory of his grandfather doing the same. Grandfather had said if he lived to be a hundred, he would never figure out women, and why his wife Josie wanted the silly city bush way out here. Even though his grandfather thought it silly, he took care of it until he died six years after his wife. Silly or not, Adam was going to take care of it from now on.

Adam sauntered over to the rickety wooden lawn chair and sat down. His thoughts turned to Mandy. He missed her. Missed her terribly. He got up and snipped off a small branch from grandma's bush. Somehow, he had to get Mandy to listen to him when he got back. She and her stubborn brother were going to sit down with him and have a talk. He stepped back, looked at his accomplishment and thought that his grandmother would be pleased with his efforts. With satisfaction, he headed back to the cabin.

Before he entered, he looked up at the blue sky and grinned. The fluffy white clouds made the heavens look soft and reachable. "Yup, Mandy and I are going to have a good future together," he said out loud.

Later that evening, he took out his grandfather's, old, beat-up tool box and fixed the weather-beaten gnarled post on the outside railing, then proceeded to fix a leg of a wobbly old end table. After a bit of lunch, consisting of a ham sandwich and a tall glass of cool mountain water, he replaced a hinge, fixed the screen in the door then swept and finished cleaning from yesterday. Standing back, Adam smiled. The old-line cabin looked almost pretty. Especially with his grandmother's added touch. He stepped towards the faded yellow curtains, undid the tie backs and let them hang straight for the night, making the cabin cozy.

He lay on the bed and stared at the ceiling with his hands behind his head and thought about Mandy and wished he could share stories with her.

CHAPTER 20

*T*he ranch couldn't be more perfect and Mandy prayed that the white rambling, cedar-trimmed bungalow, with a screened-in porch wasn't a mirage. She blinked, trying to take it all in as she focused in on the flower garden. Pretty flowers in full bloom and rich with color shaded by a mature oak. She couldn't believe what she was staring at. She turned to a solid, well-built, red and white barn. Although fairly new, the old style of the building with its familiar barn red color, and white broad x's on the doors, not only brought back past childhood memories, but it gave the place an old rustic charm look.

An elderly gray-haired, slender woman in a pair of overalls walked towards them. For someone in her mid-seventies, she had a lively spring in her step. Her skin tanned to a deep bronze and her face looked younger than her years, but her hardworking hands gave her age away as she shook hands.

"Hello, Dianne," the older woman said with a broad friendly smile.

"Hi, Bea. It's so good to see you," Dianne said then did all the introductions.

Bea patted Dianne's hand then turned to Mandy, Jason and

Richard. "It is my pleasure to meet all of you," Bea said as she shook everyone's hand then faced Mandy. "Feel free to call me Bea." Bea nodded at everyone then turned towards the western part of the ranch and the low-level ranch house. "Well, here it is." Bea stretched her arm out and swung it from side to side. "This land was my husband's parents' and grandparents' before him. When we met, we decided to settle here. Anyway, we were married for fifty-two years. The house..." she pointed, "...is thirty years old and well-built." A proud smile graced her face. "My husband built it and you won't find a weak board in it, as my Jimmy was also a wonderful carpenter." She chuckled. "Anyway, we only had one daughter who chose to become a doctor and is now married to one. They're quite comfortable living in Calgary."

Bea gazed around the property and wiped the moisture from her eyes. "This land has been good to me, but now that my Jimmy's gone, I find it lonely." Bea choked back a lump in her throat then smiled.

Mandy's heart went out to the older lady. For her age, she seemed to be quite agile and spry and it was a pity she had to move at all. But she was right, being lonely wasn't good for anybody. It hurt and hurt bad. The sparkle in her eyes when she talked about her family told Mandy she'd be happy, and she not only loved deeply, she was deeply loved.

Mandy turned towards the barn where Bea was pointing and smiled. The corral, the storage buildings and the bunkhouse, were a comfortable distance from the main house. The older lady explained that she still had a half dozen Quarter Horses that she was willing to sell with the property. They were of good breeding and well-trained. She still had a hundred and twenty-six cows and calves left and one good bull. "That's not much for a cattle ranch, but I knew I was selling out and had to down-size. Also, the new calves have not been branded, but they have been vaccinated and the young bulls castrated. It'll be a small start for you, but it's a start if you want them." She smiled. "There's two men still working full-time and want to talk about staying on if they can." She glanced at Jason and Richard. "They're both hard workers so maybe you can give it some thought. Our old foreman, Fred Borg, has been with us since we bought the place. He's the best and I must say he's a little worried about his job. He's very knowledgeable in both cattle and horses and he's an excellent mechanic." Bea laughed. "Listen to me yammer away, when you two young'uns probably want to see the house and look around."

"That's fine, Bea, we've got time," Mandy said.

"You're a dear, Mandy." She turned to Jason. "And I can see you're a fine young man." She turned to Richard. "And you, such a young man yourself must be very proud of your young'uns."

Richard nodded. "Believe me, Ma'am, I sure am." His cheeks flushed.

Mandy glanced at her uncle and smiled broadly at his flushed cheeks for being called a young man. She couldn't believe her uncle could still blush so profusely. She had to stifle a giggle when she looked at Jason. He could blush as well as Uncle Richard.

"Come on, let's all go into the house."

Mandy and Jason followed Bea into the house while Richard wheeled Dianne right behind them.

"Just wander around while I make fresh lemonade," Bea suggested.

The living room was spacious and had a large picture window that faced the striking Rocky Mountains. "Pinch me, Jason," Mandy said stepping to her left and entering a large cat-in kitchen. A breakfast nook sat at the east window making it perfect for morning coffee while the sun rose. "This is…

perfect," she said glancing at Dianne. Off the kitchen was a mud and bathroom with a large wash up sink area. "It's just great."

"Hey, Mandy," Jason called out. "Come see the family room."

Mandy left Dianne and Bea in the kitchen as she followed Jason's voice. A separate door off the dining room went into a family room. She wrapped her arms around herself when she looked out the large picture window that faced west. A stone fireplace sat on the end wall. "How magnificent." She glanced at her uncle. "It's perfect." She smiled. "More than I've ever dreamed of." Mandy followed Jason and Uncle Richard through the bedrooms and was surprised at how large they were and that they all had full bathrooms attached. She thought of Adam and wished he was with her to share in her excitement.

Everyone regrouped and sat down around the large maple table surrounded by six matching chairs. The kitchen was spacious, bright, and cheery. The whole house was absolutely perfect.

"Still want to deal?" Mrs. Turner smiled as she held up a jug of lemonade.

"Yes, for sure," Mandy said with excitement then turned to her brother and watched him nod with a wide grin from ear to ear and his eyes shone with excitement.

"I'm going to get a breath of fresh air while you talk," Dianne said and turned her wheelchair towards the front door entrance.

"I will too." Richard stood and headed towards the door.

"No, Uncle Richard. Stay," Mandy chirped. "We want you a part of this."

Jason nodded in total agreement.

"Thank you." Richard smiled. "I have been a big part of this and now it's time for you two to take over. You can talk to me and your aunt later about the experience of your first purchase."

He nodded with love in his heart, then turned to Bea and smiled. Richard then handed Dianne a plate of cut up fruit and a small cup of yogurt. "Can you handle this mug of tea too, Dianne?"

"Sure can." Dianne laid everything on the tray. "Give me your coffee mug, too."

"Okay."

Dianne held her tray securely. "I'm ready."

Richard took control of the wheelchair and headed out towards the shade tree.

Bea poured the lemonade then took her file out and spread the papers on the table then picked up her pen and pointed to everything she had listed. "When Dianne called and told me how much you were interested, I got all my papers in order, because this ranch won't last five minutes on the market." She turned the papers so that Mandy and Jason could read them. "Now, I've got two prices here." She picked up her pen and pointed to one paper. "The land includes the value of the house and all the buildings. This document includes everything, along with all the stock and machinery." She smiled. "After I talked to Dianne a few days ago..." she winked at Mandy, "...I called my lawyer and had him draw up this special deal. Dianne told me what an exceptional young lady you were. Well, just in case you want to take everything. That means lock, stock and barrel, I figured a price out." She planted it on the table and sat back with a big broad smile on her tanned face.

Mandy picked it up. The figure stunned her. Her jaw dropped then passed it to Jason and watched his expression.

Jason shot his head up at the older woman. "Bea. You've... you ah... what I mean is... if, if we uh... take everything, you'd be throwing in all the equipment, plus you've included the half ton truck and two riding mowers and..." he swept his hand over the list, "...the equipment alone is... is... I'm speechless. This is, jeez..." he passed the paper to Mandy, "...unbelievable. We won't have to purchase a thing. And you've slashed several thousand dollars off the market value."

"That's my price." She smiled. "For your family only." Bea chuckled. "Your uncle mentioned that you have a business degree so, how's it look?"

Jason's mouth fell open. "I don't know what to say. Are you sure?" he said with great enthusiasm. "This is... a dream come true." He took in a deep breath. "A dream come true," he repeated.

"I like the both of you. I've been talking to Dianne and I had a feeling you'd love this place as much as Jimmy and I have. For me, it's not just money. Of course, money is important and we all need to live, but I need to know that this ranch, that I love so much, is going to be in good hands. I want someone to buy it who will love it as much as my precious husband and I did. My daughter and her husband are fine so I want to help out another young couple with their future memories." She smiled. "Even with the deal I'm giving you, I'll still have plenty to invest."

"Oh, Bea, I'm so glad you've picked us. We just can't thank you enough," Mandy said.

"It's a pleasure doing business with you and I hope you two will enjoy the ranch as much as I have." Bea smiled.

"This is truly, a dream come true." Jason looked at his sister with a big grin. "The Twin R Ranch."

Mandy smiled then focused on Bea. "We can't thank you enough."

"It is totally my pleasure." Bea slowly stood up. "Well, I don't want to rush you, but I need to do some more packing and I need to make some phone calls and I'm sure you'll want to start talking business with your lawyers, too."

"Thank you, thank you so very much." Jason smiled.

"I'm so happy about this." Bea nodded. "It gives me a warm feeling that this place will be looked after by people who truly love the life it gives." Bea raised her hand with her palm out. "Now, you go and call both your lawyer and your bank manager to give them heads up. I'm going to do the same. If your uncle raised you like I think he did, everything on your end is organized." She smiled as she escorted them to the door. "I'm looking forward to seeing you later."

～

BACK AT THE McBRIDE RANCH, Mandy sat down in the living room with her uncle, brother and Dianne and told them everything that went on in the kitchen.

"I can't believe this day," Richard Riley said with a slap of his upper right leg. "This only happens in fiction and fantasy books." He laughed.

"I for one am so glad I'm a part of this fantasy." Mandy clasped her hands together. "I just hope I wake up tomorrow morning to find out I'm not dreaming."

"We're not, Squeak."

Mandy clapped her hands then pulled her hair up and back away from her face. "I can hardly wait until I tell Adam." Excitement rolled off her tongue. She stilled at the recollection of promising Adam there would be no more mind games. If only she had called him first. If only she had told him she wasn't feeling well, maybe he could have driven her home. Even though she wasn't well, they could have talked a bit. What a fool she'd been. Turning towards Jason, she noticed him clench his jaw when she mentioned Adam's name.

"I was a real jerk to him."

"You were, Jason."

"Adam went out of his way to try and talk to me the day I

came to the ranch to see you. I completely ignored him." Jason hung his head in shame. "It was me who threw the first punch..." he scrubbed his face hard with both hands, "...and the second. Adam was only defending himself." He chuckled nervously finding it hard to meet his sister's gaze. "He could have flattened me, but he didn't. He kept his cool while I acted like a spoilt brat ten-year-old."

"Jason, I love you and always will. I just wish you would accept the man I love..."

"Excuse me," Dianne interrupted. "I'll let the two of you talk alone."

"Yeah me, too. I have to get home to Maggie. She'll want to hear all about this wonderful news." Richard bent down and gave Mandy a kiss on the forehead. "I love you, Sweetheart." He turned to Jason and gave him a big loving man hug. "See you, son. I'm sure you two don't need me to help you work this out." He walked out with Dianne.

"Jason." Mandy grasped his arm with both of her hands. "I love Adam and I want to get to know him better. I don't know at this point where the future lies, because we haven't had enough time to see where this is going. I'll tell you one thing, he's good to me and I'm not interested in his past relationships. I'm interested in the future. Our future."

"I'm really sorry, Amanda, I'll call Adam tonight after supper and apologize."

"Thanks, Jas."

"I got to git." Jason smiled.

Mandy walked out with Jason, gave her uncle a hug, waved goodbye, then determined to find Adam, headed straight for the barn.

≈

THE NEXT MORNING while Mandy got ready to go with her family and Mrs. Turner to see the lawyers and bank managers to settle the deal of a lifetime, a tight worry wrapped around her heart. She should have been the happiest person alive, but a sadness in her heart squeezed hard. Adam hadn't come home last night and she was not only upset, she was beginning to worry that something had happened to him. Something was preventing him from coming home to her. As excited as she was yesterday about buying a ranch, today it didn't seem as much fun. She wanted Adam to be with her. Join in her excitement. Hearing a truck motor, Mandy looked out the bedroom window to see her brother waiting. It was too late to back down from the wonderful deal now, besides it wouldn't be fair to Jason. He had worked and saved just as hard as she had over all these years. He deserved this dream.

The drive to Calgary to meet Uncle Richard and Bea Turner to make the deal of a lifetime come true, was a quiet one. Mandy was thankful that her brother respected her silence and kept quiet himself. She figured he felt guilty for interfering in her life and not being able to get ahold of Adam himself, made it worse for him.

During the bank meeting, Adam was still on her mind but when she saw the bank manager's facial expression she let out a quick chuckle. Several hours later between driving and parking between different lawyers and bank offices, the deal was finally made and papers signed. The land was officially Mandy and Jason's.

Back at the Turner Ranch, they celebrated with lemonade.

"Well, it's my last day here and your first night at the ranch." Bea looked at them both. "I've got a couple of bottles of wine here." She opened the fridge door and pulled out a bottle. "I put these in here last night just in case." She gave off a girlish giggle.

Mandy swallowed hard at the sight of the three wine bottles

in the fridge and looked over at her brother. She took in a deep breath as Bea picked up the bottle opener to the one she took out. As far as she was concerned, liquor was liquor and it didn't matter whether it was beer, whiskey, or wine. It was the devil's drink and no one was going to convince her otherwise. She watched Jason mouth the words, it's okay. She glanced at the little old lady with the happy lines around her eyes, and couldn't imagine her ever hurting anyone, let alone getting behind the wheel and driving after drinking.

Jason winked at his sister and took her hand. "Hey, Squeak let's celebrate with our new friends and neighbors and order in Chinese food." He nodded at Bea. "Okay with you?"

"That's a wonderful idea," Bea said as she closed the fridge door. "I'll chip in too because I'd love to invite all of the McBride's over. They have all been so good to me and it would be nice to have them over once more. I'll call my daughter and her hubby to come join us, too."

"Okay," Mandy chirped in her best voice. "Uncle Richard, I'm going to call Aunt Maggie."

"I'm way ahead of you, Honey." He lifted his cell phone to his ear. "This is a day for celebrating." He winked. "Hey, Maggie Honey..."

Bea popped the first cork.

∿

ADAM WAS up bright and early and straightened up the line cabin then made a coffee and took it out to the porch and sat on the swing. His thoughts immediately raced to Mandy and wondered how she was coping with the few days off Dianne had given her and hoped she felt better. He missed her more than he thought possible which surprised him. He missed their early morning coffee on the porch. Missed talking to her and hearing her soft laughter. He longed to hold her and cuddle up to her warm body and tell her stories.

Leaning his head back he wondered if Mandy would like his grandfather's thinking cabin. They'd come here to have some alone time just like his grandparents did. "Yep." He nodded. "I think she would." He grinned from ear to ear then headed down to the creek to wash up. He wished he had brought a change of clothes and his razor with him, as he stroked his three-day growth. It was time to go home. First, he was going to give Mandy a big hug and kiss and tell her he loved her. Then he was going to call that twin brother of hers and meet up with him. Jason was going to listen to reason. No more interfering in his sister's life. Maybe he'd tie him to a fence post and make him listen. First, he was going to duct tape his mouth so he wouldn't have to listen to that thick drawl of his.

Later that evening, Adam pulled into the driveway and found his father's truck and Cole's family van gone. The house was in complete darkness. He frowned and took in an uneasy breath and walked into the quiet, still house and flipped on the light switch. It had been years since he had heard the silence of his family home. In fact, he couldn't remember it ever being so still. He knew Crystal and Bobby were most likely at Dianne's parents', but where was his father, the rest of the family and was Mandy with them?

Adam remembered that Kirk and Melanie and Chad and Bonnie Brandon, had invited them over for a neighborhood BBQ at their ranch, but he didn't figure they'd be getting together during a week day. Dianne had talked about her friend Rhonda and Vic maybe getting married, but, then again, a party on a week night still didn't make sense. He flipped the family calendar open. He was right, a party all right, but not until next weekend. He left the house and stood out on the porch and looked around. No sign of anyone. Weird.

He went back to the house and looked at the clock. "Eight-forty. Where the hell is everyone?" He plunked himself into his rocker recliner in the living room and stared at the clock. As he sat there, his mood darkened. For the life of him he couldn't figure where everyone had gone to.

At ten-twenty, he checked the family's phone book then picked up the cordless phone and thumbed Mandy's home number in Calgary. After several rings he hung up and stared at the phone. He found her cell number and again no luck. He carefully re-dialed her cell number just in case he had pushed the wrong number. He went out onto the porch and glanced at her empty chair beside his then sat down. Her phone rang endlessly before he hung up. He wanted his evening coffee with her sitting next to him. He needed to talk to her. He realized he wanted her in his life, not for a short period, not just cuddling and telling stories, he wanted her in his life forever.

He got up, picked up the cordless and went back inside, checked every room over again. He opened her bedroom door and stared at her neatly made up bed. He noticed her manuscript and lap top were on the desk along with her cell phone. "Oh, that's convenient. Leave your cell at home." He looked back at the manuscript. "At least she'll be back."

At eleven fifteen at night his family drove up talking and laughing, giving him reason to believe that he had missed something. Again.

"Adam, you're home?" Cole called out with sincere worry in his voice. "Where on earth have you been? We were worried sick about you. If you had been here you would have been invited to Bea's for a farewell dinner."

"Yeah, you all look like you were worried," Adam snapped at his brother.

"Come on, Adam, if you'd let us know where you took off

to." Cole took in a deep sigh, "I'm presuming you went to the line cabin, but cells don't work out there. Now if I were you…"

"Don't, Cole, not right now," he pleaded. "I've had a lot on my mind." He looked at his father. "Can we talk?"

"Sure, son." John walked to the end of the porch.

"Hey, Adam," Cole called out before entering the house with Dianne. "Maybe you should shave; you look like hell," he said teasingly.

He heard Dianne tell Cole to lay off. "Where's Mandy?" He watched his father rake his hands through his hair. "What's wrong?"

"Nothing's wrong, I just wish you would communicate more. Like Cole said, we figured you were at the line cabin, but, well, if you had been here, you would have known what's been going on."

"You going to tell me, or keep me in suspense?" Adam crossed his arms. "Did she run off and get married or did she move back to Utah?" Old fears of being deserted kicked at him like a bull being cornered. This couldn't be happening. Mandy wouldn't just up and leave. Would she?

"No, she moved into her new place."

Adam stared at his father. He wasn't sure what to think and didn't know if he wanted the answer, but he had to get to the bottom of this mystery. "What new place?"

"Mandy and Jason bought the Turner ranch."

"I'm gone for three days and she buys a ranch? I thought Dianne gave her time off because she wasn't feeling well." He shook his head in bewilderment. "Bought a ranch? How the hell did that happen so fast. Dealing with the bank should have taken a few days, let alone the legal work, meetings with lawyers and everything else."

"It was a cash deal. Papers were all in order on both sides. Extremely organized. Dianne, Jason, Mandy and their uncle went to Bea's yesterday. They looked the place over and they bought it lock, stock and barrel. They were at the bank and lawyers early this morning and moved in this evening. We just come back from celebrating."

Impossible. He unfolded his arms and stepped back. He looked towards the corral where a horse whinnied, then looked back at his father. He placed his hands on his hips. "Absolutely impossible in two and a half days?" He shook his head in disbelief. "Deals just don't happen like that."

"This one did," John explained giving Adam all the details. "And yes, it is unbelievable. But it happens. You know yourself money talks."

Adam listened, but couldn't believe it. He worked his jaw. "I knew something was off when she first drove up with that fancy red truck. What kind of nanny drives vehicles like that? She told me it was her uncle's, well… whatever. Anyway, Jason's got his sister back and they've got their dream ranch. I hope they're both very happy." He threw his hands up in the air. He grunted an unbelievable chuckle and turned.

"Adam." John grabbed his son's arm. "Stay and talk to me."

Adam shook his head and extracted his arm and left his father standing by himself on the porch and headed for the barn. His thoughts were in a turmoil. Mandy had everything, her dream ranch, financial security, and her brother to look after her. Why would she need him? They had promised each other no more mind games and after all they had shared she left him in the dark without a word. He should have been used to it, but his gut twisted with the feeling of abandonment.

He saddled his horse and rode towards the foothills needing to get lost.

CHAPTER 21

$\mathcal{M}$andy returned to work on Monday morning leaving Jason at the Twin R Ranch. Although her home was now only an hour away by vehicle, it was still her responsibility to live at the McBride ranch in case she was needed for any reason.

"Hi, Mandy," Dianne called out as she wheeled herself out of her bedroom. "I'm surprised you're here so early. I figured you'd be later since you have your own chores to do and the kids aren't back yet."

"Obviously not early enough," Mandy said with disappointment. "Jason and I got talking about the ranch hands, but I still thought I'd be here early enough to have coffee with Adam, but it looks like he's already gone."

Dianne nodded. "Adam has a lot on his mind. He's... well..." Dianne shrugged, "... he's still helping, Hank. The fight with Jason and him, didn't help, and he does have extra chores to do because of me." Dianne shook her head slightly. "Everything will be okay, in time. Trust me." Dianne pointed to a chair. "Come and sit down. I want to talk to you." Dianne waited for a moment while Mandy settled. "Mandy, I want to give you a heads up. Purchasing that ranch with your brother just made you the most eligible woman in Southern Alberta. News spreads fast among the cowboys that there's a pretty, single young lady rancher with money."

"I'll be careful." Mandy blushed with embarrassment. "I only want one cowboy and you know who he is." Her heart fluttered just thinking of him. "Do you know if Adam had his morning coffee on the porch like he usually does, because he was gone when I arrived?"

"Yes, he did. He got back last night and he was unbelievably quiet this morning. Like I said, he has a lot on his mind."

Mandy's heart sank into the pit of her stomach. She'd missed him. It was going to be a very long day until supper time rolled around.

During supper the children were wound up like springs and had a lot to say about what they did with their grandparents and how they wanted to go again soon. The noise level rose to extreme as everyone laughed, chatted and discussed the Twin R Ranch and the fun they had last evening. Wishing Adam was there, Mandy forced out a few chuckles and smiles. Down deep, she could hardly wait until she could go and wash the happy mask off her face then go to bed and sleep the hours away.

Her heart sank deeper into the pit of her stomach, when she entered the living room after speaking to Jason and realized Adam still hadn't come home. Her heart ached with a heaviness she had never experienced before and longed to have Adam share in all the excitement. She'd give anything to cancel story hour and run to her bedroom and have a good long cry.

Later that evening after the children went to bed, Mandy headed towards the barn with tears streaming down her face. "Oh, God I love him," she prayed out loud. Hearing a truck pull up before she reached the barn door, she turned. It was only Jason with her new horse, Freckles, who was a sweet little mare that was a part of the deal. She quickly dried her eyes on her sleeve and dashed towards the horse trailer. "I'll get her," she hollered to her brother then went into the horse trailer and backed Freckles out. "Good girl," she cooed then looked at her brother. "She's a beauty. I love the white blaze on her face and the three small white spots on the end of her nose. Guess that's why her name is Freckles." She walked the little mare to the barn while Jason brought in her tack. They bedded her down, made sure she was comfortable then left the barn together.

"Did you get ahold of Adam today?"

"I'm sorry, Squeak, I tried several times and left messages on his cell and called the bunkhouse and left messages with Chuck, but I haven't heard from him. I'll try tomorrow."

"I haven't seen him all day. I know he's back, but he hasn't shown his face around."

"I hope I haven't messed things up for you."

"Jas, he told me he loved me and if it's true he'll be around. If not, then I guess you were right all along."

"No, Squeak, I was wrong. He's quite the man so give him a chance. I was pretty rude to him. In fact, so rude, if I were him, I wouldn't want to be a part of this family. If I'm an example of what a Riley is and I were Adam, I'd run so fast the other way no one would ever find me." Jason hung his head. "Don't blame him, Amanda. You're going to have to give him a chance because of my mistakes. I truly am sorry and please tell him if you see him first." Jason leaned forward and kissed his sister on the forehead. "I'll call him again tomorrow, in the meantime I have to get back. See ya later."

Mandy made her way back to the house and sat down on the chair that Adam made for her. She loved him with all her heart and she was going to have him. Riley's had determination, and she was determined to have Adam for the rest of her life.

~

ADAM CAME BACK from seeing his friend, Hank, later that evening then went for a ride on Zircon to continue to mull things over. It was dark before he returned to the barn and he was physically and emotionally exhausted. When he saw Mandy come out, he backed Zircon up and stayed in the shadows so he could watch her walk with confidence towards the house. His heart ached to hold her. His body craved to be near her. He sighed at the thought of her not needing him anymore. She had touched his heart and molded it with love and tenderness. He loved her, yet a wall of emotions separated them.

Confused, he continued to watch her until she disappeared into the house. He felt his jaw tighten at the thought of how much had changed in three short days. It still boggled his mind that she had purchased a ranch and moved in. It was crazy. This just didn't happen in real life. "Damn," he said out loud. He would have liked to be involved in her dream and the excitement. Her future.

His frustration grew to a new height. He had already gone through the same discussion over and over in his mind several times today. After some time, he rubbed his forehead and carried on toward the barn. He was so unhappy he didn't stop to talk to Stacey, Dee or the other mares. For a man who took such joy and pleasure in his stock and especially the frisky little horses, he had to be depressed to just walk by. After he finished feeding and grooming Zircon, he closed the stall gate and headed out. He stopped abruptly at the new little mare and stared at it for a moment then opened her stall gate. "You're a fine one." He rubbed the mare's neck and legs. "Good breeding, strong legs, well proportioned. Where did Cole get you?" He stroked the mare's velvety nose and scratched behind her ears. "More changes around here than I thought."

MANDY SAT on the floor and leaned up against her bed with her knees up. With a pencil in one hand and eraser in the other, she desperately tried to concentrate on the final chapter where Penny the Little Painted Pony won first prize in the school town parade.

"I'll never get this done," she groaned then took her eraser and rubbed out several sentences. With Adam on her mind she continued to erase yet another mistake. Frustrated, she scrunched the paper up and threw it across the room followed by a snap of her pencil. "Focus. Think." She laid her head back and let out a heavy sigh. Her deadline was drawing near and in the last chapter Adam's name appeared in more places than the little boy who owned the pony did. She found herself drawing hearts and arrows in the margin.

Tingles raced up her spine causing her to turn her head just enough to see a tall dark figure standing in the doorway. Her heart jumped with joy. Her blood sizzled with excitement. She jumped up, tore off her support brace in a hurry and wrapped her robe around herself. "Adam, you're back." She gave him her best smile and stepped towards him but froze, when she saw the distant look in his face. His eyes dark. His jaw tight. It was the same look he gave her when she first arrived at the ranch for her interview. It was obvious he hadn't shaved in days making him look like a wild man, a predator, hungry for a meal.

Instantly, she was on high alert. "What's wrong?" She tried to keep the tremble out of her voice but failed. "I have so much to tell you." Hurt and pain squeezed her heart when he turned away from her and went to his own room. She followed him. "Adam, please tell me what's wrong?"

"I wouldn't come in my room if I were you. I have no rules

in here." His voice was devoid of emotions. Devoid of any warmth.

She glanced around the large well-kept masculine room. The double four poster bed was made with a hand-made quilt on top of it. It depicted a mighty oak tree, which dressed in full summer foliage was a sign of strength. Whoever made it knew him and knew him well.

"What do you mean?" she asked nervously. Avoiding his eyes, Mandy focused on the dresser with hand-carved oak leaves adorning it. A mirror and a matching high boy which had a strong single oak leaf in the middle of each drawer. She remembered John telling her that he had drawn up the special design and her grandfather made it for them. His stamp would be on the back and someday she'd like to look at it.

"Do I have to spell it out for you?" He took an intimidating step towards her.

She jumped back. Her skin pebbled with goose bumps. "I guess so because I don't understand."

"Fine. You stay in my bedroom, I'll take you. My rules and no regrets." He opened the top drawer, took out a handful of condoms and tossed them on the night table.

She stared at the brightly colored wrappers and felt a cold chill run up her spine. "Why are you angry with me?" she asked cautiously. The condoms were a sign that he'd be careful not to have any ties with a woman.

"Just go, Mandy, before I forget myself." He turned, dismissing her.

Mandy stepped back, staring at his back trying to figure out what was wrong. What happened in the last few days to bring this on? Her thought turned back to what Jason had said earlier. If he were Adam, he'd run from the Riley family as fast as he could. He had also told her to be patient with Adam, that he's a good man and they were a perfect match. "Adam, please tell me why you're angry with me?"

"You have everything you want in life, so why would you need me?"

She thought for a moment then frowned. "Oh, I get it. It's the money and my brother."

"You think that's it?" Adam tightened his jaw. "You honestly think that's the only problem?" His voice harsh and cold. "Money is definitely not the problem here and your brother, well... I get it."

The man she loved just stood there staring at her. His dark brown eyes filled with sadness. Her body trembled. She clutched her robe tightly in her hands. "Oh, okay. Adam, you knew Jason and I were thinking about buying a ranch. I told you that. So, what's the problem?"

"My problem," he grunted. "My problem. You told me to be patient. You told me you would talk to Jason. You told me to trust you. We promised no more mind or emotional games. You went home, because you didn't feel well. You didn't tell me. Instead, you get Cole to drive you home, so Jason can look after you? He's..." Adam waved his hand in frustration, "...to tell you the truth, I don't know what you Riley's want. I love you, Mandy. I love you with all my heart and soul. But I can't compete with your brother or your family. I don't know if I really want too." He brushed his hair back. "When I came back, I find out you not only bought a ranch, but you moved, too. So, this time, I'm asking you to give me time and be patient. Please." He clenched his fist and turned away from her.

"I made my choice, but how was I to know where you went. You never told anyone." Her voice escalated. "You left. If you had been here or at least left us a clue as to where we could have contacted you, you would have known what's been going on. I wanted you to be with me. To share in my dream. I needed you, but you weren't here."

He turned to face her. "Don't turn this on me. I had to go somewhere and think. It was you, that left and didn't tell me. I had to find out from Dianne that she sent you home because you weren't feeling well. I was worried about you." He pointed a stiff index finger at her. "You could have told me yourself. You could have left me a note, or even called me." He brushed his thick hair back with both hands. "Crap, I could have driven you home. Then at least I would have known you were okay."

"You're right. You're absolutely right. I could have and I should have. But… it just happened." She shrugged slightly.

"I realize our relationship is new and in reality, you owe me nothing. We're not engaged. We haven't made lifelong promises to each other. Then again, we promised, no more mind games. Mandy, I told you I loved you. You said you loved me, so why couldn't you have waited an extra day? Why couldn't you wait and include me in your life, your dreams, your excitement?" He huffed. "You sent me away, Mandy. Sent me away to think."

"I didn't think of waiting," she said sadly hanging her head. He was right. She could have waited an extra day. An extra week. A month for that matter. She had hurt him and by the look of his face, deeply.

He stared at her. "Didn't think. Thanks." He shook his head slowly. "The secrets we've shared. The kisses and hugs obviously didn't mean a thing to you. You didn't care what I thought. Well, Mandy, I cared. I wanted to be in your life. I wanted to share in your adventure and be a part of it." He tore his gaze away from her. "But you didn't want that."

She blinked back tears.

∽

ADAM WATCHED as her eyes filled with moisture. He hardened his heart. "Leave now, Mandy," he said with a raspy voice.

"Please, Adam," her voice trembled. Tears streamed down her cheeks. "I'm sorry. Jason talked to me and he told me how rude he was to you. How..."

"I asked you to leave." He moved towards the door holding it open.

"But... Jason admitted he was at fault. He told me to tell you..."

"I'm not interested in what Jason has to say." His voice went to an all-time low. His eyes narrowed and darkened. "I'm done. We're done."

"What? No." She stepped towards him. Her voice strengthened. "Please, no."

Adam stood still for a moment then walked slowly towards her. He stopped and inhaled the wonderful scent of her hair. He stepped back, his eyes cruised the length of her slender body. His body turned on him and hardened with need. His emotions ran wild. She was the woman he dreamed about. She had spirit. She was loving, caring and giving. There was no other woman for him and his need for her was greater than the pounding of any stampede.

Yet anger and disappointment set in. He was done with the games. They were too much for him. He would forever remember her, but a lifetime of competing with Jason for her affection was too much. He inhaled her delicate fragrance a second time. Her soft skin just beneath the light cotton pajamas was there for his taking. He leaned towards her. His hunger for her was too much to resist. His mouth brushed her slender neck. "Couldn't wait," he whispered in her ear. "Well, neither can I." He stretched his bronzed, muscled arm and pushed the door shut, trapping her in his room.

He stepped forward and turned her around to face him. His

mouth found hers. Rough and hard. His desire urgent and wanting. Greed took over. He wanted her soft firm body molded to his. He caressed her body with his calloused hands and undid her robe tie. He explored until he found her bare skin underneath her light cotton pajamas and stroked her breasts. Swelling to his touch. Her skin, soft and warm. Her breathing labored and her soft moans excited him farther. His jeans suddenly too tight. His arousal begged to be released.

Mandy allowed him to touch her, kiss her, and stroke her bare skin. She sensed his anger, need and want, yet she moaned and trembled with both fear and excitement all in one. She wanted him. But his caresses were rough. His rough unshaven face scraped her sensitive skin. She began to cry inside, but refused to stop him. His mouth crushed her soft lips. His kiss was not gentle. His kiss was fierce. A sensual passion took her a million miles away.

The predator had found his prey and was ready and willing to have him take her. She'd welcome this angry man with open arms. She wanted to sooth his pain. Mandy felt Adam tug at her robe to expose more of her skin. He undid the buttons of her cotton pajama top while his other arm kept her close. He released her mouth, picked her up and put her on his bed then straddled her. She watched his eyes take all of her in. She felt his heart race rapid and hard. His eyes narrowed. His hand went for her left side. To her surprise, she didn't stiffen or try to stop him. She was ready. Totally ready. The fear of him seeing her scars was gone. His face softened. What was he thinking?

"Adam." Tears streamed down the sides of her face. "Make love to me." She wanted him with all her heart and soul. Needed him more than anything she ever wanted in her life. She watched his eyes shift to her left side. Her heart ached at the thought of the scar she had been hiding from him. He wanted to see it and he was curious to why she covered that side of her face. She took in a deep breath as her own eyes narrowed.

Yes, it was time to show him the ugly side of her. She pushed her hair back and turned her head to the side showing him the scar. "Here, is this what you want to check out first?" Her voice was low and harsh. "It matches my leg." She lay still for a moment letting him have a good look. "Well?" She looked back at him. "Now you know why the other men don't want me." She grabbed his hand and made him touch it. "It's not exactly one of my finer features, is it?" She bit down on her trembling lip. "Still want to love a reject? Still want what other men don't?" She closed her eyes to suppress the tears that refused to stop.

Not wanting to see the look of disgust on his face, she kept her eyes closed. To her surprise she felt his fingertips stroke it gently. His warm breath caressed her temple like a soft warm breeze. Heat of his body and the soft silky chest hair caressed her bared breasts. She heard him groan as his lips kissed her temple. His kiss tender and loving.

"Adam." His body stiffened as he kissed her temple again. And again, his kiss was tender, gentle, loving. For a moment he was the man she had got to know. To love. The man who had shown her so much tenderness. To her surprise, he slowly lifted his body off of hers and got off the bed. She watched his dark eyes glance upon her exposed breasts. Yet there was a love in them she had never seen before. A love so great it made her heart flip with ecstasy. His mouth opened to speak, but words did not follow.

∾

ADAM LIFTED his eyes and gazed at the scar Mandy had said

was so ugly. He couldn't comprehend why she believed her scars would chase him away. His thoughts were confused and muddled. He didn't see ugliness. He saw a finger length scar from her temple to the top of her jaw. It was nothing. He remembered her leg scar was bad, but it wasn't something to be embarrassed about. It was Mandy he wanted. It was her heart and soul he needed. Wanted. Loved. He told her he would love her no matter what imperfections she thought she had.

His gaze went back to her perfect breasts that had hardened to his touch then, travelled to her small firm flat stomach and slender hips. She had lost weight, yet she was going to let him take her and had done nothing to hide her body from his gaze. Did she really love him enough to give herself totally? But how could someone say they loved someone, then turn around and go their own way in life? More confusion set in. He swallowed hard as he covered her with his robe, then slowly turned and left his bedroom.

In the barn he banged his fist on the tack room bench. Angry at himself for getting so carried away with her. For being rough. Adam sat on a bale of hay and closed his eyes. He curled his hand still feeling her soft warm skin under his palm. His heart ached. He had ruined everything by being rough with her. He had broken his promise to her and to himself. His precious Mandy didn't deserve to be touched by him. She deserved to be touched and cared for by a man with gentle hands.

CHAPTER 22

*A*dam tugged another fence pole from the back of his truck early the next morning. The sun was already warm on his face and by high noon the day promised to be a scorcher. It would be good to sweat out the hurt he had bestowed on Mandy. The heavy sound of hooves brought his head up. He studied Mandy as she rode up with Ryan then slid the hammer into his carpenter's belt. "What are you doing here?" He noticed her swollen and bruised lips and her cheeks red and sore from his stubble. As much as he loved Mandy with all his heart and soul, he wanted to be left alone with his emotional wounds. To heal by himself so he could carry on with his life. If he could.

"You asked me yesterday to help you," Ryan said.

"Where's the new hired hand that's supposed to be here with you?"

"Cole had another job for him," Mandy said with her chin up.

He watched Mandy dismount and walk over to the wire that lay on the ground. "This work's not easy," Adam grumbled.

"Between Ryan and me, we can pull it tight enough so that you can hammer." She lifted her stubborn chin.

"You're going to pull the wire?" Adam shook his head at her nod. "Where's your gloves?" He watched her cheeks go bright pink as she pulled her gloves out of her back pocket and put them on.

"What's this for?" she asked as she picked up the long yellow metal object with a multitude of short stubby teeth, a lever-type attachment and a handle.

"It's a fence stretcher. It helps. It also splices the wire and holds it in place." He turned away to focus back on his work.

"Oh, I think I remember my father having one of these." Mandy picked up the barbed wire in one hand and studied the yellow tool in her other. "I never realized what it was for, though." She turned quickly. Not realizing Ryan was directly behind her, she tripped over her own feet. Instinctively, her hand went out to grasp at anything to stop herself from falling. She let out a gasp of pain as the barbed wire ripped through her gloved hand and tore her flesh.

Adam rushed to her side and took her hand. "Oh, Mandy, are you, all right?" He cringed when he saw red blood run down her torn glove.

"Ouch, ow." She yanked her hand back and shook it.

He reached for her a second time. "Mandy," he said with deep concern. It hurt deeply when she pulled away from him emotionally. The pain in her face cut him to the core. "Let me help you."

"It will just be another scar and I can certainly handle the pain," she told him nonchalantly.

"I told you already, your scars don't bother me," he snapped back. "Why won't you believe me?"

She stood on her tip-toes and whispered in his ear so Ryan

couldn't hear. "Then why did you leave me in your bed after you saw the scar?" She stepped away.

"You don't get it do you?" He growled. "It's not much of a scar." He watched the puzzled look form on her face, confirming that she really didn't get it.

She grabbed her horse's reins and hid the gasp of pain as she mounted her horse. "I'm fine, I'll tend to it when I get back to the house." Without a backward glance, she galloped off.

Adam stood there for a few moments watching her leave. His heart ached with pure agony and his body stiffened up. He believed she still thought he didn't want her because of her scars and wished he had realized that before he walked out on her last night. If only he had taken a few moments to think, things would be different today.

"Uncle Adam, why are you so angry with Miss Riley?"

He turned. "Adult problems, Ryan." He took the reins of his horse. "Let's go home and check on her." He mounted, waited for Ryan then rode in silence back to the house.

DURING DINNER, Mandy went over the afternoon's conversation in her head. He had told her that it wasn't much of a scar. The look of compassion in his eyes puzzled her, yet he seemed so confused when he had walked out on her last night without a word. "I don't get it," she muttered. "Am I missing something?" She glanced at Adam who was watching her mutter to herself and blushed. "Jason and I are going to have a barn dance on Saturday." Mandy directed her invitation to Cole and John as she had already talked to Dianne. "It's only a small dance with my family and a few friends and we'd like you all to come." She noticed Adam direct his gaze to her bandaged hand. "You're all invited."

"Great, can we come, too, Miss Riley?" Crystal spoke up.

"Of course, you kids are welcome. In fact, your mother is going to let you go home with me tomorrow so we can get things organized. That's if you'd like to."

"Oh yes, we'd love to." Crystal looked at her little brother. "Want to go to Miss Riley's?"

"Me too, me too." Bobby clapped his chubby hands.

"Good and on Saturday you can meet my Uncle Richard and my Aunty Maggie."

After supper, Mandy watched the family slowly disappear from the dinner table. Cole suggested an evening walk to the kids and John agreed. They left leaving her alone with Adam suggesting that his family had planned this for them. Taking advantage of the situation, she turned to Adam. "I really hope you'll come. There will be a couple of single female friends of mine from college days you may like to meet."

"I don't want to meet any of your single female friends, Mandy."

"They're pretty and their bodies are perfect. Unlike mine," she added silently to herself. She noticed he had shaved before supper, his hair combed and he looked good. Really good. Desire for him flooded her body and filled her with need.

"Mandy," he said softly, but quietly. "I told you your scars don't bother me. Why do you refuse to believe me?" He took in a short breath. "You want to know what I think?" He didn't give her a chance to answer. "I think you're scared to take a chance with me. I think you've depended on Jason for so long you don't want anyone else in your life. I think you're confused on what real love is. You told me you loved me. Well, maybe it's about time you made a choice." Adam dropped his napkin on the table and stood up. "Think about it. Think about the different types of love." He left.

Mandy looked down at her plate. What was Adam talking

about her not wanting to leave Jason? She wondered. She shook her head. Adam's wrong. Dead wrong.

ADAM NOTICED Jason enter the stall where Mandy kept her horse as he rode up on Zircon. He dismounted and led him into the barn.

"Adam," Jason called out. "Can we talk? I owe you an apology."

Adam ignored Jason and slipped the saddle off his horse.

"Adam, I've been trying to get ahold of you for the past week." With no answer, Jason stepped into the aisle. "I was totally wrong and I know that now."

"Did your sister send you here?" Adam finally spoke as he began to brush down Zircon.

"What? No. Of course not. Mandy wanted me to talk to you ages ago, but I was angry and you took off."

Adam rested his arm on his horse's back and finally faced Jason. This conversation was going nowhere fast. He shook his head. "Do twins communicate? And what happened to your drawl?"

"What?" Jason asked looking a bit bewildered.

"Look, I'm not interested in talking. You and your sister are together and that's fine with me. Maybe that's the way it should be, because you obviously look after her better than I can. Maybe you were right, I'm not good enough for your sister. I'm too... oh, what's the use. Go back home, Jason, be happy and leave me alone."

"You and Mandy have a fight?" he asked.

"You should know. Can't you feel her pain? Her emotions? You're supposed to be able to feel her pain or something like that." Adam gritted his teeth and turned away.

"Come on, Adam, it doesn't work that way," Jason quickly shot back. "Adam, I was wrong, okay? I was rude. I can't apologize enough. I'm sorry, Adam." Jason stepped into the stall Adam was in. "You two are such a good match, I was just too blind to see it so don't blame my sister. I'm the one who was wrong. She loves you."

Adam turned. "Good night, Jason."

"Jeez, you're stubborn," Jason hissed and went to collect Freckles. "But for the record, this time... you're the one who's wrong. I hope you'll be happy in the life you choose." Jason walked Freckles out to the trailer.

SATURDAY'S open house and barn dance party had finally arrived. Now that the time was here, Mandy wanted to get the silly party over and done with and be by herself for a while. She stood back with Dianne, her Aunt Maggie, Crystal and Bobby looking at the decorating job they finished on the barn. Colored streamers, balloons and lanterns made the barn very festive and hoisted high above the doorway was a welcome to the Twin R Ranch sign. Uncle Richard, Jason, Cole, Ryan, John and a few of her uncle's friends had finished the dance floor and had gone out back to have a beer and check the beef they had put on the spit.

Mandy sat with Dianne and her aunt for a while talking about the beautiful garden furniture and picnic tables that her Uncle Richard had brought from home. She watched the children play hide-n-seek in and out of the barn and around the many shrubs, around the yard and wondered if she would ever have a family. It would never be a complete ranch without children. *Two sets of twins would be nice.* She smiled. *With Adam.* She prayed he would show up.

Guests kept rolling in until everyone was there except the

one person she wanted the most. She groaned as one of Jason's college buddies who had been hounding her for a date come straight for her. She liked Jason's friend, Vic Moor, and had known him for several years now, but she didn't want to go out with him.

"What's wrong, Amanda?" Maggie asked.

"Vic's here. I won't have a moment's peace now," she complained.

"Who's here?" Dianne asked.

"A college friend of Jason's. He keeps asking me out but I'm not interested in him, and he doesn't give up." She rolled her eyes as she watched him enter the barn. Vic was a tall, blonde, good-looking man with soft gray eyes and a warm smile. A man any woman would be proud of. Except her, and he was headed straight towards her table.

"Jason's friend may be the least of your problems." Dianne nodded towards the barn door entrance. "I see a few other fellas eyeing you."

By nine o'clock the party was in full swing. Family and friends talked up a storm about the property, horses and the beautiful house. Vic of course, was the absolute perfect gentleman and everyone enjoyed visiting with him which was fine with Mandy as she only had thoughts of one man.

One perfect man.

During all the conversations and the laughter, she kept her eyes peeled towards the barn door, hoping, praying, wishing, Adam would show up. She sat beside Dianne and watched the kids dancing with her aunt, who was having the time of her life.

"Why won't he come and see me, Dianne?" She couldn't help asking.

"I don't know, Mandy."

Mandy watched a handsome young cowboy with dark hair stroll over towards her.

"Ma'am, may I have this dance?"

She smiled and shook her head. "Thank you, maybe later." Hoping later would never come. Within a few minutes another young cowboy came up and asked the same thing. She gave the same answer. She began to talk to Dianne again when another cowboy came over. She turned to Dianne. "If this keeps up, I'm going into the house." She turned to the young cowboy and gave him the same answer.

"I have a feeling those cowboys are your ranch hands, so it wouldn't be a good idea anyway."

"I don't know, Jason looks after the men right now, however I should have taken a few minutes to meet them. They probably don't even know I'm their boss." She groaned.

"All you have to do is tell one." Dianne motioned her head to the corner. "They're all from the same group. Want to bet they're betting on who can get you on the dance floor first."

Mandy glanced over. "You're probably right, there are at least three of them from this ranch." She chucked ruefully. "Pretty sad when you don't know your own employees."

"You've been busy with me. Oh, oh, here comes another one." Dianne nodded. "I told you Jason's friend, Vic, would be the least of your problems."

"Oh, for crying out loud."

"Ma'am, may I have this dance?"

"Do you work for Mr. Riley?" She smiled and asked the young handsome cowboy.

"Yes, Ma'am I do." His smile broad and friendly.

"And you are?" she asked politely.

"Gordon Daniels, Ma'am." The clean-shaven, young cowboy tipped his hat.

She held out her hand and smiled. "Pleased to meet you. I'm Miss Riley, Mr. Riley's sister. I'll try and remember your name if I need you for anything around the ranch."

"Pleasure, Ma'am." The cowboy tipped his hat again and walked away.

"Very good, Mandy." Dianne laughed. "You handled that like an old pro."

"Wish he was your employee, I would have danced with him."

"Yeah, right you would have," Dianne grunted softly.

It wasn't long after, that Cole and Jason sauntered over. "How are you ladies doing?" Cole asked.

"Mandy's having quite a time chasing all the men away."

"I was watching." Jason raised his brows and gritted his teeth. "Sorry, we haven't had time to do any introductions."

"Don't worry, Mandy can handle herself quite well," Dianne said as she reached for Cole's hand. "Have a dance or two with Mandy. She needs some diversion," she whispered.

Cole took Mandy's hand. "You should have a couple of dances at your own party. Come on, Miss Riley." Cole escorted her to the dance floor. "I haven't been to a barn dance in years."

Mandy danced two dances with Cole, then danced with Jason, her uncle and a few with the children and finally one with Vic. But inside, she felt a void, a loneliness she hadn't felt in years. She missed Adam and it made her heart ache.

The game of playing happy hostess was extremely tiring and was wearing her out fast.

CHAPTER 23

*A*dam arrived unannounced and went straight to the barn where the music was coming from. Children ran and laughed as a young teenage boy seemed to be showing them some sort of game jumping and crawling around straw bales. He smiled. Ranch and farm kids could sure use their imagination. He focused on the barn where all the adults were congregated and thought how senseless it was to sit at home and miss all the action, like he had been doing. His family was here. And so was the woman he loved. Hopefully Mandy would forgive his class 'A' attitude, for not giving her a second chance. Forgive him for leaving her in his bed. Forgive him for being a stubborn fool. Not only that, he was tired of this foolish game they were both playing and it was going to stop tonight. This emotional game where no one wins. They belonged together, he wanted to marry her. Wanted to have a long and happy life with her. He grinned, then prayed she'd say yes.

He stood by the young ranch hands for a few moments to get his bearings. Hearing Mandy's name he turned and listened to their conversation. They were talking about the woman he loved. Each and everyone one of the young men wanted to get their hands on her and wondered if anyone of them had a chance to dance with her.

"Hey, she can give me orders anytime," a heavy-set cowboy said.

Adam clenched his jaw as he listened to the others.

"She sure is something to look at," one cowboy said, as he stared longingly at her.

Adam figured him to be the leader of the group.

"She's got a slight limp, but I'll help her straighten it out," the oldest one said slapping his leg. "Got one myself."

"Well, I'm interested, but I can't date right now." He shrugged. "I still have two more years to study and complete my university," one of the quieter cowboys said. "I'd like to settle down, but by the time I'm ready, she'll be taken," he groaned.

"Aw kid, you'll meet someone at university," one cowboy said.

Adam shot a glance at the quiet one. He looked like a decent young man. Sincere and genuine. If he had a younger sister or cousin, he'd definitely introduce him. But he wasn't going to introduce him to Mandy. As for the other yahoos, they weren't worth thinking about. They would soon find out she was taken.

"Look at that city fellah," one cowboy said, "Hah, he's dressed like a cowboy, but you can spot a city fellah all right."

Adam turned and watched as Mandy danced with a tall lanky blond-haired man. His mouth tightened into a slight line. He turned away from the babbling morons and strolled over to where Cole and Dianne were sitting.

"Adam." Cole got out of his chair and clapped a hand on Adam's shoulder. "Good to see you, brother."

Adam nodded and returned the manly slap on the shoulder. "Cole." Adam turned to his sister-in-law. "Dianne."

"It's a great party," Cole added.

"Does Mandy know you're here yet?" Dianne asked.

"Nope." He shook his head looking over towards the dance floor where Mandy was dancing with some man he'd never seen. "Who's the city fellah?" Adam asked as he removed his Stetson and threw it over to an empty shelf behind the long table. He brushed his hair back with both hands.

"A friend of Jason's."

"Just wonderful." Adam took in a deep breath trying to ease the sudden ache in his chest. He stared at the woman he loved dancing with another man. "Enough," he muttered and headed straight towards her. Adam took in a deep breath as he maneuvered between several people. He tapped the man on the shoulder. "Excuse me. I want to talk to this young lady."

"Find someone else, Mac," Vic said sharply.

"Beat it." Adam jerked his thumb towards the exit. "And for your info, name's Adam."

"It's okay, Vic." Mandy held up her hand and gave him a half smile. "I'll talk to you later."

Adam took Mandy's arm and led her out to the back of the barn away from the crowd of people. Away from his meddling family's curious eyes.

"That was mighty rude of you. He's a close friend of the family."

"Yep, I was rude. But we need to talk about this silly emotional game we're playing and if he's a friend, he'll get it." He took in a deep breath. "First of all, before we get into anything, Mandy, I'm sorry about the other night. I'm sorry I left you." He released her hand and stroked his hair.

"Sorry, because I'm dancing with someone else. Some other man is interested in me and has been for some time now and doesn't mind dancing with someone who isn't perfect."

"Enough," Adam said sternly as he cut the air with his hand. "I've had enough of you talking about scars, being a reject, being a gimp, or how you think your damaged goods. I'm sorry for what you had to go through to get them. The accident, losing your family, it had to be traumatic. I can't even wrap my head around the tragedy of it all. But, Mandy, your limp and scars never bothered me. God knows how much I love you." Adam took a breath and stroked her arm gently. "We have to stop hurting each other. Blaming each other. Playing games that neither one of us likes. We got to talk and..." He touched her cheek with the back of his knuckles. "I love you, Amanda Joy Riley. I've done my share of running, too and blaming, but I'm not running anymore. I'm not running to the barn, to the tack room, or to my grandfather's line cabin, unless you're with me. I've been in love with you since the first day I saw you. I want to spend the rest of my life proving that to you."

He lifted her chin up with his finger. "I love you. I love you with all my heart and soul. You're kind, sensitive, educated and hopefully forgiving of my mistakes. I believe we were made for each other. I believe God brought us together."

Adam swallowed the emotional lump in his throat. "You were ready to give yourself to me that night, even when you knew I could have been rough. Honey, I didn't leave because of your scars or your limp. I left because I didn't want to take you when I was so frustrated, so confused. I couldn't handle hurting you. I'd never forgive myself if I did."

His thumb touched her lips. "I want you to enjoy making love with me. I want to make you happy." He watched her cheeks warm with color as he pulled her close to him. "I love you." He felt her soft hand take his. Her bright eyes filled with love. His heart swelled. She loved him and he felt it. Saw it.

"Should we go sit over there?" She pointed to a large tree with a knowing smile. "I want to apologize too. I should have waited at least until you came back. I..."

"Shh. Dance with me." He squeezed her hand. "No more apologizing. We're both good."

"I'd love to dance with you, but I don't dance very well."

"I was watching you." He grinned. "You dance beautifully." He wrapped his arms around her and slowly danced down the moonlit path behind the barn. "I've been absolutely miserable. I can't sleep. I can't do anything without you on my mind. I want..."

"Adam, it's my turn to tell you to shush." She put her finger to his lips. "Just hold me."

They danced in silence and cherished the moment in each other's arms. After several dances, they walked down the moon lit path away from the noise and crowd. Adam stopped, took her into his arms and lowered his head. Slowly, deliberately, he took her mouth. She accepted him. The kisses were hot and wanting. Soft moans created embers to ignite into flames of passion. Suddenly giggling rang out in the darkness of the bushes.

"Ohh, Bobby, look. They're doing it again," Crystal said.

"What daa do?"

"You know... the kissy, kissy, stuff."

Little whispers, snickers and soft giggles came from behind a hedge close to the back of the newer barn. Adam released her. "We have an audience," he whispered out of breath.

"I heard," she whispered back as her hand touched her beating heart. "Adam…"

"What are you two doing hiding behind a bush?" Ryan's voice was loud and clear.

"Ryan," Crystal said in a low whisper. "Look, Uncle Adam and Miss Riley are kissing again."

There was more rustling in the bushes. Adam chuckled quietly. "Let's find someplace else." He stepped in front of her to shield her from the kiss he wanted to give her. He covered her mouth with his and pressed his hot lips against hers.

"I think they're French kissing, Crystal," Ryan said.

"French kissing! Uncle Adam or Miss Riley aren't French," Crystal's whispers were louder.

Adam stopped and shook his head. "Let's go. This audience isn't going away." Just as he took Mandy's hand they heard Ryan speak up.

"Uncle Adam took French in high school."

"Did Miss Riley?" Crystal asked her brother.

"No, she took Spanish, because she's American."

"How do they kiss?" Crystal's voice went higher yet.

Adam laughed. "Come with me, I want to find out what you did in Spanish class."

"Adam." She blushed. "I took high school in Alberta." She laughed. "So, I took French."

"All the better." Adam smiled. "But I know you also took Spanish, in Jr. High, in Utah." Adam brought her closer as they walked to his truck and away from the giggles. He reached in and pulled out a large package wrapped in brown paper with a big red bow. "This is for you."

"What is it?" She took the package from him.

"Open it," he said as he led her to the back of the truck and let the tail gate down.

Mandy undid the wrapper. "Oh, Adam, the quilt from your bed. It's beautiful and the stitches around every oak leaf are so even and perfect." Her fingers traced the tiny stitches.

"I knew you'd like it," he said laying his hand on hers.

"Absolutely, I love it. Who made it?"

"My mother made one for me and one for Cole."

"She knew your strengths." She spread out the quilt and looked at the mighty oak tree in full summer foliage.

"It's a house warming gift I want you to have it. I want you to think of me when the sun goes behind the mountains and the air becomes chilly." He took the quilt and wrapped her in it. "I want you to remember the bedtime stories I told you while you were in my arms those few precious nights." He brushed her hair back and gazed into her whole face. "I want you to feel warm and secure in your bed until our wedding night." Adam smiled at his precious Mandy and the love in her eyes for him.

"Our wedding night?" Her eyes widened.

"Yes. I love you, Honey. Will you marry Me?" Adam's fingers gently traced the left side of her face then bent his head and trailed soft kisses down the scar.

"Yes, oh yes, Adam, I will. I love you to." Mandy wrapped her arms around his neck. "I've thought about you from the moment I walked up your porch steps. I loved you then, and I love you now."

Adam combed her hair with his hand. "I love the way you've cut your hair. It brings out your delicate features." He wrapped the quilt around her and brought her close to his chest and held her tightly. He would never let her go. He would never again run.

God had brought them together forever.

EPILOGUE

$\mathcal{M}$andy and Adam were married in a small church in Longview followed by another barn dance. They chose to move into the McBride family home where Adam's masculine bedroom was redecorated. Just a tad. A few ruffles here and there made a nice touch to a couple's bedroom. The beautiful mighty oak tree quilt lay on top of their bed.

Mandy had finished her book before the deadline while Adam was out on the range and sent it into her editor and continued to write other stories.

Jason was the second happiest man in Alberta. His family was growing and he loved having Adam as a big brother. With his love for fine carpentry, Jason decided to keep the Twin R Ranch on the small scale and raise quarter horses, more as a hobby. He built a new furniture shop on the ranch so he could continue working and being a part of the Riley Fine Furniture Business. That way their dream was complete and he continued to do what he loved and that was carpentry.

Hank was doing well and returned to his old job as second foreman. Adam had been right, he had found some good supports in his group. And a woman that he was falling in love with.

Eighteen months later, Mandy presented Adam with a girl and a boy. Twins. Adam was thrilled to be living his dream with the woman he cherished and loved.

For everyone, it was - A Dream Come True.

～

If you have enjoyed A Dream Come True,
you can help others find this story by leaving a short review on
your favorite book site,
review site, blog or your own social media properties, and share
your opinion with the other readers.
Thank you.

ABOUT S.L. DICKSON

 S.L. Dickson writes romantic suspense, mystery and contemporary romance. She focuses her stories in small towns and rural settings, although some of her characters are city dwellers. She is passionate about her writing with the support of her husband, Bill, family members, beloved friends, and all her writer friends from CaRWA and ARWA.

To relax after finishing a story, and needing a few days to think of another one, Shaa will often set up her acrylic paints and paint on smooth river rocks, old plates and flat paint stir sticks. A fun hobby she shares with her family. Shaa and Bill have lived in Manitoba, Alberta and now reside in northwestern Ontario with their sheltie mix dog, Lacey.

Throughout the years, Shaa has worked in a variety of careers, with addictions being her main focus. Shaa decided to decrease her work hours, so she could pursue her dream of being a full-time writer.

Bill and Shaa enjoy outdoor activities including canoeing, swimming, hiking in the forest, sitting on a dock listening to the call of the loons, and watching bald eagles soar in a blue sky. A bonus when their grandchildren can join them between their studies and busy schedules. A favorite family time, is gathering around a camp fire, roasting marshmallows, whether it be summer or winter.

To learn more about S.L. Dickson:

Visit her website at: https://sldickson.com
View her author page at Amazon.ca: S.L. Dickson
Send her an e-mail at: Shaa@sldickson.com

Made in the USA
San Bernardino, CA
14 June 2018